Test of Faith

TEST OF FAITH

Christa Allan

Abingdon fiction
a novel approach to faith

Test of Faith

ISBN-13: 978-1-4267-3326-0

Published by Abingdon Press, P.O. Box 801, Nashville, TN 37202

www.abingdonpress.com

Library of Congress Cataloging-in-Publication Data has been
requested.

Printed in the United States of America

2 3 4 5 6 7 8 9 10 / 18 17 16 15 14

To Ken,
keeper of the faith

Acknowledgments

This novel was a test of faith, persistence, and Mike and Ikes. I think I passed all three tests; well, except for the Mike and Ikes. We formed a study group.

This was my first opportunity to work with the ever-patient, ever-prodding, and ever-positive Jamie Chavez, my developmental editor. As evidence of my card-carrying membership in The Jamie Fan Club, I'll admit that I was delighted to receive her eleven-page, single-spaced editor letter. If you need to make order out of chaos, Jamie is your woman. I'm so looking forward to working with her on future projects.

Volunteering to share life's experiences with honesty, openness, and sometimes pain requires courage and trust. I'm humbled and grateful that Allison so generously spent time with me to develop this story.

One person I've neglected to mention along the way is my forever friend Claudia Schulz who provides me with medical-related information. She's not at all shocked to receive a phone call from me starting with requests such as, "I need a disease, not cancer, with a sudden onset that could happen to a man in his 30s and cause him to die in less than a year." Our husbands ignore our conversations about different ways characters can die, but I'll bet most nights they're sleeping with one eye open.

I appreciate my posse of writing and reading friends who provide me some time to whine and some time-outs because I do. Many thanks to Jennie, Kristen, and Sibella for their e-mail rah-rahs. And to Shelley, Carrie, Michelle, and Carole who ground me.

Of course, cheers to Abingdon Press and Acquisitions Editor Ramona Richards and agent Sandra Bishop.

To my brother John and his husband, Ricky, thank you for the meals you cooked and all the ways you helped as deadlines neared. My children, Michael, Erin, Shannon, Sarah, and John, are endless sources of entertainment when I'm frumpy and forgiveness when I'm snarky. And then there's earth, water, air, fire, and Ken. My life essentials.

And I'm grateful that God gives me endless quizzes to prepare me for the greatest test of faith that awaits me.

1

Since I couldn't kill my husband's mistress, I settled for toleration. As long as Logan agreed to reserve at least one night for me, I'd endure the other nights alone.

Well, at least I didn't suffer the agony of deceit. Election day was six months away, and the all-consuming political campaign that seduced my husband would end. I'll deal with the "then what?" later. For now, I'll add it to the "then what" collection and wait for it to decay like the others.

Tonight, though, she beckoned him away to another hand-shaking, wide-smiling, campaign-promoting event.

For too long, our physical relationship languished on the Logan Butler, Candidate for State Representative, "to do" list. Matt Feldman, his campaign manager, probably slotted it in on his calendar:

> 10:20 P.M. Make love to wife
> 10:25 P.M. Sleep

I told Logan weeks ago, after another night of my hand returning with empty hope after reaching across the bed to him, I'd never have to worry about another woman taking him away.

"And why is that?" he asked. The words bounced back to me from the wall he spoke to. A wall that saw more action than I did considering the number of times I'd painted it in the last two years.

"Because the campaign's already your mistress. You don't have time for anyone else," I said and crunched my pillow under my head.

He rolled over, scooped me into his arms, and in a voice as smooth and soft as the sheets, whispered, "You know I love you."

"More than . . . ?" When he didn't answer, I thought my pillow had suffocated my question. But his breathing was slow and measured. He had fallen asleep. My sadness spilled itself out in quiet, hot tears.

By morning, I'd tugged on the good wife costume again. And by lunchtime, I'd sat across from two silver-haired gentlemen who double-teamed me at checkers at the East Haven Home for the Elderly while Logan surprised the ladies' Zumba Gold class as their bodies convulsed to the calypso beat of Harry Belafonte's "Jump in the Line."

And that was my life as the wife of a politician running for office. Smiling, playing checkers, smiling, and hoping to have a reason to unwrap my ivory, lace-appliquéd satin slip.

But since the meeting with his staff tonight didn't start until seven o'clock, I knew not to expect any more than his arriving home in one piece.

"It'll be over soon. I promise." Logan grabbed the back door handle and tossed his farewell over his shoulder like an old, nubby sweater. The state of Louisiana was not to be denied. Just me.

He paused, the door still open. "I love you. You know that, don't you?" he said in a voice that seemed wrapped in silk.

I closed my *Southern Living* magazine and looked into those eyes of his that caressed me and pulled me in as if he'd reached out his arms. The eyes that made me shiver with anticipation. "It's what saves you every time," I said.

Logan left, but captured in the residual flush of his "I love you" was the Logan of long ago. He didn't look much different now, maybe bulkier shoulders and more expensive clothes. The scruffy beard replaced in the name of politics by a clean-shaven, only slightly stubbled look. But the J. Crew jeans and T-shirt he wore tonight erased the years between then and now.

It was disconcerting to have a husband more handsome than I was pretty, which had made his marriage proposal all the more surprising. He knew even then the track his career would race on. Why not pick someone who would be a photogenic ornament on his arm? Logan joked that he didn't want an "eye candy" wife. "Once she's gobbled up, there's nothing left," he told me. I figured I'd have to be someone with substance, like gourmet granola. With panache. Someone to be reckoned with, not devoured.

Logan told me I had a "classic beauty." In my universe that translated to "You're a woman who can pull off wearing your mother's clothes." My parents' professional careers did nothing to improve my pedigree to win the Blue Blood Ribbon in Martha Butler's status contest. My mother, Nancy Claiborne, didn't claim membership in Daughters of the American Revolution, and neither she nor my father, John, could have been considered even remotely related to landed gentry.

But something about the first Mrs. Butler made me wish I'd been born with a rearview mirror attached to my shoulder. Her physical presence alone intimidated me. Any woman see-sawing between the ages of sixty and seventy who could have been mistaken as my husband's older sister made me want to avoid looking in a mirror. If her features had been cosmetically induced, I might have felt less insecure. And she and I stood eye-to-eye until someone brought up the topic of the homeless, taxes, or the New Orleans Saints. Then, as if the heat of her righteous indignation ignited some turbocharger under her feet, she seemed to hover three feet above everyone else during her rant.

It was that startling aspect of her personality that made me wonder why she didn't pursue politics after her husband's unexpected death. Logan and I were in college then and had just recently rediscovered one another. Daniel Butler, his father, had been a state representative in Louisiana for over two terms. Daniel's charisma and charm endeared him to his New Orleans constituents as evidenced by their outpouring at his funeral. Logan said his mother refused to finish out his term. The city adored the Butlers, so that would not have been improbable for her to accomplish.

"She doesn't have the heart for it, does she?" I asked him.

"No," he'd replied. "She said she didn't have the stomach for it."

We didn't speak much of Daniel. The mention of him twisted Martha's lips into a figure eight, and Logan had little to say that could be considered positive remembrances.

My mother-in-law waited over four years before nominating me for membership in Junior League. "I needed to be sure," she had told me the day we had lunch in the Tea Room. She sipped her coffee, but from under her sparkling plum-shaded lids, her eyes pinched my composure. Logan may have inherited his mother's soft sable eyes, but his weren't comfortable in the Arctic tundra.

"Certainly," I purred. "As did I." My voice surprised even me.

Her eyebrows rose and met one another like small peaks on her forehead. The retort from her daughter-in-law had thrown down the gauntlet.

After that, I became Martha's project. At first, I questioned her motives because for four years she played on the team of doubt and expected to be declared a winner while I sat on the bench and waited to play. When Logan decided to run for city councilman, she told me, "Let's start with the one goal we have in common, and that's Logan winning." We did, and he won, but she continued to chip away at my veneer of self-confidence. Suggestions meant to be followed were disguised in questions beginning with "don't you think it would be better if . . . ?" It didn't take too long for me to learn the basic lessons: hemlines down, necklines up, perfume probably not, smile probably always, and Logan first always.

Now Logan was campaigning for state representative, and Martha was still as snarly; still as overbearing, and still as persistent. I was still as compliant because if Logan lost, it wasn't going to be because I wore short skirts or a plunging neckline.

Tonight's reprieve due to Logan's meeting meant I could devote time to assessing the requirements I needed to fulfill for my provisional membership in the local Junior League, one of Martha's recent victories. I kicked off my flip-flops, rested my feet on the chair across from me, and when I leaned back, remembered why I regretted not buying upholstered chairs. Ladder-back chairs stained Tuscan Walnut appeared stylish in the furniture store. And they were. But, like most things I discovered in my journey up the social ladder, comfortable and fashionable were generally mutually exclusive.

I opened my laptop and found the folder I'd labeled JL Stuff. I scrolled through the list of requirements. Welcome reception? Check. Provisional education meetings? Check. Two community agency visits. Check one. Four general meetings? Check two. Service hours? Not even half of the almost ninety-two hours needed. Somewhere, I had to find almost thirty days to squeeze in two hours of volunteering a day. The Art in the Park Camp for special-needs kids and adults was the last week in June. If Logan didn't have me scheduled to kiss any babies or dance with grandfathers that week, that would work. In fact, I might even ask him to leave me off the calendar and consider inviting Martha to replace me. She'd pounce on a chance to be indispensable.

Ever since my last year of high school when I realized my friend Jenn's beloved sister lived in a group home for disabled adults, I'd looked for ways to be involved with special-label kids too. These kids taught me we're all retarded—it's just a matter of degrees. I thought the term was misunderstood because I was always the one who walked away feeling special for having been with them. I went into occupational therapy and focused on special-needs kids because I loved teaching them skills to help them achieve independence and enjoy their lives. Like Jenn's sister. I focused on children with the alphabet-soup of conditions. Autism, low birth weight, premature birth, fetal alcohol syndrome, congenital anomalies, neurological disorders. But building a politician took priority over building a practice, so I retired early. I knew, though, that the list of kids and conditions that qualified for services never shortened. It wasn't how I wanted to have job security, but I never doubted returning to the profession would be difficult.

I blocked off the week on my calendar and sent Logan an e-mail with the dates for an Art in the Park appearance and a suggestion to schlep Martha along if he wanted company.

After working through a schedule of sorts, I'd traded my laptop for laundry and was folding a hill of towels that covered the kitchen table when Logan plowed through the back door. His limbs flailed as if a mini-typhoon blew behind his back. He blinked as fast as a camera shutter, and I pictured what his eyes had captured. My hair swirled into a banana-sized clip, my freshly three-step cleansed, toned, and moisturized face, and my scrubs that sometimes doubled as my painting attire. I was Victoria with a megaphone, clearly not with a secret. He must have recovered in another blink because the excited glow on his face could not have emanated from the sight of me.

"He might be withdrawing from the race." Logan grabbed a bottle of water from the refrigerator, then sat at the table across from me.

"Who 'he'?" I moved a folded stack to the side to be able to see him.

"Chad Wiggins." He pulled his cell phone out. "I'll tell you why. I'm calling my mother so you can both listen at the same time, and I won't have to repeat the story."

Chad was Logan's opponent in the primary. If he dropped, then Logan would automatically be the candidate for his party. And one less opponent to battle in the media would give our finances time to breathe before the big race. But "might" suggested he might not. Huge territory between "be" and "not."

I heard Logan say, "Walk over," and decided I needed to divert my attention to the conversation. A year ago, in what I'm still convinced was a strangely fortuitous happening, a house three doors down from ours went on the market. Martha bought it. Those two words together crashed into my brain as "brace yourself for the diatribe" or, when given more lead time, "feeling urpy. I need a nap."

My husband shook his head and mouthed, "Not coming."

I stopped holding my breath now that I'd been granted parole. But what he told us both was not anything to celebrate. He ended the call with his mother, and the enthusiasm that propelled him through the door had the decency to dissolve into seriousness.

Logan finished his water, then spoke to the table as if it, not I, waited. "Martha said the news about Chad was an answer to prayer," he said.

"Really?" Steam rising from the indignation boiling in my gut burned my face. "Did she pray that his wife would be diagnosed with cancer and he'd decide to withdraw?" I grabbed the laundry basket like it caused Martha's insensitivity. "Your mother needs to be careful what she prays for. She just might get it."

I learned that lesson what seemed like a lifetime ago. It taught me at least one thing. To stop praying.

2

I thought I'd outgrown naiveté in eighth grade. I discovered the startling truth of Ben Franklin's "three can keep a secret if two of them are dead" the day Jason Knight, the hottest kid in the school, sauntered past me in the cafeteria and said, "I hear you want me to invite you to the spring dance."

But I guess not, because the next night was supposed to be our politics-free time, and Logan informed me between my serving the salad and the lasagna that Matt, who managed the campaign, was coming over later to vet our personal histories. Again. Chad had dropped out officially this morning, and this politics thing had just leaped to the next level.

"Didn't we do this already? How many times do we have to submit ourselves to these interrogations?" I stabbed an olive in my salad that seemed to be eyeing me with suspicion.

"We did do this, but since Matt wasn't around then, he wanted to meet with us himself. Plus, he said he has some other papers for us," he said. "At least the inquisitor is a friend."

Matt and Logan met their freshman year of high school. Two awkward-limbed kids who made the junior varsity football team, then bulked their way onto varsity. Matt played offensive tackle, and Logan quarterbacked the team. Later, he served as Logan's best man in our wedding. And his job continued to be making sure Logan wasn't blindsided. When his wife gave birth to their twins two months ahead of schedule, he asked Logan for a campaign sabbatical so he could be around to help.

"You're right. It is good that he's a friend because he won't mind that the kitchen smells like garlic and that his shoes might stick to the floor." I wagged my fork in his direction. "You'd better hope that one of his questions isn't how much advance notice you give your wife about guests."

Logan held up his hands in surrender. "Guilty as charged. I promise no more surprise vettings."

"Holding you to that one," I said and started clearing the table. "Now I'm going to be vetted by our campaign manager who will use important vetting documents to vet me? It sounds ridiculous."

Logan handed me his empty dinner plate on my way to the dishwasher. "Well, yes, it does seem ridiculous when you say it that way."

But the process was as far from ridiculous as I was from transparent. Which explained why I scraped most of my dinner into the sink where the disposal could chew it up more than I did. I knew when Logan dipped his toe in the political pool he'd have to dive in sooner or later. I hoped for later. I wanted to ease into the water, not experience the breath-sucking shock of leaving what was comfortable.

I flipped the switch to send the uneaten lasagna and salad swirling into the garbage disposal. Bits of food shot out of its black rubber mouth accompanied by a grinding, clanging ruckus in its belly. It was a weirdly riveting performance of what I felt going on in my stomach.

Logan shut the disposal off, and when the noise wore itself out, reached in and pulled out a teaspoon gnawed by the metal teeth. "Are you okay? Why didn't you just turn it off?" He handed me the disfigured spoon and pulled the faucet toward him to wash his hands. "You need to relax about tonight. Matt's our friend, and it's going to be fine. Unless . . ."

"What? Unless what?" The wood floor beneath me shuddered.

He leaned against the counter and smiled at me. "Unless you ever killed someone. You'd have told me that, right?"

The hands that had clenched my lungs let go. I returned the smile. "Right. Absolutely." Later I wondered if that might have been easier to share than my secret. At least dead is dead.

Matt sat across from the two of us, his hands palms down like paperweights on the two manila folders in front of him. "Here's how we're going to look at this. The two of you are in the confessional, and it all stops with me. We don't want to do damage control, especially now that we're getting ready to go head-to-head with the other party." He slid one folder to Logan and one to me. "The questions are the same for both of you. Some are just simple yes or no. Others may need more explanation."

My stomach crawled into my throat and collapsed. Logan's hand patted my knee. An unusual display of affection from him, especially now. But when the pat became a firm press, I realized my left leg had been bouncing up and down, up and down, up and down. Whenever I felt trapped, smothered, or on the verge of a primal scream, I tried to bounce the anxiety out of my body. It was why my wedding shoes were pearl and glass-sequined ballet slippers and not stilettos. Logan, that day, I was sure about. My mother, left alone with Martha, was potential for disaster.

"It's not like you don't already know most of my life," said Logan. He nodded in my direction. "And Elle's, too."

"Look, man, I knew before I came here tonight that you're what this state needs. Otherwise, I'd be sitting in someone else's kitchen. But it's my responsibility to scare the skeletons out of the closet before the other side finds them. I'm not judging either one of you. Just asking you to spill it all out now. If you popped a few Adderall to pull all-nighters before exams or smoked pot, I need to know before your opponent accuses you of being a drug dealer or user or both. I don't want to read the morning news and see a list of people you've slept with or sent inappropriate texts or pictures to."

I opened the folder and scanned some of the questions: Were you a member of a fraternity/sorority? If so, what hazing was there? Were there racial or religious restrictions? What was the fraternity's/sorority's reputation? Were there any bizarre rituals? Did the fraternity/sorority engage in sexual harassment? Did you ever use drugs? Sniff glue? Take your parents' prescription medicines? Attend parties where drugs were used?

"These questions reek of witch hunt, don't you think?" I looked from Logan to Matt and waited for an answer.

"The difference is this isn't designed to punish you. We're doing this to make sure you don't get punished," Matt said on his way back to the table after fixing himself a cup of coffee. "You don't have to finish this now. Of course, if it takes you days to complete this, then we have bigger problems than an election."

He stared at us as he stirred. "That was meant to be funny."

"Okay, the two parking tickets, the speeding ticket"—Logan closed the folder—"the time in college when I may have been over-served and tried to catch a goldfish in one of the ponds . . ."

Matt laughed. "I remember that night. And, if that's the worst you have, I suppose the bad news is your opponent can't depend on character assassination to deflect voters." He paused. "Elle?"

My conscience bit its fingernails and reminded me this was not the time or place to dredge deep. I recrossed my legs and made sure to hold on to my knee so I'd be less tempted to bounce. "I stole a pair of earrings," I said.

They made eye contact with one another before Logan leaned back a bit and looked at me as if I'd just dumped a bowl of cereal on his head. "Earrings? You stole earrings? When?"

"The summer after eighth grade." A flash of memory. Julie stood next to me and pretended to admire a pair of large gold hoops while I slipped a pair of the silver ones in my cargo pants pocket.

"Whew," said Matt. "My brain was already wondering how we'd spin this one."

Logan refilled Matt's cup and returned with one for himself. "You never told me this." He sounded more apologetic than I did.

I released my leg, gulped some water, and shifted in the chair. "It was before we met."

"What happened?"

"My mother dragged my friend Julie and me to the grocery with her because she didn't want to leave us alone." I stopped doodling on the outside of the folder and looked up at the men to acknowledge what I already knew they must have been thinking. "I know. Absurd, right?" I returned to my scribbling. "At least the store was in a neighborhood strip mall. Julie and I went to the little gift shop next door while she went to the grocery. We looked at the earrings, and I thought I couldn't live without this pair of silver hoops. But I didn't have any money with me. Julie told me that wasn't a problem. At first, I thought she meant she'd pay for them. But when the sales clerk walked to the register to check out the customer already there, Julie handed them to me, pointed to my pocket, and that was that. I just slipped them in. We stood there for a few more minutes, spinning the display and pretending to be interested. Then, when the other customer left, we walked out after her."

"What are we talking about here, twenty dollars?" Matt almost looked amused. "Stealing is stealing, but as long as we weren't talking about diamond earrings or something equally expensive, it's not that damaging an issue."

"Then you'll love this part," I said and put the pencil down. "That night my mother asked where the new earrings came from. At first I told her Julie, but then she wanted to know why she gave them to me because my birthday was four months ago. She wouldn't stop asking questions. I broke and told her what happened. Next thing I knew I was in the car with her and headed back to the gift shop. My mother paid for the earrings, and I apologized to the sales clerk who told us she wouldn't press charges. I paid my mother back by cleaning the house for a month, and I couldn't hang out with Julie for a few months."

"I think Martha would have threatened some Old Testament justice, like chopping off my hand," said Logan. "Good for your mother. She taught you an important lesson."

"Not the ones she intended, I'm sure."

"How's that?" Matt asked.

"I learned to not cave in to my mother, and I learned to not get caught."

"We'll just need to make sure your mother doesn't bring that up in any interviews," said Matt. "Sometimes parents don't think of the big picture when they're telling those sorts of stories."

I looked at Logan and hesitated. *How honest should I be here?* His silence was my answer. "Actually, I don't think that will be a problem," I said as I focused on the pencil I twirled in my hands. "My mother and I don't talk much, and we don't see her that often. She still lives in Lafayette and, since my father died, she stays busy helping my sister, Cam, with her son." I set the pencil back down on the table. If he missed the shade of sadness in my voice, I didn't doubt that he'd see it when our eyes met.

"Elle, this might be a good time to call your mother. You know, just to touch base. It would be a nice gesture, and it would give you a chance to give her some advance warning in case she gets any calls. You never know," said Logan.

"Logan has a point," said Matt. "And I know this is personal, but that's what tonight's about. Is there something going on between the two of you that you don't communicate much? If there is, we need to deal with it now."

Where was I going to start with this one? I had no doubt my mother could keep a secret. She and I learned that about one another years ago. But, I couldn't tell my husband or Matt that. Not now. "No, we're fine. I mean, we're not exactly best friends. Since she and my sister only live about five miles away from each other, it's much easier for the two of them to spend time together. Driving three hours one way to visit us isn't an easy weekend for her. She's a dentist, and she does some relief work when she can. I don't demand much of her time." And she's probably grateful for that.

"Still, I'd appreciate if you'd take Logan up on his idea of calling her. Maybe even plan a visit. You could drive to see her, right? We'll find time in your schedule."

Not what I wanted to hear. I thought Logan would see the pleading in my eyes to save me from Matt's suggestion to visit, but he didn't dive in to rescue me. I still had time to wiggle out of that one, though. Or, I could use my commitment to the center as a valid reason to stay home.

"Sure, we can see if that works. But between my volunteer work for the Junior League that Martha graciously invited me to be a part of and trying to pull together plans for the center that I've adopted as my project, it might be difficult. At least for now."

Logan reminded Matt about my idea to build a center for adults with special needs, someplace they could hang out during the day and where businesses could bring work to them. "Elle's already talked to the Diamond Recycling Corporation. They put together information packets for their clients, and they're willing to turn that over to be done at the center. The state tourism commission puts together Mardi Gras bags for companies inquiring about conventions, and they'd be willing to turn that over too."

"I've been making plans for a fund-raiser, but with everything happening with the election, it's been pushed aside. That's another thing I really want to devote my time to," I said, still hoping to schedule a fun run and a golf tournament to raise money.

Matt explained the fund-raising itself wasn't an issue, but we had to be sure to avoid accepting money from special interest groups entirely unrelated to what we were trying to do. "The lobbyists for the gambling and alcohol boards might show real interest. The kind that would be reflected in large contributions. But you don't want someone supporting you that Logan wouldn't support. It could make him an easy target for being accused of compromise and lying."

I reassured them both I would handle raising funds with the utmost propriety. "And if I ask Martha to be involved, I'm certain she would be careful to avoid anything that could jeopardize votes for her son."

Before leaving for the night, Matt suggested we shut down any personal social networking sites and let the press relations coordinator take care of communicating. "We don't want any Twitter or Facebook controversies. Sometimes an innocent comment can be misconstrued, and even if we take it down, someone's captured it. The exponential effects of that instant access are almost impossible to control."

"Let's hire someone just to navigate social media. It's too important, and just keeping up with the print and other media keeps her in a frenzy," said Logan and made notes on his iPad.

"Were you two aware that Martha has a Facebook page and a Twitter handle?"

Matt and Logan looked like two men who just heard the pin pulled out of a hand grenade.

I pulled Logan's iPad over and opened her Facebook page, then clicked over to her Twitter page. "She uses the handle 'PoliMom,' because 'I'm the mother of the best candidate for State Rep!'"

Logan reached for his cell phone. I tugged his arm. "What are you doing? You can't call her now," I said.

Matt nodded. "No, dude. Not over the phone. She'd probably tweet about it. Just talk to her in person. She'll understand." He tapped his pen on the table. "I hope."

My husband's face reflected the same doubt Matt expressed. "Maybe you need to tell her, Matt. She'll listen to you with your campaign manager hat on."

"Especially if she thinks she'll lose voters for him." I patted Logan's arm. "Take heart. I can get her involved in my adult center, and if you know anyone in the local theatre group, maybe they'll pick her for that part she wants. And that'll keep her busy."

"Part? She wants a part?" Surprise lifted Logan's eyebrows the same way it did Martha's.

"You have been disconnected, haven't you? The next production is *A Streetcar Named Desire,* and she wants to play Blanche."

"Is she crazy? I'm running for office, and she wants to play an oversexed, tragic woman who gets taken advantage of by her brother-in-law?"

"Honestly, I think she just wants to utter the line, 'I've always depended on the kindness of strangers.'"

I woke up early the next morning after catching sleep between the horizontal aerobics of tossing and turning from the streaming video of the night before and things left unsaid. I scrunched my pillow and rolled over to see if Logan was awake. Not there. It was still dark outside, which meant he hadn't left yet for work. No doubt I'd find him in his office doing his morning devotion. Sometimes I wished he'd have studied me as faithfully and fully as he did his Bible. He was committed even when it meant setting the alarm clock to wake up earlier than usual to read Scripture passages and write in his prayer journal.

I untangled myself from the sheets and slipper-shuffled my way into the kitchen to make coffee. I filled his mug and brought it to him. Knowing he probably didn't see me, I stood at the open door for a moment just to frame the picture of him in my mind. His chair pushed back from the desk, his open Bible rested on the crook of his leg. The pen he held tapped the open page as he read. Unguarded moments were rare for Logan, and I experienced a calmness watching him. It was the kid who wouldn't fight back, the person who refused to engage in the argument, the peace that eluded me, that let my fingertips brush up against its softness, but wouldn't fill my hands.

3

Neither Logan nor I mentioned anything to Matt about how we met and how long we'd known one another. I followed Logan's lead, and since he never introduced it in the conversation, I didn't either. Even after Matt left, we didn't discuss our not having discussed it.

But we hadn't talked about that summer we met at Leadership Camp for a very long time. Of course, that summer was a very long time ago.

The last time it came up was a few months ago after I discovered Melody Loeman's office building spotlighted on one of the sites I'd found while cruising the Internet for landscape architects. "Well, baby, look at you now," I said to her picture, my voice two parts stunned and one part envious. Melody, my roommate at the camp, could have posed as the poster girl for Nerdville at the time. On the geek thermometer, she registered in the high fever range. Plaid shoelaces often tied her braided pigtails together, she wore stretch pants under her shorts, and t-shirts with "Obey gravity. It's the law," or "Actually, it IS rocket science." On her hot pink Converse sneakers, she'd written the last names of her favorite scientists. Melody sometimes referred to herself as Willow, the equally nerdy, computer-savvy character in *Buffy, the Vampire Slayer.* I didn't mind hanging out with her because, next to her, my own dorkiness came off as cool.

That summer before my junior year at Washington High School, my high school counselor, Mr. Hargrave, selected me to attend Leadership Camp at Louisiana State University in Baton Rouge. In my small town of less than four thousand people, with only one high school that could pick only two students to attend, I couldn't wait to spend time on LSU's campus. Especially for four weeks. Four parentless, sisterless weeks. Of course, some discontents claimed I was the choice because my mother was the town's only female dentist and my dad, the principal at the middle school, had just been elected to the Board of Deacons. The grumblers would rarely mention the fact that I had a 3.998 grade point average, was president of the National Honor Society and Student Council, and played on the varsity soccer team. It did, though, provide my parents some bragging rights among their friends and annoy my older sister Camden by trumping her having been voted Homecoming Queen when she was a senior.

The second day at camp I met Logan when we were placed in the same small group for the duration of the week. He'd just graduated from Montgomery Prep, an exclusive academy in New Orleans, and made himself known when he challenged my idea for creating music therapy for kids with disabilities as the group's social action plan. Logan thought we should investigate the possibility of providing learning centers for homeless adults.

After he pitched his idea, the short-shorted, long-legged, Meg Ryan-haired clone—her name was Carole—sitting next to him rolled her eyes, then tossed a few blades of grass she'd been snapping out of the ground in his direction. They fell as

I turned off the late night news and set the remote on the arm of the sofa. "I'm officially tired now. You?"

"Almost." Logan, sitting in the recliner, his feet resting on the ottoman, looked up from that day's crossword puzzle. "What school's motto is *Lux er Veritas*? Wait. Never mind. Yale."

"Light and Truth, right?" I impressed myself by remembering that one from Yale's application.

"Now are you ready for bed?" I slid my feet into my flip-flops.

He scanned the puzzle. "In a few minutes. I'm close to finishing," he said.

"We both know 'in a few minutes' means at least thirty." I leaned over and kissed his forehead. "Just wake me up when you get there."

We also both knew that was code for "wake me up so we can have sex."

"Sure," he answered.

And, again, we both knew "sure" meant, "maybe, but probably not."

Logan's enthusiasm for having sex seemed diminished by his constant campaigning. And, when we did, whatever passion I'd felt was eroded by his unwavering decision to not want children. When I thought our lovemaking might, eventually, result in actually making something . . . like a baby . . . it seemed to elevate sex to a level that was beyond physical. Even with my fringe belief in God, I never doubted that we were participating in an act of creation beyond ourselves. Now, having sex was, well, having sex. Logan, before we married, didn't equivocate about not wanting to be a parent. But I loved him, and the fear of losing him again far outweighed, then, the pain of our being childless. I was to blame for my own disappointment. I buried it far under the mounds of hope I'd built, convinced that, in time, Logan would relent. But he didn't, and those constant waves of truth eroded my foolish expectations.

"It's not like politics, Logan," I said to him one evening when I asked if he'd consider us going to a therapist. "We can't reach a compromise and have half a child. Maybe if we just talked to someone—"

"Why are we even having this discussion? Didn't you agree with me you could live with this choice? We talked about this the first time we met. Remember?"

The last week of Leadership Camp we spent most of the hours between dinner and curfew alone. We'd eat at one of the food courts at the Student Union, then walk to the quad or Indian mounds to talk. One night we went swimming at the apartment of a friend of Logan's who'd graduated the year before. On the way back to the dorms, we stopped at the lake and spread out our towels next to one another.

It wasn't quite dark yet, and the lake still glowed like polished silver, but the sun had settled enough that we could enjoy the shade under the trees.

We'd been talking about his father being in politics. Actually, I'd asked him if he'd expect his son or daughter to follow him into politics like his father did.

"No," he answered as he traced the letters of his name on my back. "I don't think that will happen. I wouldn't be a good father—I might treat my kids the same way my father treats me." He kissed the nape of my neck where my bathing suit halter-top had been tied, and I trembled. Not from his finger moving like warm honey across my back or the softness of his lips. But from the trail of crushed ice along my spine left by his words.

"What do you mean the way he 'treats' you? Are you saying . . . ?" I waited.

He rolled on his back, his arms crossed underneath his head, and stared at the dark ceiling of night that blanketed the trees. "No. He doesn't hit me. But sometimes I wish he would. . . ."

Neither anger nor frustration filtered through Logan's voice. But that absence of emotion left me more, not less, uneasy. I rested my hand on his chest, his T-shirt still damp from his having pulled it on after our swim. "You really wouldn't want your father to hit you. Right? And, honestly, how could you hit him back?"

In the same even-toned voice, Logan answered, "At least if he physically abused me, I'd have proof. But the crap he slings at me almost every day about how I'll never be as successful as he is, how much I disappoint him, and telling me I'm too sensitive and I should have been born a girl . . . that doesn't leave scars. Not the kind that show on the outside."

And that's when he told me he didn't ever want children. I heard him that night. I just didn't listen.

I didn't believe an adult would weld himself to a conviction made before he was old enough to vote. I was wrong.

I brushed my teeth, washed my face, and applied the moisturizer that promised I'd be wrinkle free. I slipped on a black lace and satin sleep shirt, more appealing than my flannel jammies, though not nearly as comfy. I woke up in the still dark room from a nightmare fending off human-sized spiders. When I rolled over into empty space, I figured Logan had fallen asleep in the den.

He had. He was already snoring trumpets. I pulled the afghan from the back of the sofa, covered him, and turned off the light.

4

I awoke to the tip-tap-tip of rain on our bedroom windows followed by a sudden blast of light and a voice asking about a cell phone charger.

"Have I seen it in the past thirty seconds since you just flipped on my lamp and I first opened my eyes?" I pulled the sheet over my head. "Did you check your office, your briefcase, your car, and the kitchen counter near the coffee maker? And why are we awake this early?" Logan flipped and flopped the bed comforter. "You didn't sleep with it last night, why are you looking there?" I surrendered the comfort of my pillow and the notion of a slow morning rise, leaned against the padded headboard, and watched him.

"I might have set it there when I came back for my tie," he said to the floor as he checked under the bed. "Jenny's daughter has an orthodontist appointment this morning, so I told her I'd open the office." The rain stopped its dainty, polite, staccato dance and thundered its way into a bass drum crashing. Logan, his tie draped around his neck, looked outside, then back at me. "How many orthodontic appointments are necessary for kids with braces?"

Jenny had been Logan's paralegal since before her daughter was born. He'd actually driven her to the hospital the day her labor started because her husband's car had a flat tire on the Mississippi River bridge.

"Maybe you need to find that out when Jenny gets back today." I walked over to an electrical outlet by the bedroom door and unplugged Logan's charger. "Here, and the umbrella's in the hall tree," I said. "I'm going to make coffee. Finish getting dressed so you won't be late, and I'll make you a to-go cup. Save you a trip through the drive-through."

Logan wrapped the cell phone cord around his neck too and walked to the closet to pull a pair of navy chinos off the hanger. "The baristas might send out a search party."

A joke, but one closer to serious. No telling how many days Logan's car found itself at the PJs drive-through. He believed in supporting local businesses, so he drove one mile past the store with the iconic mermaid logo to order his morning latte from the hometown franchise.

A cup of coffee later, Logan, his umbrella, and his cell phone charger walked out the back door.

I was headed to BoraBora for a long overdue appointment for a mani/pedi when Logan called.

"Hey. If you forgot something at home, I already left."

"It's, well, it's something I wanted to talk to you about last night. But I wanted you to hear it from me first, and not in front of Matt."

He asked if I planned to be home for lunch. The driver behind me saw the light change to green before I did because she leaned into her horn to let me know. I pulled into the nearest parking lot to finish the conversation and avoid being the subject of the next accident report.

"Honey, it's not even ten o'clock, and you expect me to function for two hours waiting for that conversation?" I shook my head. "I'll call to reschedule this appointment. Nails aren't an emergency. Can you be home sooner?" *Or could you have just called later?*

"Wait. Let me talk to Jenny. She just walked in."

A garbled conversation later, he said he could be home in the next half-hour. "And, Elle, I love you. This isn't about us, together. I mean you don't have to worry about that."

At least there's that. It's not about us. Someday it would be. But not today.

I rescheduled my appointment, then I sat. I stood. I perched. I paced. I walked around the family room in every geometric shape I knew. I counted the number of times my heels hammered the wood floors. I wished, instead of buying the crisply painted model home in the gated community, we'd opted for the 1930s redo. At least it had stairs I could have climbed. I checked my face in the mirror over the fireplace to see if I looked presentable, which was my mother's equivalent to unembarrassingly passable. My complexion was mottled, like I'd blushed in all the wrong places. Thirty minutes with a cosmetics artist at Sephora last month and still I applied makeup like a three-year-old. At least the bags under my eyes were lunch-bag and not full-blown, grocery-sack-size. Kudos to my lipstick because it lived up to its promise of light stain and shiny fullness. "Okay, we can do this," I muttered to my not-so-convincing reflection. I finger-combed my hair, then landed on the edge of the white leather ottoman and stared out the open shutters where I could watch Logan's BMW turn into the driveway.

His estimated arrival time passed. The slow march of minutes reminded me of days spent mentally pushing the second hand on the classroom clock forward, synchronizing—every tick an inch closer to bolting from the desk at the end of the school day. I dreaded this conversation with Logan. I had a heart made of glass and a hammer for a conscience. One day, the fractures would shatter from the truth, and I didn't know if I would survive.

Three minutes later. Still no silver car curling into the driveway. I re-examined my cuticles, but my hand-wringing did nothing to improve them. I checked my cell phone for a text message. None. If I'd been a campaign stop, he would have been early. And taken me to lunch. But Logan practically scripted conversations at restaurants after what we called the "Beth Bomb." The wife of one of Logan's other-party opponents had been overheard asking her husband over dinner at Tujague's if he thought the mayor's wife was pregnant or on her way to lap-band surgery.

"I'm sorry. It seems all I have to do sometimes is say that I'm leaving early, and people I've needed to talk to for days suddenly find the time to call," Logan said after finally walking through the back door. "Let's go to my office. The papers I need to show you are there."

Papers? He has papers? I mentally chewed my nails all the way down the hall.

He pulled a file from his desk, and we settled into the chairs across from it.

"After talking to Matt, I realized that it's hypocritical of me to promote myself as someone running a transparent campaign, only for you to find out I wasn't being transparent at home."

I could bear filmy. Streaks. Slightly opaque. "What exactly does that mean?" My fingers tightened around the chair arms.

"It was never my intention to not tell you about this, especially when I first became involved. Why would I want to keep an investment that could benefit us from you?" He opened the folder on his desk and spread out the pages.

Investment. My angst waved a white flag and retreated. "You forgot to tell me you invested in something that would benefit us? I wouldn't have been upset to find that out from you. Or anyone else, I suppose."

He winced as if I'd crunched his bare toes with my platform shoes. "It's not just the investment I wasn't transparent about. The project didn't move as quickly as we thought, and Sidney Carlyle, the developer, said we, meaning me and the other four investors, needed to come up with more money." Logan shuffled through the papers to show me an architect's drawing. "This is a city block downtown. The area around it is coming back, and Carlyle proposed building condos that looked like French Quarter doubles above first floor, high-end retail stores. We've butted heads with the historical commission on almost every aspect of this. They're insisting on changes like wrought iron instead of wood railings, special casement windows . . . it goes on and on. I still think it's viable, but the delays and the changes are killing us."

I heard the worry pulling his voice taut. "How killing?" I asked, controlling my anxiety to avoid straining an already tense discussion. "As in slow, painful death? Or immediate annihilation?"

He stared at the plans in his lap. When he looked at me, his eyes bore the weight of his apology. "I took a second mortgage out on the house. That kind of killing. And I took advantage of not needing you to sign off on it because the house is in my name," he said. "Added to not telling you about something that had the potential for a great return was not telling you about my taking money out of the house. I've invested—"

I put my hand on his mouth. "Don't tell me how much. You don't have to be transparent about that. Not now." I wasn't one of those wives completely oblivious to our finances, but I didn't have experience with developments like this. I had no basis of comparison for whatever amount he told me. I took the plans and looked them over. "With the added investment, will this happen?"

"Well, we're closer now, so, yes."

"Then we're not in danger of losing our house?"

"No, but we're talking about a chunk of money that, if we went to sell, we wouldn't see as profit," he said. "I guess, if everything blew up in our faces, we could move in with Martha." He managed to maintain a serious expression after he said that. I managed not to slap him.

"In that case, you might have to ask about a third mortgage." I returned the plans to him. "You've never done anything financially to put us at risk. I trust you. I'm sorry you worried about it."

"After borrowing more money, I realized that if I'd told you in the beginning, it wouldn't have been as difficult to be honest about everything else that happened." He closed the folder. "What's that saying about putting truth in a grave, but you can't keep in there?"

The truth rose in my throat. The words had been scripted, practiced, an endless loop of apology that waited and waited and waited. He would understand how one unexpected thing led to another and how, all those years, I meant only to protect him. I did what I could. Who could have predicted this?

"Logan, I want you to know . . ." I closed my eyes. If I didn't see him, it would be easier. I wouldn't have to watch the pain or anger overtake his expression. I wouldn't have to see the first strike of damage. I pulled my hands away from the comfort of his. "I've meant to . . . " Nothing. The words refused to release themselves. After years of being imprisoned, they wouldn't escape.

"Elle? What's wrong?" His words were as gentle as his fingertips that tucked my hair behind my ears, then lifted my chin until my face met his.

Not now. After the election. Let him have his dream.

"A year ago, this wouldn't have been such an issue. . . . I mean, I was working then, and we hadn't remodeled the house, and then your campaign . . ." After what he'd just shared about the money he'd invested, this seemed silly, even to me. But I was too far in now to back out.

"Okay . . ." he said. "Tell me where this is going."

"I bought a pair of Christian Louboutin shoes last week."

"And that's something to be upset about?"

"The shoes aren't. The price is."

He smiled and patted my hand. "Really? For one pair of shoes?"

"They cost $700.00. Before tax." I spoke softly to cushion the blow, but Logan's skin had already turned as pale as the peep-toe pumps in my closet.

"Really? You did say $700.00 before tax? I'm in the wrong business." He sighed. "Okay, you just made one of those spontaneous buying decisions. Honey, just return them."

"I can't return them. I already wore them."

The color that had seeped back into his face was flushed out again. Logan inched forward on the couch and settled his elbows on his knees, grasping his hands in front of him. The prelude to a serious discussion.

"Please tell me you didn't wear them to a political function. Or, if you did, that women wouldn't recognize how expensive they were. I'm talking to people who haven't worked in months or years, people who already think the divide between classes grows wider every year, people with hospital bills beyond what they earn in a year. If my wife is at my side in a pair of ridiculously expensive shoes, that sends a mixed message, don't you think?"

"I wore them to the Junior League fashion show and lunch. I haven't worn them as Mrs. Logan Butler, politician's wife. But, yes, they'd be recognizable to people who know Louboutins have red soles."

"It's not just the politics of it, Elle. You're not working. . . . It's just not the time."

"I didn't know at the time I bought them that you'd collateralized the building for a loan since you didn't bother to tell me until five minutes ago."

"You're right. I take full responsibility for that. That's why, from this point on, we have to be open with one another. It's not about the shoes. Well, maybe somewhat, considering . . . That was the whole point of that paperwork, Matt coming over, the vetting."

"I've got it. I've got it. But I wasn't comfortable telling you in front of Matt how much money I'd spent on something so impulsive and expensive."

"But that's exactly why Matt needs to know first. If some reporter asks why the candidate's wife is splurging on fashion while I'm encouraging financial responsibility, that's a problem. My opponent will use anything he can dredge up to his advantage. His side is vetting us too."

His side is vetting us too. If Logan heard the news from the other camp first, nothing would ever be the same between us. Ever.

Not long after I gave Matt all the written responses to everything everyone needed to know about my life, he called to suggest I step away from the fund-raising role of the center. "Since we met, I've been thinking about what you said about raising money for the center. Be the chairperson in charge or whatever title you want to give yourself, but ask someone in the committee you're forming to be responsible for all aspects involving money. The more distance between you and the funds, the better."

I explained I didn't have much of a committee yet since I'd just had the idea from working with the Junior League. Martha was involved, but then how could she not be? My mother-in-law would have immersed herself in campaigning to support the bubonic plague if she thought it would gain votes for her son. "And I suppose it's a no-brainer that Martha's out in that chairperson role as well?"

Matt laughed. "Not just out. But way out. As far away as you can push her, and I know that won't be easy."

The problem with finding someone wasn't that I'd decided to give legs to the idea or even that I hesitated to let go of the financial aspect of the project. The problem was since marrying Logan, moving to New Orleans, and role-playing Mrs. Butler, candidate's wife, I didn't have close friends.

I didn't share my friendless existence with Matt, though he knew by now almost all the details of my life. It sounded so pathetic, I didn't even want to hear myself say it. My two best friends from college moved right after graduation. One to Denver, the other to Boston. Stacey, Lauren, and I e-mailed, sometimes even Skyped, but none of the online chatting compensated for that person who called and asked, "Lunch?" and you knew without saying where to meet. Or the one who pulled three dresses out of the closet and said, "Ditch these," and you'd be grateful. Or the one who didn't need to ask why tears puddled in your eyes when a baby cried.

Logan thought I should or could make friends doing church-y things. I'd seen some of those "friendships" at work in my parents' church.

Our lips would be barely finished forming the "Amen" that ended grace before dinner when my mother would announce the news heard at Sunday school that morning. Most of it sounded like sanctioned gossip in the form of prayer requests. "Jane requested prayer for the Higgins family because their daughter Franny is having some problems with drugs, and Laura's husband might be losing his job soon. And Mary Beth asked if we'd pray for her and Warren. . . ." She'd pause to make sure my elbows weren't on the table before she finished telling my father whatever marital discord had befallen the poor Hamiltons.

I may not have known then how to answer the "what would Jesus do" question, but I knew what He wouldn't do. And that would be hang out at one sinner's house to talk about all the other sinners.

In my teens, I used to wonder what families like Jane's and Mary Beth's might be hearing about my own as they drank their iced teas and buttered their bread. My mother requested prayer so often, my father said he'd heard one of the church deacons wanted to propose a moratorium. But even with all the ways I'd sinned, as my parents frequently reminded me, it seemed my sins must have been either too ordinary or too detestable to grab Jesus' attention. My prayers went straight to voice mail, and I never knew if they'd even been heard.

I attended church with Logan often enough to not be labeled a heathen, but not too often for my name to have appeared on the Women's Prayer Group roster. The notion I'd ever find friends there was as likely as Angelina Jolie calling me to go shopping. Even the wives of the men helping Logan with his campaign treated me like the new girl in school who captured everyone's attention like a shiny Christmas ornament. Until the season ended, and then they were off to the next new glittering person. Why would I need to be included in playgroup scheduling or in strategizing ways to vault to the top of the pre-school admission list?

But, given a passion worth pursuing, I knew I could summon what and who I needed to make it happen. Teachers didn't nominate me to Leadership Camp for me to become a leader. I went because I was one. All I needed to start was a match to light the fire. Martha.

5

Martha surveyed the post-meeting kitchen clutter. "For the record," she always pointed her finger and smiled when she said that, like it was a photo op waiting to happen, "I think we had quite a successful first meeting."

We? I called twenty women, ordered and picked up antipasto and hummus platters, made two dozen avocado deviled eggs, baked two batches of caramel brownies, served coffee, hot tea, and mango peach tea. Martha arrived five minutes before everyone else and asked if she could help.

"I think so, too. I didn't expect that many members would show up," I said as I carried a stack of dessert plates to the sink. Even dirty, the vintage, hand-painted set that belonged to my grandmother looked pretty. I happened to be home between semesters when my mother added them to the stack of garage sale items because they were "such weird, artsy things. Who could stand all those colors and patterns when they're trying to eat?"

My mother worshipped at the altar of practical, slaying anything "crazy-cockeyed," which meant not black, white, or beige. That her own mother could own such bohemian-inspired, richly colored plates amused me, and it also reflected my grandmother's spirit of playfulness. I rescued the plates at a time in my life when I needed to rescue myself from life's dullness. And maybe because I knew my using them would drive my mother all routes to crazy. "Do you think we'll have enough people buy-in to get the center off the ground?"

Martha handed me a basket of used silverware. "Well, I'm worried we'll have too many. You probably should have talked to me before you called all those ladies."

I opened the dishwasher, avoided the knives while she stood nearby, and started loading in plates and forks. *This isn't the hill you want to die on, Elle. Not even the one for sustaining an injury.* I breathed in, a cleansing breath, and exhaled, imaging my aggravation surfing out on puffs of air. By the time I constructed a response that wouldn't be grounds for slander, she'd returned from the den with an almost full tray of brownies in one hand and a platter of antipasto remnants in the other.

"Whatever are you going to do with all this food?" She slid the trays on the table and looked at them as if she dared them to move.

How many hills are in this battle? I don't tell her there's a little dollop of egg stuffing on the long sleeve of her coral silk blouse because she'd have said I should have told her to wear a short-sleeved blouse or one that was a muted yellow. I sidestepped my prepared question about the next meeting and asked if she'd like me to send some food home with her.

"No, not tonight. It's the third Thursday of the month, remember?"

It didn't sound like a question. More like a recrimination. The question mark on my face cued her. "Girls' night out. We're all going to LaMancha's for Mexican Margarita Madness night. Though, I tell you," she lowered her voice as if her voice resonated beyond the house, "some of those girls need to slow down on the eating and the drinking."

"We'll talk later about organizing committees? I'm anxious to get a plan together—"

"Of course. It's better to let ideas marinate for a time, you know. Daniel always encouraged his people to not act quickly. He said the important things will rise to the top if we let them sit long enough." She walked away and returned, a coral Coach purse that matched her blouse, of course, on her arm and a smidge of impatience on her face.

"Whoa. You're in a hurry. It's not even five o'clock yet," I said as I continued to wash sticky platters.

Martha walked toward the door. "I know, but I have to pick up Deena on the way. Joe won't let her drive at night anymore. He told her he's tired of buying new mailboxes for everyone in the neighborhood." She pulled the door open. "Sometimes that man is so cheap."

I stopped, dried my hands, and participated in one of those stiff-bodied hugs as if we feared bruising one another. "Be careful. And have a good time."

I peeked through the shutters and watched her back out of our driveway. Martha hadn't endangered any mailboxes, but she kept the tire store in business grazing concrete curbs. She made it to the street without a blowout, and I returned to kitchen duty.

Martha was right about the meeting being a success, and like I'd hoped, she provided the hook I needed to reel women from Junior League into the project. She knew which families had children or adults with special needs, and being asked by the widow of the former state representative and mother of the hopeful state representative helped. Her influence made a difference, and I appreciated her support, even though she could be a human cactus. I just had to get past the prickly spines to value what was underneath.

———

I made sure Logan and I avoided LaMancha's for dinner that night and opted for shrimp po-boys at Dolese's, one of those generational family restaurants where the owners remembered when Logan was too young to see over the tops of the tables. What it lacked in ambience, unless walls decorated with neon beer signs and framed magazine pictures had become upscale, it made up for in heaping portions of near perfect, batter-fried seafood, layers of melted cheese with enough macaroni to be a legit side dish, and waitresses who called everyone "Baby."

Eating there was an unofficial campaign stop for Logan. We'd walk through the door, and before we even sat at a table, Papa Dolese wrapped his thick arm around Logan's shoulders and steered him around tables until he'd been introduced to everyone there. Customers' political affiliations mattered not to Papa D. He'd tell them, "I don't care if you vote donkey or elephant when you get in that booth. You just vote for my boy, Logan, here. He's a good kid. Known him since before he could talk. Makes up for it now, though. You listen to him. He'll do us proud." Depending on how busy the restaurant was that night, Logan might spend a half hour making rounds. In the meantime, I'd usually catch up with Tanya, our waitress, who'd show me the latest pictures of her grandkids and her two Pomeranians. Since it wasn't a weekend night, Logan returned in under fifteen minutes.

"One of these days, we'll come here and actually come straight to the table," Logan said as he unrolled his silverware.

I gave him one of Martha's pointed-finger-for-the-record gestures and said, "You better hope not. That might mean you lost the election." I fanned my napkin on my lap. "Besides," I said, squeezed his hand, and smiled, "you know you enjoy being courted by Mr. Dolese."

He grinned, but his eyes didn't. "I do. He's a great guy. Always has been," he said in a way that made it seem as if he apologized. "It's almost embarrassing to admit that he's treated me like a son." He tore off a chunk of hot French bread and passed it to me. "Then again . . . ."

I slathered butter on the bread and waited for him to finish the sentence. Logan didn't share much or often about his father, but I didn't want to fill in the blanks for him. I knew years of that kind of pain never spilled out all at once. If it did, I'd be a jellyfish, with nothing left to hold me up. But, if I siphoned it out in bits, I could heal. With time.

Logan moved his spoon through the dark, thick bowl of gumbo. "After my high school graduation, my father said we could go anywhere in the city to eat. 'You pick the place. Commander's Palace, Galatoir's . . . wherever you want to go,' he told me. I said I wanted to come here." He stopped to chew. "It wasn't the place he expected me to name. He said something about my taste being in another part of my anatomy, not in my mouth. At first, he refused. I told I him I wouldn't go anywhere else. Before we left for the ceremony, I overheard my mother tell him if he kept his promises to his voters, the least he could do is keep them for his kid." Logan smiled. "Martha actually had my back that day. Didn't happen as often as I hoped, but I really appreciated it. My mother trotted out some excuse that my father didn't like Mr. Dolese acting like I was his son."

I squeezed my lemon into my iced tea, and over Logan's shoulder I watched as the waiter moved a table away from the wall to accommodate the baby bump of a woman clearly close to delivery. Her husband held her chair until she was seated, and because he stood behind her, she couldn't see his expression of raw joy as he looked at her. I felt like I'd trespassed on a private moment. I diverted my attention from the couple to Logan. "Maybe it wasn't that your father didn't like Mr. Dolese acting that way. Maybe he didn't like that you enjoyed it," I said.

"That's another reason I decided I could never be a father. I never felt as if I really had one to learn from."

"But can't learning what not to do teach us what we could do?" I thought of my mother and Martha, who maybe thought of me the same way.

"I don't know, Elle, but . . . " He stopped when the waitress appeared at our table. He moved his empty gumbo bowl aside, and she set between us a fried seafood platter holding a small mountain of golden-brown shrimp, oysters, soft shell and stuffed crabs, and catfish, all finely dusted with golden-brown batter.

"Coming back with your coleslaws, hush puppies, and tartar sauces soon as I get their order," she nodded in the direction of table with the pre-parent couple. "Y'all get started while it's hot."

Logan winked at me and smiled at the waitress. "You don't look old enough to sound like my mother," he told her.

Every wrinkle and crease in her face smiled back. "Shame on you. Flirting with me with your pretty wife sitting here." She tapped him on the shoulder with her pencil as she walked off.

Witnessing her reaction, I chastised myself for assuming Logan was turning on his politician persona with his comment. They both knew he was teasing, but she clearly appreciated his effort in being charming. And just as clearly, I was rebuked by the question I'd just asked my husband.

Logan started dividing the seafood onto our plates. "Anyway, to finish what I was trying to tell you before. I know I don't have to be my father. But I'm not going to take that chance. Not with someone's life."

"I understand," I said. I didn't add that I disagreed. I wanted to say the difference for him would be that I wasn't Martha. I wouldn't allow the cycle to repeat itself. But I didn't know how willing I was to take that chance.

The Junior League volunteer hours I needed weren't happening, and the whole thing was beginning to remind me of homework or the dreaded research paper. All very albatross-y.

Too bad I couldn't count hours spent with Martha because I came away from every meeting with her feeling as if I'd sacrificed part of myself. The morning after her dinner out, she sent me a text at 8:00. "I'M COMING OVER." All caps was her preferred method of communication, which wasn't surprising for a woman for whom attention was as much a requirement as her daily vitamin D and calcium. Within ten seconds after the text, she rang the doorbell. I didn't have to open the door to verify she waited on my porch. Every time she pushed the doorbell button, it was as if I'd been transported to the center of Casino Royale with its constant dinging.

I shoved the stack of clothes and towels I'd been folding back into the dryer, made sure dirty dishes weren't lounging in the sink, and opened the door. "Hi. Come on . . ." But she was already in before the word dropped out of my mouth. "This is a surprise," I said, daring my voice to be anything less than gracious.

"Surprise?" Martha set her now navy blue purse, designed to coordinate with her jeans, I guessed, on the coffee table.

"Weren't we supposed to be discussing yesterday's get-together and strategizing our next course of action?" She pulled her iPad out of her purse and waved it as she spoke. I guessed she meant it as some magic wand to start my neurons firing or she imagined herself slapping me with it. She flipped open the cover and showed me her calendar entry for the day. "See? There you are."

Yep. Right there. I still didn't understand how or why, but with Martha those questions were inconsequential. "I must have been confused yesterday. I thought we were going to talk today about when we could meet next. But, no problem." I allowed myself one tiny sigh for effect as I looked at my watch. "I promised the PTA president of the new elementary school that I'd help get the classrooms ready, so we won't be able to talk too long."

Her eyes narrowed at the word "won't," but the gods of favor had already smiled on me, and I was prepared. I offered the raised hands apology shrug. "Have to keep working on those League hours." Score one for Team Elle Butler.

She nodded, her suspicious glare replaced by our mutual understanding of the demands of the Junior League. "We'll just do what we can, save the rest for later," she said. She looked toward the kitchen. "Do you have coffee?"

"Of course. Why don't you help yourself to a cup? I'll grab my notes and meet you in the kitchen."

Three cups of coffee and two bagels later, Martha and I came up with a plan for fund-raising, a design plan, and publicity committees.

"There's one problem. None of this will work without land. We don't even have possible locations," I said.

"For now, I'll handle looking for property. You'd be surprised what's for sale in this little town," Martha said. "And some of it isn't property, if you know what I mean."

I'd finished my coffee seconds before she finished her sentence, which saved me from choking. My mother-in-law with an edge. Maybe I didn't know her as well as I thought. "I'm guessing you're not referring to the car dealerships, right?" I smiled.

She closed her iPad and stared at me with that same look of concentration I saw on Logan's face when he read briefs. "No, not car dealerships," she said like she soaked the words in vinegar before she spoke them.

Martha missed the cue that smiling meant I got it. Why did she think I wouldn't, and why did conversations with this woman have to be tennis matches? All we lacked was a line judge shouting, "Fault!" anytime we went out of bounds. Maybe we needed one of those.

"Oh, I knew that. I thought, well, it doesn't matter. I appreciate your scouting for a location for the center," I said.

After Martha entered the date for our next committee meeting in her calendar and set up e-mail reminders for both of us, she left. She didn't volunteer information about where she was headed, which was uncharacteristic. Martha often shared her daily agenda as evidence of her importance or notice of her availability. No doubt a text or phone call was in my future to provide details she neglected.

It's not like Logan hadn't cautioned me before I met his mother. "Try not to take what she says personally. She's one of those people with no filter between her brain and her mouth. It's as if she uses what spills out to build walls between her and people who might invade her personal space. The only person she didn't do that with was my father. Whenever he was around, she bit her lip. And I mean she really did."

Her lips seemed perfectly fine now.

My cell phone rang on the way home from the school, but I didn't recognize the number and I let it go to voice mail. It's what I was instructed to do, and I did. When Logan asked Matt to manage his campaign, one of the first conversations we had was about conversations. "If you don't know who's calling you, don't answer the phone. If it's important, they'll leave a message. We don't want to wake up and hear a private cell phone conversation on the news, or worse yet, YouTube. And we also don't want some idiot calling with threats."

Idiot, stalker, wrong number didn't leave a message. Which reminded me I hadn't talked to my mother in weeks. Of course, she hadn't called me either, but I always lost that fight. "Children should call their parents. Camden calls, and she lives three minutes away. You're three hours away," my mother said months ago when we had the verbal volleyball about who should call whom. Camden, my older sister, moved back to Lafayette after dental school, then opened an orthodontic practice. She married Nick Fortunado when he came to her office to sell medical supply equipment right after she opened her practice. Their barely potty-trained son, almost three, was deposited at my mother's house four mornings a week by one of his parents. My mother had brought on two other dentists because she only wanted to work part-time. She decided that she could afford to help with her grandson until he started school.

When I'd relayed the phone call mandate with Camden, she responded with, "I'm glad she finally said something. I lost track of how many times a week she said, 'Elle never calls me,' and 'I suppose being a politician's wife is more important than being my daughter.'" Sometimes my sister would text me, "CALL HER," when mother's whining was at full-scale pitch.

6

The gate was open when I turned into our neighborhood, as it often was during the day, to allow construction and service trucks access. According to Martha's real estate agent friend, Dootsie, who sold us the property, just the presence of a gate, open or closed, increased our home value. But even in real estate, security wasn't always what it seemed.

Small oak trees planted ten feet from one another lined each side of the three-mile drive to the Timberlake Country Club, which was the first sign of bricked civilization after entering the gates. Logan joined the club, but that was a given from the beginning. I think the club wanted him on their membership rolls as much as he wanted to be a member. Politics survived on symbiotic relationships, and this one had an affluent ecosystem.

I hesitated to describe where we lived as a neighborhood. While we had neighbors by virtue of homes on either side of us, most of the residents were not neighborly. Most of them weren't home during the day because they were working. The ones who were home didn't venture beyond their own driveways. Streets looked like abandoned Hollywood stage sets. If

I hadn't lived there myself, I'd wonder if some of those house exteriors were propped-up facades.

As the garage door groaned its way open, my cell phone rang again, the same number that showed up thirty minutes ago. The area code indicated Baton Rouge, but I hadn't been there since college and what friends I had, moved away. I checked, and still no voice mail.

Before I started weeding the garden, which provided cheap therapy as well as a neat landscape, I threw on my mismatched sweats. Just in case that number showed up on my phone again, I logged online and Googled it. That, and a check of the White and Yellow Pages, turned up nothing. Probably a wrong number or persistent crank caller. *Speaking of . . . my mother. I need to call my mother.*

I punched in my mother's number and picked at the small feathers that hatched out of the variegated tan and white linen weave of the sofa. A hand-me-down from Martha, but its age didn't make it any less comfortable. Just as I hoped the call would switch to her voice mail, my mother answered.

"Hold on, Elizabeth. Nick is finishing on the potty." Family legend has it that when they brought me home from the hospital, Camden decided the name Elizabeth was "too long to say or spell or write." She anointed me "Elle," and for everyone in the family but my mother, the name stuck. Her tone melted and honey poured out in the direction of my nephew. "Aren't you, sweetheart?" I pictured the two of them in the gray and pink tiled bathroom that, in the span of time my parents lived in their house, had gone from contemporary to outdated and now to fashionable retro.

"I can call back." (*Yes, yes, please.*) "Or you could call me at a better time," I offered. (*Is there ever?*)

"No. I can handle a two-year-old and talking on the phone."
Again in her lilting, candied tone she told Nick, "Grammy is
very proud of you. Here's your cookie."

"A cookie for a poop. What a payoff," I said.

"He didn't *poop*, at least not this time, and Camden said I
needed to reward him whenever he used the toilet."

"I didn't mean it to sound as if I was accusing you. I meant it
to be funny." Maybe I should schedule my calls in the evening.
After a glass of wine. For me or her or both of us. "Anyway, I
didn't call to discuss Nick and his bathroom visits. How are
you?" I prepared myself to find out.

"Doing better since you called me a month ago. I had a
miserable sinus infection, the central air unit died, and Larry
the serviceman came out to fix it. We've been doing business
with him for years, but he still charged me a small fortune to
replace it, and then the anniversary of your father's death was
two days ago. I thought, since you hadn't called me, you might
have sent flowers to his grave. I didn't see any there."

I had failed. Again. Yet, again. I walked to my office, grabbed
my planner, and checked the date. I had the twenty-fifth circled,
but nothing written down. *Good grief, Camden. Why didn't you
remind me?*

"Are you there, Elizabeth?"

"Yes, I'm here." I sat in my desk chair, my legs crossed, like I
could stop my stomach from plunging further down my body.
"I'm sorry I didn't call or send flowers. I don't know what happened . . . but it has been fifteen years." I didn't want to forget
or to remember that year. She knew that. "Look, not sending
flowers doesn't mean I don't miss or didn't love Dad."

Nick Junior pleaded, "More cookie, Grammy, pa-leeze and
tank you." Nick Junior had his dad's scowl and my sister's tem-
per. What saved him from eternal time-outs was his entirely
adorable grin.

Smart kid. Already working the politeness in his favor. In the background, the familiar rattling of that nerdy yellow Happy Face ceramic cookie jar, the top glued together after I dropped it on the kitchen floor trying to sneak out a few Oreos before dinner. I wasn't much older than Nick, and Camden tried to fix it, but we were both caught in the act and banned from cookies for two weeks.

"I'm sure you were busy doing all those important political things you need to do. I guess you had no idea what you were getting yourself into," she said.

I bit my lower lip.

Oh, God, I'm becoming Martha.

I yanked my garden gloves on and marched to the front yard, a human tank propelled by frustration, disappointment, and resentment. I yanked weeds out of flower beds with a vengeance. Every one became some memory, some sin, some shame buried in my life. *Enough. Enough. Enough. You will not own me, you will not kill all the good I've planted, you will not take over my life.* Some plants had roots longer than they were tall, and I used both hands to trench underneath to remove them. Other roots didn't resist, but they crawled under the soil in every direction. I wondered which of these my mother thought I had been and maybe still was in her life. I was pulled out easily and quickly. But I don't think she suspected that she'd have to deal with all those parts of me slowly pushing their way through and learning how to thrive.

When my fingers felt arthritic from weeding, I left my gloves in the garage, pulled off my sweatpants that were muddy and soggy where I'd knelt, and kicked off my shoes. I put on a pair of clean shorts in the laundry room, caught a whiff of my sweaty self, and decided to head for the shower instead. On the way to the bathroom, I checked my cell phone for messages. The first one was from Logan reminding me he'd be late that night because he was scheduled to speak at the Rotary Club's annual banquet. The second message was from the mystery number that had called twice before.

"I'm trying to reach Elizabeth Claiborne Butler. If I have the correct number, would you please call me as soon as possible as there's a situation I need to discuss with you. My name is Holly Taylor and my private cell phone number is . . ."

I felt as if I'd been smashed between two steel doors, then subjected to full-body acupuncture. The last time I experienced this nightmarish fear was, of all places, in Disney World. The summer after my second year in college, my friend Tammy's family invited me to join them on vacation. Her teenaged brother dragged us into some alien invasion attraction, and I spent every second in claustrophobic terror. Harnessed and restrained in my seat in suffocating darkness, the hot steamy breath of an escaped monster wet the back of my neck as my seat rumbled and warm water spewed on my face. The shrieks and screams vibrated and pulsed in the circular chamber, and not even Tammy, trapped next to me, could hear me beg for someone to get me out. Until that day, I didn't know my heart could pound as if it would break through my chest wall.

I folded my hands over my heart as if I could have mashed it back into my body if it pushed its way out of my chest. But this ride might not end because the monster that was regret usually invaded without warning.

—◦◦◦—

My mother hadn't approved of my marrying Logan. She exhausted herself attempting to convince me to end the engagement. When I set the wedding date, she said she wouldn't be there. When Camden agreed and told my mother that not attending would probably be best, she changed her mind. "I'll be there, but don't expect me to be happy." I explained to her that I didn't expect her to feel happy, but I sure expected her to look happy. I knew her capacity for impersonation. I'd seen it after my father died before the end of my junior year.

How she pretended we were all "fine and adjusting and glad to know he was with the Lord." My mother, at some point, turned on the televisions in the family room and in her bedroom and blasted the sound. Our neighbors may have wondered if Oprah had actually dropped in to visit. At first, people in the church brought food. Enough food that it didn't matter if my mother stayed in the same clothes for days and curled up in the fetal position so long and so often that I thought she might give birth to herself. When the food ran out, I found her credit cards and went to the grocery. Sometimes ordered in. Two months later, she resurrected herself but not her relationship with me. Not fully.

When I told my mother Logan had asked me to marry him, she turned off the red beans and rice she'd been cooking, walked past me into her bedroom, and closed the door. I called Camden, who said if Mom hadn't surfaced by 5:00 to text her and she'd call after her last patient. "Just let her be for now, Elle. She probably just didn't want to say anything she'd regret later. Give her time to think through this." By 5:00 she was still thinking because she hadn't left her room, and she wouldn't respond to Camden's calls or texts.

"I've waited two hours to talk to you," I said to my mother's bedroom door. "I almost can't believe I'm going to say this, but you're acting like a spoiled brat with the passive-aggressive behavior."

I leaned forward, my forehead and palms pressed against the door as if I was readying myself to push it open. Not only didn't I have the physical strength, my already exhausted emotional strength refused to prepare for another round in my mother's fight. "Whoever said this was supposed to be one of the happiest days of my life lied. Again. I thought you Christians were all over that 'Jesus forgives us, then we should forgive others' vaudeville act you trot out." My hands beat the door until my palms throbbed and burned. I squeezed my eyes shut and demanded they forbid the tears that already burned them to fall. "Where is your forgiveness?" With each syllable, my hands again hammered the door.

I dried my eyes with the hem of my blouse. A new silk blouse I'd bought to visit her. A blue the color of the irises she loved. She might never know.

"Okay, you win. I'm leaving now," I told her, my voice as weary as my spirit.

I'd already taken a few steps down the hall when the latch clicked.

"Elizabeth." She called my name the way lovers do after they part, as if it could travel through the air and wrap itself around the person leaving and pull him back.

I stopped. I counted to ten. I'd waited over two hours, she could wait less time than it took to cook an egg in a microwave. I turned to face her. My hands clenched, and I felt the crescent moon each fingernail pressed into my palms.

"I can forgive. I have forgiven. But Jesus didn't say we had to forget." Her words fell to the floor. Too insubstantial to bridge the gap between us.

I never knew how long she stood in the open doorway. Or maybe she didn't. Maybe she shut the door and returned to her cocoon. Maybe she walked through it and stood on the other side.

I left. We didn't see one another for months afterward. But sometimes I allowed myself to imagine that she called my name that day until she was breathless.

—⊸∞⊷—

I cradled my cell phone as if the bomb squad would storm in soon and detonate it. How had Holly Taylor found me? But even more disturbing, why? And what did she have to say as soon as possible? That was somewhere between "call at your leisure" and "your urgent attention is needed or it may be too late." She hadn't said, "As soon as you receive this message." That would have been a level closer to urgent, so if I don't call within minutes after hearing the message, I'd still be in the acceptable range. *Right?* Right.

I sat on the floor outside the bathroom, hugged my knees, and rocked back and forth. I hadn't heard Holly's voice for fifteen years. Back and forth. And even with all the time and miles between us, I knew she wouldn't have contacted me unless there was no other choice. Back and forth. Orphanage syndrome. Logan's press secretary and her husband were in the throes of an international adoption. They were told by the placement counselors at the adoption agency that they might witness many of the children rocking back and forth, a behavior known as *orphanage syndrome*. It was a child's way of soothing himself when afraid or hurt because he didn't have parents to comfort him. Sitting on the floor of my house, I was all of those things—hurt, afraid, relatively parentless, and trying to calm myself.

The phone call had to be made. And, just in case Logan might decide to come home early, I knew one place where I could ensure my privacy. I went into the bathroom, locked the door, and reclined in the empty bathtub. If the God I hadn't

60

paid much attention to considered a do-over on praying, would "help me" count as a pin-sized hole of communication? Even though my finger trembled as it punched in Holly's number, this was one call I didn't want to go to voice mail.

Five rings. Six. Seven. Eight. Nine rings. She answered after the tenth.

"Holly?" Please let it be her.

"Hi, Elle." Her voice still had that fuzzy blanket softness. "It's been a long, long time, I know."

I nodded just like Nick Junior who thinks his mother can see him when they talk on the telephone.

"Are you still on the line, Elle?"

"Sorry, yes. I was agreeing with you. You just couldn't see me. Because I was nodding my head." She must have thought my mind had deteriorated if she judged by my conversational skills.

"I'm going to get right to the reason I called because I suspect you already know it wasn't to catch up on the last fifteen years." She took a breath. "This is the most unusual case I've had in all my twenty years. In fact, I think it's the only one."

She paused and every muscle in my body contracted.

"Faith's parents died two days ago in an accident. I'm calling because her only option now is foster care, unless she can live with you and Logan."

7

If. Faith. Can. Live. With. Me?" I heaved every word out of my brain and into my mouth. I felt like someone regaining consciousness in an unfamiliar room or house or life.

"Yes, but—"

"But? But? There is no but," I said. "I'm in a bathtub in my bathroom. A bathroom. A locked bathroom in case my husband comes home while I'm talking. Do you know how ridiculous this is? I mean, could you have given me some warning in your voice mail? What sane adult locks herself in a bathroom to have a conversation?" By this time I had maneuvered myself to the toilet, where I sat and braced my forehead on the sink. "Granite. We had to have granite. It's cold and I misjudged the distance and now my head hurts and Logan will want to know how and why I have a bruise on my forehead, especially from the sink, and what am I supposed to tell him? What, Holly, am I supposed to tell him?"

She might not have understood the last few words because they were punctured by deep-breathing, spit-producing hysteria. I grabbed the end of the toilet tissue. The holder spun like a roulette wheel and yards of soft tissue draped on the floor.

I didn't bother to tear any off. I wiped my runny nose and moved on to the next section.

"Elle, I understand—"

"Oh, really, you do?" I paused. "Ha!" I patted tissue underneath my eyes. "Oh, and I suppose you know what it's like because somebody asked you to take back the baby you gave up fifteen years before?" I shook my head and pointed at invisible Holly in front of me. "No! No, you don't. How dare you pretend that you do."

Silence. I shook my cell phone to make Holly reappear the way I shook my Etch-a-Sketch and waited for what I'd drawn to disappear. Still silence. "Holly? Are you still on the phone? Holly?" My slobbery, hiccupping crying waned, but a fleet of goosebumps traveled the length of my shivering body.

"I'm here. Let's meet for lunch tomorrow. Can you do that?"

"I-I'm not sure. Wait. I'll have to check my calendar, but it's in my office." *Office. I have to walk to my office.* I located my planner. "Okay, Holly. Can you meet me at Marigny's Restaurant by noon tomorrow?" I'd be less likely to run into my husband, mother-in-law, or any friends or foes since it was on the other side of town.

Once again I planned to be where I might not be seen.

Over fifteen years ago, I had gone through yet another day where I suspected, once again, my period was not going to arrive. I told my mother I needed to attend a workshop for student council that wouldn't be over until noon and the officers and I were going to lunch after that. She worked half-days on Saturdays, so she'd be occupied instead of trying to call me.

"That's fine. But don't forget, the deacon installation program's tomorrow, and you told me you'd go shopping with me at the mall. For once, it's your father who has nothing to wear," she said as she dusted the toast crumbs from breakfast off the front of her navy blue scrubs. "And be careful."

Probably too late for that. "No worries. I'll be back in time." It would have been nice if my period were too.

Before I left my house, I had looked up drugstores in Jefferson, a city an hour's drive from home. Not only was I not going to risk being seen buying pregnancy tests, I planned to buy five kits to compensate for any false positive readings. And I refused to buy them all at one store. That would be more embarrassing than Will Arnold, who sat next to me in geometry, checking me out at the grocery with my boxes of tampons and pads with wings. He had grinned as I loaded them all on the belt, which made me want to step on my own toes. But, no. Instead, I waved my hand over the collection and said, "These aren't just for me. They're for my mom, too. These," I stopped and separated all the extra large variety, "are hers." Will leaned over as he scanned the last box. "TMI, Claiborne, TMI."

I walked into the drugstores wearing my sunglasses, and I stretched my 5'8" self, counting the two-inch platform shoes, as if someone above me pulled a string attached to the top of my head.

On the way home, having spent over a hundred dollars of my birthday and Christmas money to buy sticks to pee on, I stopped at Starbucks and PJs coffeehouses along the way. I knew they had single bathrooms, which would make the awkward fumbling and three-minute waiting I anticipated less humiliating. By the third Starbucks, I knew there'd be no more studying needed for this test, but I forced myself to stop at one more. Three minutes later, I'd passed another one with plus signs. I threw the unopened fifth one in the trash can, and I drove us home.

Who knew that opening a bathroom door would forever divide my life? The woman I was when I opened the door would forever be a shadow of the one who closed it after my conversation with Holly.

Breathing became more of a priority than dinner. My lungs felt twisted inside my chest, and yet I felt this weird compulsion to run. Run until the current surging through the circuit of my veins shorted itself out. But Holly's call just flipped the switch I thought I'd turned off over a decade ago. I retreated to the backyard deck to escape the confining walls of the house. I sat in the glider that hung from the upper beams of the pergola. White jasmine vines curled around the cedar beams and spilled over the sides, tangled curtains of leaves and flowers. I watched the sun melt into the evening sky, and I wondered if my future was sinking with it. Drowning in a past I thought I'd drained from my life.

The lights from the streetlamps blocked the stars. I hated that about the suburbs. The smell of jasmine surrounded me and saturated the lazy evening air. It wasn't fragrant, it was flatulent. A text from Logan interrupted my garden reverie. "Be home in 1 hour. Love u." The man's campaigning for a congressional seat and pressing "y" and "o" was exhausting his pointer finger? One of those vetting things Matt should have caught in case an opponent ever hijacked Logan's iPhone.

An hour would give me enough time to shower and be in bed, and if not sleeping, at least pretending to be. Survival meant I had to will myself to be numb, to replace the chaos in my brain with order and logic. I counted each time the glider shifted back and forth. I counted the cedar planks on the three steps that led to a benched seating area and table near the built-in grill. I counted the years and months and weeks since that day. The day I was scared I'd remember and afraid I'd forget. The day I last looked at my daughter's face, breathed in the just-bathed scent of her, kissed her forehead, and whispered in her ear the line from *I'll Love You Forever* that my mother read to Cam and me, "I'll love you for always, and as long as I'm living my baby you'll be."

And then she was gone.

No one had informed the baby of the due date. Every morning that passed after it, I woke up thinking, "This could be the day." Then at night I lowered myself onto my bed thinking, "Maybe tomorrow." When I found sleep impossible at night because of the little gymnast in my belly, I rocked in my grandmother's bentwood rocker. Sometimes the rocker's graceful S-shaped curves calmed both of us and swayed us into sleep.

Four crossed out days on the calendar later, I woke up with Braxton Hicks contractions, which I'd experienced for almost a month. When they first started, I thought I might be in labor too soon. But my doctor explained they were false contractions and told me the name came from the doctor who first described them. "Just be happy the doctor's name wasn't Poindexter Finkleburg." I loved Dr. Phillips. She and my sister mothered me through my pregnancy. But when the pains radiated around my swollen belly and came at regular intervals, I called Camden. "I'm having contractions. Well, I think that's what they might be."

My labor lasted almost ten hours. Camden and I had been to pre-natal and Lamaze classes together. She was the only family member I wanted in the delivery room. That night, when Faith slipped out all red and glistening, I waited to hear her first cry, watched them dry and poke and prod her, and then closed my eyes. I repeated to myself, "She's not mine. She's not mine." It was an endless loop I had been chanting from the day I felt her first flutterings in my womb.

The next morning, when the nurse wheeled her in, I only saw her little apple face because the rest of her was wrapped snugly in a soft pink and white blanket that reminded me of an ice cream cone. The nurse asked if I wanted to hold her. I felt the uncomfortable tingling in my breasts because the milk my body wanted to produce had nowhere to go. I shook my head and looked away. "Are you sure? She'll be going home soon," she said. I knew she was only trying to be kind, but I needed to lash out at someone. Swollen with grief and sadness and anger, I wanted to push all of those feeling out of me like I'd pushed out my baby. Overnight I'd aged from 16 to 106, and yet my heart sobbed like I was a two-year-old. I didn't even face the nurse. I stared through the slatted blinds at the bits and pieces of buildings and sky. "Of course I'm sure. I've been sure for the past six months. Please take her away. Now. I don't want to hold her again. I don't want to see her." I waited until I heard the bump as the door met the jamb before I dressed and waited for my mother. She was at the hospital already, making sure her grandchild went home with another family.

The family that was now giving her back.

8

When I heard the chime after he unlocked the front door, I checked the clock on my nightstand. Logan smelled like stale beer and a fresh ashtray when he walked in the bedroom an hour after the hour he said he'd be home and kissed my forehead. Since those weren't scents of any colognes he owned, I suspected he'd stopped by The Office after the meeting. A clever name for what was billed to be an upscale bar, but the upper case deception only succeeded until the spouse of the missing spouse realized no one was in the lower case office. Eventually, only visitors or newcomers cackled and knee slapped about the bar's name.

I wished I had fallen asleep because a slideshow of images of the past wouldn't stop playing against the backdrop of my closed eyes. But only an academy award performance would have enabled me to have a conversation with Logan that night. Since I wasn't capable of that, I feigned sleep. He mustn't have been inebriated or else he'd have toe-snubbed and wall-hugged by now. He opened and closed his dresser drawers as if the slightest sound would have triggered an alarm, turned off his lamp, then he eased himself into bed. When Logan moved next to me, he whispered, "I love you, Elle." His lips pressed softly against my shoulder, then he pulled up the sheet and tucked it under my chin.

What have I done? What am I doing? All the years I held the truth hostage and waited. Years I convinced myself that protecting Logan was honorable, for the greater good. Especially since I didn't see him for years after that summer. I believed the words of T.S. Eliot's poem I memorized my senior year, "There will be time, there will be time to prepare a face to meet the faces that you meet." Except there won't be time. I was Montag on the beach, filling a sieve with sand. No more beach. No more sand. No more lies. *How far can forgiveness stretch?*

I woke up hung over with guilt, shame, fear. My body felt like a toxic waste dump of putrid emotions. I rolled over, no longer able to avoid facing Logan, and prepared to look happy. Even prepared for what we hadn't shared in a while, and that was making love. Instead, I must have looked surprised because wherever Logan was, it wasn't in bed. I sat up and tried following his tracks. A white T-shirt collapsed on the floor by the closet, a damp towel decorated the closet doorknob, and three neckties, one orange, one blue-green paisley, and one navy and gray striped, lounged on the back of the slipper chair. I left the comfort of bed and found a half-full mug of coffee on the bathroom counter near his sink and a note taped to the mirror over mine.

"E—Forgot about Community Prayer Breakfast this morning at The Scrambled Egg. Will call you on my way to office. Might need you to pick up a few things if you're planning to be out today. My mother left me a message for you to call her??? Love you, L."

I pulled the paper off the mirror, tossed it in the wastebasket, and wished I could have trashed my irritation along with it. I hadn't even brushed my teeth yet, and I already felt overwhelmed. Fear and stress roiled in my stomach. Thinking about the day ahead reminded me of watching the news, years ago, as Hurricane Katrina gained strength, and we waited and braced ourselves for catastrophic winds and tidal waves. The hurricane we hoped the city would never experience, like the phone call I never expected to get. Destined to wreak havoc and slam into the shore of my life. We knew we'd never escape destruction. The question was the extent of the devastation. I braced myself as I hung my head over the sink. Tears burned my eyes and bile rose in my throat. I'd survive. But at what cost?

Take one small step forward, Elle. One small step. I washed my face. I brushed my teeth. Two small victories.

Agenda: call Logan, breathe. Call Martha, breathe more deeply. Confirm with Holly.

Logan sent me a text while I stood in the closet trying to decide between my white swing dress or a green eyelet sleeveless one, as if the choice might influence the day's outcome. He asked if I'd stop at the print shop to pick up the new campaign signs. I messaged back that it wouldn't be a problem. I then realized I needed to not have him and Martha calling or texting me during lunch. If I failed to answer either one of them the first time, they persisted and persisted and persisted because "something might have happened to me." I finally had explained to both of them one day that if the something that happened was my being kidnapped, held at gunpoint, profusely bleeding, or some other atrocious event, it was unlikely I'd answer anyway. But, it was an exercise in futility. That's when I learned to be proactive. I always told one or the other of any events that might necessitate my going off the radar. I called Logan's office and chatted with Jenny for a few minutes about the woes of orthodontia and teens. I asked her to please tell Logan I'd be meeting a friend from high school who happened to be in town and I'd call him on my way home.

Back to my fashion crisis. The times I experienced this total inability to select something to wear was one of the times I most missed having a friend, an I'll-always-tell-you-when-you-have-broccoli-in-your-teeth kind of friend. Someone who wouldn't be at all surprised to have a Skype conversation with me while I stood in my closet wearing only a T-shirt and my uncertainty. I decided the eyelet dress looked far too optimistic, so I opted for the white dress with cap sleeves since my arms were about as toned as Jello. I slipped it on, turned to one side and then the other in the full-length mirror long enough to determine my rear didn't look like the continental ocean shelf and my knees weren't exposed. I wore the black onyx necklace from Tiffany's, a birthday present from Logan, and spritzed perfume on my neck.

I called Martha. She wanted to pick me up so we could look at potential properties for the center that Dootsie, her real estate friend located for us, and "it wouldn't take long." In Martha-speak, that meant maybe less than four hours. As anxious as I was to view the possible locations, I couldn't risk being late for lunch.

"Can we plan another day? I already have a lunch date today," I said and wiggled my feet into white sandals.

"Oh," she said sounding confused. "Someone from the League?" A hopeful question.

"No," I said. My toes looked like refugees from pedicure camp. "It's someone I knew in high school who happens to be in town." I kicked off the sandals.

"Well, that's nice." She said it the way I heard Camden praise Nick Junior after he showed her his scribbles in his coloring book. "What brings her our way? Is she going to be here long?"

A disaster. That's what brings her here. "Business. She works for . . . " I stared at the ceiling as if an answer would materialize there. "She works for, um, a wholesale supply company. The name escapes me right now." My flair for generalities was impressive. "I'm not sure when she's leaving." I located a pair of black, closed-toe flats to replace the sandals.

"I'll contact Dootsie and reschedule us. Any day I shouldn't set this up?"

Sure, with my stable of friends, I'm overbooked. "No . . . wait, I need to make an appointment at the nail salon. How about Saturday? Logan may even be able to get free to come with us."

"Great idea, Elle. I'll call her now."

I think I heard a smile in her voice before we ended the call at the notion that Logan might join us.

I checked my makeup and swiped on lip gloss. One final, full-length mirror check. Would Holly recognize me? Or would she look at the woman standing before her and see the young girl with the fractured heart?

<hr>

The sticks didn't lie, and I had to tell my parents. I sat on my bed, cross-legged, elbows propped up on knees, and held my head in my hands. I was terrified. My teeth chattered while the rest of my body shivered in the sweaty, sweltering August sun that baked our house from the outside.

I called Camden, relieved she answered. She said I'd caught her between classes.

When I tried to say her name, my words cracked into syllables and I sounded like a wounded animal.

"Elle, Elle, what's wrong? Are you okay? Did something happen to Mom or Dad? You're scaring me."

"I . . . I'm," I sniffed, one of those loud, wet sniffs that sends everything phlegm to the back of your throat. "Oh, God, Camden, I'm . . . I'm . . . preg—"

She finished the word for me. "Pregnant. You're pregnant." Her voice flat, clinical. "How far along are you?"

"Two periods. I've missed two periods. That's all I know."

She asked me the date of my last period and told me to hold on while she did the math. She said, "The end of March. That's about when the baby would be due."

Due? I hadn't thought of due. "Are you sure?"

"Well, I'm in dental school, not medical school, but I can go on the web later and find a due date calendar to figure out a more exact date. The baby's probably not much bigger than a grape at this point."

I looked at my stomach. Something the size of a grape was making my jeans difficult to zip? I blew my nose. Camden mumbled something, and a door closed in the background.

"Okay, I'm back. That was someone in my study group asking about lunch. Just asked her to bring something back for me. You're more important than a platter of nachos. That should brighten your day, right?"

"Of course. Sure, bright enough that I'm about to need sunglasses." I sniffled and smiled. A real smile for the first time in the past few days, and it took some of my chest pain and smoothed it out as if it were a rumpled sheet. "Cam, you're not mad at me? Or disappointed?"

"Elle, Mom and Dad are going to be enough of that for both of us. I'm your sister, not your judge. I'm surprised. As in shocked surprised. And mad or disappointed won't change the fact . . . you're pregnant. Here's the deal. I'm willing to help you, but you're going to have to put your big girl panties on since you, well, decided to take them off."

I flinched. "But it was one time, Camden, one time. I know girls say that a lot, but it's true. It's really true. We weren't planning to have sex. It just—"

"Stop right there. We don't have time to talk about all the emotional crap. Wrap your brain around this. Your one time involved millions of sperm. It only takes one strong swimmer. At this point, you have three choices, abortion, adoption or . . . Wait, haven't you been dating that guy Jake recently? Are you planning to marry him?"

"No, I'm not marrying Jake. I don't want to marry Jake. And, no, I haven't told him. And, abortion? Really? I can't even believe you mentioned abortion. It's a baby, even if it's only a grape big. I'm not going to kill it just because I did something stupid."

"Calm down, Elle. I just meant anyone in your situation eventually has to choose. You need to know what you want to do before you talk to our parents. Especially if you think you want to keep this baby."

"Keep the baby? How could I even live here? Dad, Mr. Deacon of the church, would confine me to the closet. Mom would have to resign from her garden club or bridge club or whatever she's in. Cam, I can't even support myself. How could I support a baby? And finish high school?" My hysteria thermometer rose with every question.

"Then you realize the only choice left is adoption, right?" She asked in a way that suggested she understood, that perhaps we both understood, it really wasn't a question.

I didn't want to answer. I didn't want to hear myself acknowledge that to give my baby the best life possible would mean giving it to people I didn't know. Strangers. Even with knowing I had a life inside my body, I felt hollow at the thought. "I don't know. I just don't know if I can do that. Let someone take my baby from my arms and give it to someone else." I curled on my bed and pulled the quilted comforter around me. "How am I going to do that?"

"Elle, you don't have to know how today. But you do have to tell Mom and Dad. The longer you wait, the harder you're making it on yourself. Now, listen, you're still kind of early in the pregnancy. Sometimes there are problems before the fourteenth week and women miscarry. They usually wait to see if they're going to make it through that before they announce they're pregnant. You have about two weeks. We'll wait and see what happens, but either way, you're going to have to make a doctor's appointment. You need to spend time deciding what you want to do. But if you decide on adoption or on keeping the baby, you still have to tell the father."

"What if I don't want him to know?" I said.

"You'll have to tell him because it's the right thing to do."

I looked around my bedroom as I listened to her. All the things that used to matter. I slept in Cam's four-poster bed since she couldn't take it with her, and she'd found this crazy colorful bohemian quilted comforter that she left behind for me. The antique roll top desk I stripped and painted white, and changed all the knobs to pink ceramic butterflies. The two butterfly throw rugs, one hot pink and the other lime green, I found one summer when I visited Cam in New Orleans. Everything about it screamed teenage girl. But, now, talking about abortions and adoptions and pregnancy, I felt like I didn't belong in this space. It seemed young and fresh and innocent.

Everything I no longer felt I was.

9

Two weeks before I first met Holly Taylor, the ultrasound had revealed the baby was a girl. I stared at the screen, watched what the technician called my little "avocado" because she said that was about the baby's size. I saw the baby's heartbeat, how her tiny arms swayed. How each finger was so distinct that, when she reached her hand to her mouth, she started to suck her thumb. At that moment, I turned my head and squeezed Camden's hand. "I can't do this, Cam. I can't look anymore. It's too painful," I said, my voice wet with tears.

When I last saw Holly, she was probably close to the age I am now. I never expected that we'd ever have a reason to see one another again, though not a year passed that I didn't think of her. As a teenager, I saw her as someone with wisdom, someone who had much to teach about life. I thought, then, that when I reached her age, I would have grown to be someone like her. But, today, I didn't feel wiser. I doubted I had the ability as an adult to be to a teenager what she was to me then.

Since Logan and I moved to the suburbs, I hadn't eaten at Marigny's Restaurant in years—the very reason I wanted to meet Holly there. And since they were only open for breakfast and lunch, the small restaurant tended not to attract people who needed to be seen more than they needed to eat.

Even as I drove to the restaurant, I wondered why I didn't, when she called yesterday, refuse to entertain the thought of Faith returning. Several times along the way, I reached for my cell phone, considered calling her to tell her I'd changed my mind, delivered myself from the fog I must have been in, and decided the idea was beyond ridiculous. Beyond sane. But not beyond totally destroying my life and the life I had with Logan. It wasn't just my marriage that might not survive. Everything Logan had worked for in his political career could be damaged. The risks were social, emotional, political, and even financial. And, yet, I kept driving.

I pulled into a parking space and was digging in my purse to find lip gloss when my cell phone rang. It was Holly. *Maybe she's calling to tell me that we don't need to meet. That something miraculous happened, Faith's parents were misidentified or Holly decided to adopt Faith herself.* But what if she was calling to tell me she had to cancel our lunch? I'd have to relive this day all over again. *You're being idiotic, Elle, just answer the call.*

"Hey, Elle. Running about ten minutes behind schedule. I didn't want you to wonder if I would show up. Oh, and I'm wearing a red dress. Figured you couldn't miss me even if you might not recognize me."

"Okay, and I'm wearing a white dress and a black necklace. I'll get a table for us." I dropped my cell phone in my purse and found some tissues shoved in the center console to wipe my sweaty palms. *Turn off the car. Open the door. Step out of the car. Close the door.* Little victories. By the time I sat at the table, I felt like I'd crossed the finish line of a marathon. In my mind, I stood on the table and shouted, "Hey. I did it. I did it. Way to go, Elle." But when I recognized Holly weaving through the tables, I realized I'd only just heard the gun starting the race.

Her blonde hair was now shoulder length instead of cropped short, and the loose curls softened her face, which hardly showed evidence of having aged fifteen years. The wrinkles at the corners of her eyes were obvious only because she'd replaced her square, black-rimmed glasses with contact lenses. Otherwise, the Holly Taylor of today who wrapped her arms around me after she said hello, was the same one who wrapped her arms around me after telling me good-bye as she left Cam's house.

We sat, not in awkward silence for the first few minutes, but in that silence needed as your mind zipped along the time-line of years, bridging the gap between yesterday and today. I had forgotten what it felt like to be with someone who knew me almost as well as I knew myself. Ironically, the one person responsible for bringing us together had been absent from both of our lives. Until yesterday.

Holly knew more about my family than I did of hers. She asked about Cam and my mother, wanted to know if she'd remarried after my father died. She smiled, I supposed, see-ing my expression, which would have not been any different if she had asked if my mother decided to buy a Harley and join a biker's club to ride cross-country. "I guess that's a no," she said. "When your dad died, she was, what, in her forties, right? Certainly young enough to start over. You know, grow old together, and all that jazz."

"My mother was anything but jazz. More like the blues," I said. "That hasn't changed since you last saw her. Though Nick Junior does make her tap dance sometimes."

We laughed. I asked about her family. I didn't remember or maybe never knew her husband's name or anything about children, existing or not. As she talked about them, her eyes sparkled and her face became so animated that her crow's feet smiled and her enthusiasm pulsated in her voice. I thought those reactions were generally reserved for Disney movies or reruns of Seinfeld. Her husband owned an architectural design firm and their two children were in college. One in Texas, the other Florida. "I tried to convince them to consider colleges on at least the same side of the map. Obviously, my social worker charms hold no influence over my own children."

At the mention of her job, I sensed a pending segue into the real reason we met today. I didn't think she'd scripted the dialogue, but we both knew we weren't going to mosey down memory land, enjoy our meal, and then agree to meet in another fifteen years. After our waiter took our drink order, I checked my cell phone to make sure the volume was off. I settled my hand-me-down Coach purse, a bright blue one from Cam who bought purses like I bought books, as if they'd suddenly disappear from the universe while we slept. She gave it to me after I'd admired it shelved in her closet between a scrambled-egg-shaded satchel and a screaming violet carryall.

"Here, it's yours," she said as she settled the strap on my shoulder. When I protested, she tilted her head, the way she did when she thought before she spoke, and looked through me. "Elle, it's a purse. Not my kidney. What is it with you and this aversion to being nice to yourself once in a while?" She eyed her collection. "Maybe I'm nice enough for both of us."

I felt like an anorexic who deprived herself of stuff instead of food. The guilt I experienced after splurging on an expensive dress or jewelry or a spa day overwhelmed whatever enjoyment I expected from it. The idea that giving up something material somehow compensated for giving up a baby was irrational. My head knew that, but my heart couldn't get past the pain. At times I allowed myself an indulgence. I treated myself with a pair of Louboutin shoes. That didn't work out too well for me. But every time I carried that purse, it tugged on my conscience, a reminder to be nice to me.

I scooted my chair closer to the table. I ironed the napkin on my lap with my fingertips, my head bent as if I was about to say grace. Close enough. I was about to ask for it. "Holly," I said, "I owe you an apology for screaming at you on the phone yesterday. It wasn't kind or mature, but—"

"Stop right there," she directed and held up her hand as if to shield my words from reaching her. The waiter, standing behind Holly, his arm outstretched with a glass of iced tea, froze. "Oh, goodness, not *you*," she turned to him and said, his shoulders visibly relaxed as his placed the two drinks and a basket of bread on the table.

"I'll give you more time to look at the menu and come back later to take your order," he said, his voice sounding as if he sensed lunch was the least of our concerns, and he headed off to another table.

"If you hadn't been upset, I'd be concerned you might be overdosing on Valium," she said, her spoon clanging against the glass as she stirred.

"What I meant to say was, but I don't know how you could have expected me to react any other way."

"Honestly, I prepared myself for your directing me to a multitude of places I might take my butt, hanging up on me, blocking my phone number, or never answering one of my calls again. That was one phone call I never, ever expected to make. And I hope I don't ever again. For your sake or for Faith's."

At the sound of Faith's name, the butter knife in my hand quivered for a moment. I set it and the warm chunk of French bread on my plate. "Well, if you've never done this before, then why are you doing it now? Why me?" I sat back against the chair. "How can you even be asking me to do this?"

Tommy, our waiter, hovered, so we paused to order, then Holly began to explain what led to her call, starting with Jay

Wyatt, Faith's adoptive dad, winning a trip to Las Vegas in a sales contest for the pharmaceutical company he worked for. Faith had stayed with friends of theirs.

Holly stopped, took a drink of her tea, and stared at the vase of daisies on the table as if she expected them to finish the story. She swept the bread crumbs by her plate into her hand and deposited them in the bread basket.

I waited, feeling the emotional rumbling in my chest and anticipating the roller coaster free fall of events.

She cleared her throat and continued. "They left Vegas on a tour bus going to the Grand Canyon. On the way back to Vegas that evening, they think the driver might have suffered a heart attack. The bus swerved, then hopped the median near Hoover Dam before it overturned. Eight people died, including the Wyatts."

10

Holly's words drifted to the table, cradled by the silence between us, and my sadness tied itself into a knot in my stomach.

Tommy placed our salads in front of us and ghosted off as quietly as he came. I added salt and pepper to mine to keep my hands from grabbing my purse on my way to running out of the restaurant. I wasn't much older than Faith when my father died, and I didn't want to imagine losing two parents at once. Maybe she feels like she lost yet another set of parents. The ones where her grief wasn't memory, but the absence of it.

I flashbacked to when I searched through dozens of parent profiles. Sometimes my sadness for the couples wanting to adopt caused more pain than my self-pity. Too many hopeful faces stared at me. I'd find myself whispering, "I'm sorry," as their folders moved to the stack to be returned to the attorney. When I opened the Wyatts' folder and saw the cover photo of the two of them, I laughed. They stood next to one another and held an empty picture frame over their faces. Just that pose set them apart from the carefully orchestrated pictures that most couples used. And though they both flashed wide smiles at the camera, I saw in Kim's eyes what I saw in my own when I looked in the mirror. A whisper of sorrow. The second page showed Jay standing behind a rocker where Kim sat holding a baby, wrapped in a blue blanket, but tubes sprouted from different parts of his body and ended in a monitor not far from the rocker. Underneath the photo, they'd written: "We don't pretend to know how you feel, but we did want to share that we know what it's like to lose a child. We experienced four early miscarriages, and then finally a pregnancy lasted longer than three months. But, our son Nathan was an impatient little boy, and he decided to arrive two months early. He died three weeks later. His heart was broken, and so were ours."

Kim said she became a pediatrician because she wanted to know when and why their children would be sick. I loved that this couple didn't attempt to gloss over their weaknesses. She admitted she compensated for her atrocious culinary skills by making expert dinner reservations, but her husband Jay was an extraordinary cook and he wasn't giving up on teaching her how to boil water. They were both only children in their families, and each of their parents had been married over forty years. Unlike some of the other profiles, they didn't gush about wanting to adopt a barrel of children. Jay said they'd be blessed with the gift of one child's life.

I imagined Kim and Jay, in that swallow of time between life and death, thinking of Faith, pleading for her safety with whatever God they worshipped. I grieved for them, for Faith, and for myself. All victims of a stranger's heart attack. But I'm also ashamed because I'm angry and bitter about the unfairness of it all. I'd grieved for fifteen years for the baby I'd given away. Would I now have to multiply that grief with the loss of my husband, my marriage, my future?

I rearranged the strawberries and chicken in my salad and waited while Holly dabbed the corners of her eyes with her napkin. Another sip of tea and she continued. "I didn't know about the accident until I received a phone call from the Wyatts' attorney. He said that my contact information was in their file. Which, by the way, it might not have been except that we exchanged Christmas cards every few years. The Wyatts had named guardians for Faith in the event something happened to both of them—"

"So, why am I here?" My almost sigh of relief caught in my throat when it occurred to me that naming other parents was a version of human regifting. "Who's this family they chose? What if they're not the right people for Faith to grow up with?"

Her expression couldn't have been any different if I'd just asked how many times a week she and her husband made love. "Elle, the Wyatts were her parents. It was their decision who could best raise their daughter if they weren't around, just like it was your decision to choose them. They didn't owe either one of us an explanation. But none of that matters because I didn't finish telling you about my conversation with their attorney." Holly lowered her fork. "That couple died in the accident with the Wyatts."

A Greek tragedy. I'm a walk-on in this play. "Grandparents?"

Holly shook her head. "They all died within the last fifteen years."

There it was. The only two characters left on stage. Me. And Faith. I pushed my salad to the side, my hunger diminished by the news I suspected would soon be served.

"Kim contacted their attorney just days before their vacation. She wanted to make sure, he said, that they'd covered all their bases 'in case.' She told him that the two of you have been corresponding on and off since they adopted Faith. It was only because they were vacationing that she and Jay established what's called a tutorship by will. It essentially allows you to care for Faith, like a parent, until she's eighteen." As she talked, she reached over and removed a file folder from her tote bag.

I stared at the folder. A treasure or Pandora's box? "It *allows* me to care for Faith?" I pushed my straw up and down in my almost empty tea glass, the ice noisy, like rocks in a tumbler. "Might they have checked with me first? Rather presumptuous of them."

Holly's back straightened, and her lips and eyes narrowed as if controlled by the same circuit breaker. She spent a minute aligning her silverware, and when she stopped, I sensed a cool breeze about to blow in my direction.

"Can you remove yourself from the center of the universe for a moment? Let me qualify everything I'm about to say with the disclaimer that I have no clue what it's like to be you, then or today. But this I do know. No one has consulted Faith in any of this either. She's a fifteen-year-old whose parents died two thousand miles away. In her last conversation with them, they joked about losing all their money, and they told her they didn't want her to be disappointed when all they brought home for her was a T-shirt. She has no siblings, no grandparents, no extended family. An attorney she doesn't know is handling the details of her parents' bodies being returned, their funeral, and the rest of her life. You want to talk presumptuous? You're taking for granted that *she* wants to live with *you*."

When she'd started talking, her hands were clasped in front of her. By the time she finished, her palms were smacked down on the table. She probably wanted to smack me. Instead she relied on the outrage in her voice to pummel me. It did. The bruises to my ego were well-deserved. Though terror and confusion still flowed through me like lava, they paled in comparison to the seismic eruptions in Faith's life. "Does she . . . do you think, she wants to live with me?" When I spoke, my voice sounded as small as I felt.

"I don't know. She doesn't know yet about the tutorship by will. I wanted to talk to you first. I didn't ask the attorney what we'd do if you refused," she said and stabbed a cherry tomato in her salad. "Because her only other option would be foster care. At least until something else could be worked out. But I have no idea what that something would be."

Foster care relieved my marriage of the burden of reinventing itself, assuming it survived. Plus, we wouldn't risk the possibility of the campaign exploding into fragments of impossibility. What it didn't guarantee me was the ability to close my eyes to sleep peacefully because forever etched on the inside of my eyelids would be this day. This day when I chose expediency over decency. But still.

Holly told me she'd need to know within the next two weeks. "I need to be able to tell Faith the next step."

I debated calling Cam on the drive home. She knew about Faith before my parents, and she'd been a part of every decision I'd ever made about her. But I couldn't have half a conversation while she was between patients. I'd wait until the weekend. At least it was a decision that wouldn't involve our parents. A decision that was made when I wasn't much older than Faith was now. The last time my parents and I played tug-of-war with my decisions, I lost. They were wrenched from me, my parents pulling the rope of power that left me raw and burned from trying to resist.

When I had passed the fourteen-week mark, my sister and I decided it was time to break the news. At first, I suggested we go out for dinner because a restaurant wouldn't be the place for high drama and screeching. Cam didn't want to take that chance unless we could drive fifty miles in one direction or the other to decrease the odds of being impromptu performance art for people we knew. We settled for Sunday evening. Cam and I devised our plan during her drive home that Friday afternoon. I'd survived another week of school without any displays of morning sickness or dressing out for P.E. since I lucked out and my first semester was Health. My parents weren't due home for another two or three hours. I carried a jar of peanut butter and a bag of apple slices to my bedroom, dipping and chewing while we talked.

"No way are we saying anything Saturday or Sunday morning. Too much after-time to deal with. Sunday evening they'll be all churched, fed, and relaxed. We'll break the news, and eventually everyone will have to go to bed. I'll drive back Monday morning," said Cam.

By Sunday morning, anxiety rippled up and down my spine, and I felt like I'd been on a whaler during high seas instead of my house. I don't know how my parents didn't suspect something when Mom asked at breakfast if we wanted to eat after church or go out later for dinner. Cam and I had flashbulb eyes as we both answered, "After church." Dad took a sip of coffee, then glanced at Mom. Cam and I had witnessed those almost imperceptible exchanges where his eyebrows tilted toward one another in disbelief, and Mom responded with an eyebrow raise that wrinkled her forehead and a tiny shrug of her shoulders.

Dad nodded at Cam. "You don't even attend church, at least not when you're here, and you," he turned to me, "always rush us home after church because you have homework." He left the table and emptied the carafe of coffee into his cup.

The toe of Cam's sandal tapped against my shin. Our sister signal for me to shut up and she'd take over. "Elle has just two years left of high school, so I thought it would be cool if we did more family things. Soon she'll be away, and who knows how often the two of us will be able to be in town together?" She finished her last bite of bagel and was probably not finished chewing when she said, channeling her best martyr voice, "But if you two would rather not make a day of it and eat later, that's fine." She looked at me and asked a question she pretended she didn't already know the answer to. "Elle, what do you think?"

"No problem. Whatever Mom and Dad want to do," I said, keeping my voice as airy as a sheet drying on a clothesline.

We stopped for lunch at Lola's. That was one of the last pleasant meals I had with my family.

Maybe the two of us shouldn't have blindsided our parents at forty minutes into *60 Minutes*. We at least waited until a commercial before we told them we had something important to tell them. Dad adjusted his recliner to make himself less parallel to the floor. Mom folded the page she had stopped on and closed her *Dentistry Today* magazine. They looked back and forth from me to Cam and back again like we were balls whizzing over a tennis net.

I'd practiced this moment in my bedroom mirror until I tired of seeing myself. I changed my inflection, my tone, made sure not to look too somber, but yet not allow the corners of my mouth to suggest anything smile-like. I didn't want the announcement to sound like a death sentence or an announcement for a party. Declarative statement with a hint of apology? Or with a subtle regret? Not guilt. Definitely not guilt.

Cam and I sat on the sofa that mostly served as a place to fold towels while we watched television. Seeing Mom and Dad, I realized too late that I should have practiced with pictures of my parents taped to my mirror, not my own reflection. I closed my eyes, gave myself a fast count from one to three, opened them, and said, "I'm pregnant."

The room was silent. And still.

Camden had already coached me to stay quiet after I told them. "Give them time to react. That way you'll know what you're up against. Try, try, try not to yell or walk off. Remember you've had over three months to process something they're just finding out."

As frozen as they appeared, my parents had to be boiling inside. It was just a question of how soon they'd thaw. I'd counted up to thirty-four bricks on the fireplace chimney when Mom said, "You're pregnant. Pregnant." She rolled the magazine in her lap into a baton, but her hands continued to curl it as if she couldn't twist it tightly enough. She stared at my father, whose stunned expression grew as tight as the magazine wound in Mom's hands. "John, did you hear your daughter?"

"Yes, I heard her. But I wished I hadn't," he said, his voice on the tipping point of anger. "How could you do this to us, Elizabeth?"

"I did this to *you*?" I shook my head, my hand settled on my stomach. I half smiled in disbelief and turned to Cam and held up my hands in confusion. "I don't get it."

She patted my knee. "I've got this one," she whispered. She faced our parents. "If Elle wanted to upset the two of you, don't you think she might have picked something less life-changing than a pregnancy? Like failing a class. Discussing the 'how' isn't going to be productive—"

"Camden, I . . . we," my mother said and pointed to my father, "don't need you to tell us how to parent. And if Elizabeth thinks she's old enough to be in this situation, then she's old enough to speak for herself."

"She's not speaking for me. She's speaking with me. I wanted Cam here." I inched a smidge closer to my sister, kicked off my shoes, and pulled my legs up on the sofa. "It is what it is. I'm pregnant, and that's not going to change—"

"Well, of course not." My mother spit the words out like curdled milk. "Your father's a deacon in the church, for God's sake. An abortion is entirely out of the question. One sin is sufficient."

"Wow, that was harsh," Cam said. She looked down as her cell phone vibrated and flashed on the coffee table. Actually an Amish hope chest with its worn patina of blues, greens, and reds. When I was seven years old, I filled it with my Junie B. Jones books, a few nightgowns, and my dance recital costumes because I'd decided it was time for me to find another place to live. Somewhere without television and bed-time rules. That afternoon Cam found me, both of my hands wrapped around the antique brass handle, tugging the chest and accomplishing nothing except brush burns from my feet treading the carpet. She convinced me not to leave home until she had her own house. "Then you'll always have some place to go," she'd told me.

My parents' eyes followed my sister as she left the room and then made their way back to me. Had I been a bug specimen about to be mounted, they wouldn't have needed pins. Their eyes were sharp enough.

"Do you realize this isn't just your shame? It's something you're bringing on all of us," my father said.

"Elle, you and Jake . . . you two have been that serious? You're both good kids. I had no idea . . . no idea," said my mother, but this time her voice drifted off into something closer to confusion.

"This isn't about Jake. It's about me." I wanted to avoid their questions about the father as long as possible.

"If he's any kind of man, he should be responsible. Not a coward leaving you here to defend yourself." My father started pacing, hands in his pockets, his keys clinking in one and his change in the other. He talked to the floor, his reading glasses still perched on the end of his nose. He stopped and sat on the ottoman near my mother's chair.

"He didn't leave me anywhere. And I'm not defending what I did." I chose my words with care, on the high wire between truth and lie. "I'm due at the end of March. That's less than six months away, and I wanted to talk to you about my, um, options." Anxiety tapped on my shoulder. *Okay, Cam, where are you?* I rearranged myself on the sofa and spotted Cam standing on the outside deck. Still on her phone, she pulled dead bulbs from the camellia tree and tossed them into the grass. She must have sensed the heat of my laser stare shooting through the window because she lifted her head and gave me the one-finger, I'll-just-be-a-minute signal.

I needed to pee, my waist and the top button of my jeans were engaged in a territorial battle over my body, and my back-up was on bud patrol. I had five chapters to read in *Things Fall Apart* for my AP English class, two chapters to outline for anatomy class, and not a clue what I'd be able to squeeze myself into for school without looking like I had an unresolved gas problem in my gut. *For something now the size of a bell pepper, you're causing watermelon-sized problems, kid.*

11

I set the to-go container with my salad from lunch on the seat next to me, along with the spinach salad I'd ordered for Martha and the Mediterranean paella for Logan. One less dinner to cook and one more opportunity to show Martha I could be thoughtful. Our waiter insisted I take my lunch, since, he said, "You ate two pieces of lettuce and an olive." I couldn't, of course, explain to him that my emotions had commandeered every available space in my body, so my stomach probably flattened in self-defense. I knew it would likely be wilted, a victim of the sun and stops I needed to make before I reached home, and I'd toss it in the trash. Even if it survived the ride home, it would be infused with too much lunch memory for me to digest.

I turned the volume up on my cell phone and listened to the voice mails. Logan reminding me to pick up his campaign materials, Martha to set up a time to see the property and, oh, by the way, did I have a copy of *A Streetcar Named Desire?* And my mother called to remind me about Nick Junior's birthday party, which was months away, and she hoped she'd hear from me. *Maybe I'd be more eager to call if I detected even a ripple of enthusiasm in your voice.*

But the seismic shift in our relationship after she heard I was pregnant proved too catastrophic. That Sunday afternoon when I told my parents replayed in my mind like a classic movie reformatted in high definition. The striped orange and fuchsia sleeveless tank top I wore because it slipped over my hips, my father's worn khaki green slacks that ballooned out at his knees when he paced, Cam's musky violet scent that followed her when she left the room. Even the way my mother pressed her temples with her fingertips and scooped her hair into a ponytail and defiant tendrils twined around her ears.

The discussion of my options ended in my parents' inform-ing me that my only option was adoption. They refused to listen to any other possibilities. "We're not going to raise your child while you finish high school and college. It's selfish and irresponsible to think you're capable of parenting and continu-ing your education. Your father and I will talk to our attorney and look into information about private adoptions."

It's not that I believed keeping the baby was the best deci-sion for the baby or for me. But I wanted to arrive at that con-clusion myself because for years after Faith was adopted, I blamed my parents for the phantom pain of loss. And nothing then or since has sealed that open wound. Cam and I were always close. But I gained, though, the unwavering support of my sister the day I threw the switch that derailed my parents' lives.

Cam abandoned me during the conversation to take a phone call, and I didn't understand why or know who she was spending time talking to while she pruned an unmoti-vated camellia bush outside. During Cam's absence, Mom started a new rant. The rant in which the words seemed pulled out and knotted together like magician's silk scarves.

"Iknowweraisedyoubetterthanthis . . . andwhatwereyou
thinking . . . nevermindifyouwerethinkingthisprobably-
wouldn'thavehappened . . . andnowyourfatherwillhavetotell-
thechurch . . ."

My father's silence bruised me more than my mother's
waves of anger. He avoided eye contact with me until Cam
returned, and when he looked at me, I wished he hadn't.
Disbelief and disappointment were no longer there; they'd
given way to indifference. And that rejection didn't require
an emotional investment. By then, I couldn't stop the tears. I
knew he'd never see me the same way.

Cam walked in, perched on the arm of the sofa, and called
a time out. "You know, if you're going to talk about God providing a way . . . that's what you've preached to us, right?" She
nodded, but Mom and Dad didn't. Cam shrugged her shoulders. "Anyway, I don't know if you remembered that Lacey's
wedding is in January." Lacey lived with Cam in New Orleans
in our great-grandmother's house. It was one of those fortuitous happenings in the family my father always referred to as
evidence of God's great wisdom and timing. I think that also
fended off those who might believe his grandmother moving
out of a home his daughter needed to move into might be a
calculated serendipity.

Mamie, who had just turned eighty-five, moved into Blue
Bayou Assisted Living after a number of visits during which
my parents would find her purse in the refrigerator, the spare
eyeglasses she thought she'd lost hanging from a chain around
her neck, and her dining room stacked with empty boxes from
food she'd had delivered. Yet she still remembered to wear her
Saints and LSU jerseys on game days, would call my dad after
the games and tell him the plays the coaches should've run
"if they had the sense God gave a woodpecker." She ate rocky
road ice cream for breakfast sometimes, but Cam and I figured

Mamie knew exactly what she was doing there. My parents convinced her that at Blue Bayou, she'd have more of a social life, meals she never had to cook, and her home well-cared for by my family. All of which also meant they didn't have to visit (translate, check on her) as much. Her house was within bike riding distance from the school. Cam started dental school two months after my parents drove Mamie to Blue Bayou wearing her oversized "Who Dat?" sweatshirt over black leggings. Blue Bayou hadn't been the same since she arrived.

"Lacey's moving out in December after the semester ends, which means Elle can move in. Actually, she can move in tomorrow if she wants to. The third bedroom has a few boxes scattered around, but there's enough room for a bed. And," Cam stopped and looked at me, "if you did decide to move early, it would only be temporary. We'd be able to have you set up in Lacey's old room the same day she moves."

I wiped my wet cheeks with my hands, and something that resembled hope fluttered in my voice. "What about school? Will I have to transfer to a high school there? Do you think I'd still be able to graduate on time next year?"

"Lacey's checking into that. She was the reason I needed to answer my phone. I'd talked to her before I left, but I wanted to make sure she didn't have a problem with your coming before she moved out. Assuming that's what you want to do," she explained as she moved to sit next to me on the sofa. "And a friend of hers is a teacher, and she told Lacey that you'd be able to take some online classes." She hugged me. "We'll figure this out."

"And what are we supposed to tell people when Elle just disappears?" My mother didn't seem to be buying in. Dad had relocated to his recliner, but he stared into some space beyond where any of us were.

"It doesn't matter to me what you tell them," I said, thinking my mother would understand she could invent whatever worked for her and not worry about what I thought. Um, no.

"Of course it doesn't matter to you," she said. "If what people said mattered to you, we wouldn't be having this discussion right now, would we?"

My mother had a way of drilling into people even without her dental equipment. She hit a nerve, and though the shock radiated through me, I refused to give her the satisfaction of flinching. Or of responding. Without the backlash of anger, her words were swallowed by the silence.

Cam spoke first. Calm and assertive. "Mom, tell them I need help with Mamie. That she's had some unexpected situations," she said. "I think Elle qualifies as an unexpected situation. And, honestly, visiting Mamie can be time-consuming, especially when she drifts in and out between decades. It would be a relief to know Elle's there to help."

Mom walked to the steps leading to the screened porch off the deck. From there, she could see the trampoline, still surrounded by the safety net, though none of us had used it in years. Except for one night, I'd stayed awake until almost midnight working on a research paper. I'd forgotten a book I needed, and when I walked over to the bookcase, I noticed the landscape lights still burning in the backyard. As I started to flip the switch to turn them off, I heard a low rumble of conversation followed by a woman laughing. My parents were stretched out on their backs next to one another, their arms folded underneath their heads. It was startling and yet comforting to witness this casual intimacy, even if it had started with the almost empty bottle of red wine and two glasses left by the back door.

Watching my mother now, I wondered if she might have been thinking about that night with my father. Or maybe even other nights like it. But her arms were folded, her body at military attention. Not the posture of a woman softened by memories of intimacy with her husband. "You understand, both of you, that moving doesn't alter the decision about adoption? No phone calls in a few months that you've changed your mind and that you, Cam, and the baby are going to be a little happy family in Mamie's house. Because that won't happen. Living there is a privilege, not a right. Don't take it for granted."

I started to respond, but Cam stopped me. She shook her head and mouthed, "No."

My father roused from whatever mental cave he'd escaped to and spoke to my mother's back, "I suppose we'll pay for her to live there, since Cam's roommate's moving out." It sounded more like a question. Almost as if he was asking permission, which considering it was his grandmother's house and not my mother's seemed strange.

"I assume we'll have to do that. I don't think she's going to be able to work, do you?" My mother relieved her folded arm stance only to pull her falling hair back into a ponytail of sorts.

By this point, I wearied of participating in the conversation. I'd been rendered invisible for a while, so I stopped squirming and announced, "I'm going to pee. I'll be back."

Later, Cam said that my father drilled her about the baby's father. The longer she insisted she had no idea, the shorter his patience held. My father finally ended the interrogation with, "I don't know if she's protecting some guy or she's embarrassed. He'd better not be some married man. I've had shame enough."

She said Mom just patted his arm and said, "She'll have to tell us one day."

By the time I told them, it didn't matter.

12

Fred loaded dozens of yard signs and posters splashed with "Vote Butler for Honesty, Integrity, and Experience" in the back of my SUV. He pressed the button to lower the back, then resettled his glasses on his nose. "Thanks, Mrs. Butler. And good luck."

"I'll bet you say that to all the candidates," I said and smiled. Fred was probably closer to Martha's age than my own, but he still had one of those round faces I imagined had been subjected to years of cheek pinching.

"Got me on that one," he said and laughed. "Man's got to stay in business, you know?"

"And you can stop calling me Mrs. Butler anytime now. You've known me for almost ten years. Besides, I might think you have me confused with Martha."

"I don't think that would happen." Fred shook his head as he opened my car door, then as if he'd just heard himself, said, "Oh, I didn't mean that Mrs. Butler isn't a handsome woman because she was a head-turner in her day."

"It's okay, Fred. I was kidding. Besides, you can always tell us apart because I'm the taller one." I patted his arm in what

I hoped was a gesture of good humor. The realization he saw Martha as both handsome and a former head-turner suggested I might need to turn back time and dredge up some old photos of my mother-in-law in her heyday.

"It's Elle. No more Mrs. Butler, well, except for the other Mrs. Butler. Thank you again, and you tell Logan to let me know if he needs anything else."

I was about to leave when I thought about Chad Wiggins and his wife. "Fred, have you heard any news about Lucy Wiggins lately? When Logan told me she'd been diagnosed with cancer, I . . . I was shocked. I'm sure they were, too. I thought you might know how she, they are doing."

"Last time I talked to Chad, guess it was about a week ago, he said they were going to MD Anderson in Houston. He didn't tell me much more than that. Lucy's parents came from Dallas to stay with their kids." He stopped and nodded hello to a couple walking into the store. "The baby, she just made two, and their little boy's in first grade." Fred shook his head. "Sad. Real sad."

"Is there anything, any way we can help? Can we send some meals or something?" After my father died, I learned that any tragedy plus food equaled comfort. The equation was not to be violated, questioned, or ignored. Whether or not the family needed or wanted or consumed meals was irrelevant. Grief didn't stand a chance against Mindy's yellow mustard potato salad, Mrs. Ferguson's artichoke casserole, and J.B.'s chicken gumbo. The strategy was to feed the monster until it couldn't fit into whatever clothes your grief dressed it in. It stopped making a grand entrance when you weren't prepared for it to fling open the door of your heart at its whim. It just buried itself deep inside where no one could see its nakedness. Except for the times it went skinny-dipping in the pool of pity.

"I think their church emptied the grocery store shelves with all their cooking. Lucy's folks will need a new freezer soon. But that's nice of you to be thinking of them. I tell you, the best way you can help is prayer. Gives people hope when they know they're being lifted up in prayer."

"Thanks, Fred," I said. "I'll tell Logan to give you a call if there's anything else he needs."

A casserole or cupcakes for the Wiggins, I could manage. But prayer? I wanted to tell him that praying for Lucy to be healthy was a no-brainer, and why would I need to pray for something so obvious? Having me on the prayer team was a liability. I supposed cheering from the sidelines counted for something. God's win/loss record in my life hadn't yet convinced me that I wanted him as my coach.

Martha's car was in her driveway as I headed home, and before I questioned the sanity of what I was about to do, I turned in. Minutes later, I stood on her porch, a yard sign in one hand and her food in the other, and pushed the doorbell. Avoidance. That's probably what my therapist would have labeled this. An unexpected stop at my mother-in-law's house was the Magic Kingdom compared to the *Les Misérables* production that awaited me at home, wandering around my empty house with only myself as company where I'd be visited by the ghosts of regret, confusion, and uncertainty. No, this was much better. An opportunity to bankroll good behavior tickets, since the almost certain possibility of relationship bankruptcy loomed in my future.

Martha's silk door wreath of flowering wild dogwoods twitched as she fought with the deadbolt. "I declare. This safety lock is going to be the death of me yet," she said, her exasperation more successful coming through the door than she. Sometimes Martha sounded as if she'd stepped off the set of *Gone With the Wind*. Seconds later, the door swung open, the wreath applauding against it. "Elle, now it's my turn to be surprised. I knew it was you before I opened the door, of course. I never unlock the door without checking the peephole first. A woman can't be too careful."

"I'm surprised too," I said. "That you were home, I mean." I held up Logan's sign. "I thought you'd want to see this. Be the first person on the block to have one."

She took the sign, opened the door wider, and walked away. I supposed that was my cue to enter.

Martha held to the tradition that one's home decor should reflect the seasons. Her living room had already been dressed in its buttercup-yellow houndstooth prints on some pieces of furniture offset by white linen on others. A few pillows, some electric blue and a few neon green, made themselves at home on the milk-white sofa, which was where Martha carried the sign for inspection.

She sat on the end and patted the space next to her. Another cue to sit. Martha may have missed her calling as a dog trainer. That may have said more about my ability to follow instructions than hers to give them. I placed my purse and container on the clear, acrylic cubes that served as coffee tables and sat.

"I wish Logan had talked to me before bringing these to Fred. Don't you think the lettering should have been red and the background white?" She flipped the sign from one side to the other as she held it at arm's distance. "Maybe he can try switching the colors on the next order."

"Maybe," I said. I knew there was a way to make keeping it a non-issue. "If you'd rather wait for one of those . . ."

Martha moved it out of my reach. "That would be appalling for his own mother to not show her support." She leaned it against the sofa, patted it as if commanding it to stay, and followed her sigh with "This one will do until then."

Thanks, Elle, for bringing this over. You're so welcome, Martha, happy to make you a bit less critical.

"I brought you a spinach salad from Marigny's. That's where my friend and I met for lunch, and I know it's your favorite. I thought you could have it for dinner tonight. Or lunch tomorrow."

Her eyebrows hiccupped enough to suggest I'd caught her off guard. *Bravo for me.* A celebration enough to rouse my Guilt Grinch, who shamed me for having enjoyed a Martha moment.

"Elle, that was kind of you," she said. "I'll have it for lunch tomorrow. Auditions for *Streetcar* start tonight. A few of us girls are trying out." When she said the word "girls," she made those air quotes and grinned. "It's nice to have something to do besides grow older. The Seasoned Theatre group is new here, and we want to make sure it stays."

The enthusiasm in Martha's voice both surprised me and belied her age. Dressed in a polka-dot cardigan, fuchsia linen pants, and peep-toe shoes, Martha didn't look like a woman eligible for a Seasoned Theatre group. Until she pulled up the sleeves of her sweater. Her hands reminded me of Mamie's. Wrinkles etched in every finger revealed her age like growth rings on trees. I remembered the silky softness of Mamie's skin as my fingertips stroked the backs of her hands. Like Martha's hands, Mamie's veins rose under her translucent skin. Mamie never cared that her veins looked like tree roots reaching toward her fingers. She said they grew stronger with age just like she did. "Those gnarly veins gave me hands to feed my babies, heal them when they were sick, drive them all over creation and back again, hold their little cheeks when they kissed me good night," she told me.

In my mind's eye, I saw Martha's hands, shaping Logan into the man he would become. In that instant, a tidal wave of loss surged and my heart cracked open. And I knew. I knew what I wanted to do.

After leaving Martha's, I called Holly. I said yes.

Holly was not as happy to hear from me as I was to call her.

"You've already discussed this with Logan?"

"No. Not yet." I felt like a six-year-old scuffing the floor with the toe of her shoe waiting for her mother's scolding. "But I know this is the right thing to do, and I thought you wanted to know something as soon as possible." I moved a bag of grapes on their way to becoming raisins, a plastic container of aged rice, and wilted celery in my refrigerator to make room for my leftover salad and Logan's paella. "Holly? Are you there?" I walked to the bedroom to change into something slouchy. Maybe I'd take a walk instead of collapsing on the sofa.

"Yes, I'm here. But I'm . . . I can hardly even think of a word . . . dumbfounded, perhaps? We didn't discuss Logan specifically, which I'm thinking now was a mistake, but I assumed you understood this decision needed to be made by both of you."

"I don't think Logan would be so heartless as to disagree. Of course I'm going to talk to him. It's not like I can hide her." *At least not physically.* I flipped through a stack of yoga pants. Black. Pink. Blue. Grey. Which one? Flipped again. I swayed from one foot to the other. The agitation churned and coiled and reached out through my fingers. I pitched one pair of pants after another onto the floor. *You're talking to someone who can't decide what pants to wear. Pants. I'm not exactly the poster woman for assertiveness and self-confidence. I'm going to talk to him. I will.*

I will. I pulled out a pair of jeans and left the pants in a tangled, colorful mess on the closet floor.

"Of course, Elle," said Holly, but it sounded as if someone had clipped her words with scissors. "If you and Logan need me to, I can come to your house, and we can talk there."

I wiggled one of Logan's campaign T-shirts over my head. "Sure. I'll let you know." *Unlikely.*

I ended the phone call, turned off the closet light, and stretched out on my bed. I closed my eyes and watched Holly's last words stream across my mind. *This decision will affect the rest of your lives, and Faith's too. Don't just think about what to do. Pray about it.* The same words I'd heard over fifteen years ago.

13

Most New Orleanians wouldn't know the difference between January and April without a calendar, but the rebellious January day Cam and I first met Holly required a total wardrobe revamp. My sister and I searched for a coat that zipped over my baby bump and settled for one of Mamie's old ponchos, a purple wool turtleneck. I looked like an overripe blueberry with legs. Swathed with scarves that hid our noses and mouths, we battled the blustery weather into Suis Generis for brunch. For someone whose body temperature ranged twenty degrees higher than everyone else's, I appreciated the brisk, clean cold. It was like walking into an outdoor freezer without worrying about defrosting its contents.

The Bywater area restaurant lived up to its meaning of being in a class alone. With its upside-down, red Solo cups ceiling, salt and pepper shakers glued to little toy cars, and ever-revolving menu, the place was entertaining and the meals delicious. The last month, my appetite increased, but the baby's tolerance for my food choices hadn't. An issue that also complicated eating at school when I forgot my lunches from home. But not long after I enrolled at City High School, I became friends with

Hillarey, whose mother worked in the cafeteria and offered as much special dispensation as possible in my meal choices. Hillarey, along with her friend Kendra, and I gravitated toward one another. We recognized and embraced ourselves as social misfits. Hillarey, by virtue of everyone seeing her mother wearing a hairnet as she scooped green beans adrift in a sea of watery butter into red, divided cafeteria plates. Kendra's bi-racial Japanese ethnicity left her on the fringes of white, black, and Asian students, and her National Merit Scholarship qual-ification intimidated even the brainiacs. Both of their mothers had given birth to them before graduating from high school, and they saw me as just Elle. Not as Elle, the new student, an unwed pregnant teen who moved from home to live with her sister. They had become my family. I even considered asking Cam if they could be invited to our "meet the social worker" brunch.

Social worker Holly came into our lives via Cam's room-mate, Lacey, whose mother knew Holly's mother. One of those connections close enough for my sister to trust her, yet dis-tanced enough to not be emotionally involved. Holly arrived at Suis Generis before us, and she and I had one of those half-handshake, half-hug moments. I expected her to be my mother's age, but she looked Cam's age. My anxiety level rat-cheted down a bit seeing Holly and feeling like I wouldn't be talking to my mother.

Cam made sure that she prepared me as much as possible for this first meeting. We read websites about adoption, writ-ten by birth moms and adoptive parents and parents of birth moms and even adopted kids and adults themselves. There were nights I'd be on the way to a calculus headache or read-ing more adoption stories while "Peanut," as I called her then, would perform somersaults, her fists and feet tapping against the walls of her little home. To soothe both of us, I'd play

Michael Bolton through my headphones, loosely attached to my belly and on the lowest volume. As much as I chanted to myself, "She's not mine. She's not mine. She's not mine," I'd wander into Cam's room, my hands cradling my belly, dragging my sadness like iron shackles, and she'd give me the gift of silence. Holding her arms out, she'd pull me toward her and rescue me from the undertow of pain with her hugs.

No matter what happened that day with Holly, I knew Cam was my life vest and I wouldn't drown in my decisions. I sat between these two older, professional women who were going somewhere in the world other than a delivery room and squirmed under my skin. My failure, my weakness, my disgrace an unavoidable physical presence. While other girls my age lounged in coffee shops after school, cruised the mall on weekends, planned dates for dances, I'd be reading parent profiles. Deciding on the couple who would meet me at the hospital one day and walk away with my daughter. And this meeting with Holly was the first step toward that inevitability.

Cam placed our orders for breakfast burritos while I forced the salt and pepper cars into minor head-on collisions. I expected her and Holly to engage in catch-up chat before they turned their attention to me. But they didn't. Instead, Holly's lukewarm hand covered my own, the one that steered the rust-eaten Corvette, and stilled it. "How are you doing, Elle?"

The honesty in her voice caught me off guard. Even more so when I looked up from my Hot Wheels entertainment and saw she meant it. I'd vaccinated myself against that question since my body started to out me with this baby. My parents asked how I felt as if it was on their list of "to do" items during their weekly phone calls. At school it was a one-stop "hello and see ya" from other students as they slammed their locker doors and drifted off to classes. One of my teachers, Mr. Theriot creeped me out, and not just because he could have walked off the set of a scary cartoon movie as one of those stick-legged, almond-eyed, gangly characters. He'd always stare at my belly when he asked, "Elizabeth, how are we feeling today?" in a way that made the words ooze out of his mouth like tree sap. I answered with "Great, Mr. Theriot," as I escaped into the hallway and lost myself in the throng. What I wanted to do was slam my backpack at his feet on the scuffed floor, jab my finger into his sunken chest, and say, "How am I doing? I left home to save my parents from suffering my disgrace. I'm in high school, and I waddle from one class to the other. I can barely squeeze into a desk. Instead of laughing with the cheerleaders or buying prom tickets or running varsity track, I'm shopping my baby around. And in April, I'll be back at school with a flat belly, no baby, and enough guilt, grief, and doubt to serve it at lunch time to the entire school."

I packaged everything I ever wanted to say to Mr. Theriot and gave it to Holly, but I wrapped it with sincerity, not anger or frustration. Her eyes, framed by her square, black glasses, registered understanding, not feeble pity. She didn't mouth empty platitudes or ask me inane questions. She waited until I stopped talking, and even after that, she let the silence have its space against the humming ceiling fans and kitchen clatter.

Just minutes into Holly dissecting the types of adoptions, she stopped as if an offstage director had just shouted for the scene to end. "Wait." She glanced at the table as if searching for a lost word, drummed her manicured fingers, and said, "Before we talk about any of these options, is this fully your decision? What does the birth father say about this? He is supporting you in wanting the baby to be adopted, right?"

Yes. Nothing. I don't know.

I stopped picking the sausage out of the scrambled eggs and set my fork down. I wanted a sip of water, but my hands were too limp to hold the glass. I moved them to my lap where

I clutched one with the other. Cam and Holly didn't speak. Without moving my own eyes from examining each curve of the looping design on my plate, I sensed their stares. Even if I hadn't been physically trapped between them in the pseudo-leather booth that made the backs of my thighs damp, I couldn't escape the emotional ambush. I closed my eyes and imagined excusing myself to go to the bathroom, finding a back way out of the restaurant, hailing a taxi, and . . . and what? *And nothing.*

I opened my eyes, pulled off the jersey headband that had grown too small for my head in the last minutes, and doubled it around my wrist. "Here's the thing," I said. "The birth father doesn't know about this baby. And I'm not going to tell him."

14

Still sprawled on my bed after talking to Holly, I wondered if being electrocuted felt much different from the electric currents that radiated from my spine into every part of my body. The source of the voltage was likely regret surging from my conscience, generated by years of postponing what was unavoidable. Drawing lines in the sand, and now there was no more desert. Until today, I'd succeeded at compartmentalizing my life. I built emotional firewalls of protection, but I couldn't prevent something unexpected, like the Wyatts' death, from penetrating those shields.

And now what? I focused on the swirling patterns of the ceiling and considered the possibility of spontaneous combustion. Logan arriving home to find the charred outline of my body on his beloved 1600-thread count sheets. The medical examiner would describe how energized particles like zillions of pinballs ricocheted through molecules in my body, ignited my clothes through my skin, and the rest was ashes. But I shivered too much for someone about to be consumed by her own body heat. Even with my body fat as fuel resources, I couldn't transform into a human wick.

I wanted to crawl into myself and disappear. Whenever I felt that way, I imagined myself transported to the day before whatever crisis had happened. I'd breathe in that innocence, where I wondered what I'd wear to school the next day or the time of the next football game or if I wanted a chocolate or raspberry snowball. But like Truman in the movie coming to discover his world wasn't at all what he thought it was, the wave would be gone, and I'd collapse on the shore of reality.

Then I did what I always did when I didn't know what else to do. I called Camden. Her office wasn't closed yet, so I left a voice message asking her to call me on her way home. My other coping mechanism was playing in the dirt. I forced myself to abandon the seduction of sleep and went outside to plant things that weren't green. That actually flowered.

Cam called about a dozen plants later.

"Hey. What's up? I almost called sooner because you sounded pathetic."

"And you sound like you're in a wind tunnel. Am I on Bluetooth?" I said.

"Yes, but I'm alone. The only other person who'd be in the car with me is the baby, and I think we're still safe with him. Well, except for the Tabasco-in-your-mouth kind of words. What's going on?"

"More than you'll believe. But for now, just listen and don't ask questions until I'm finished." I told her about Holly's call, our lunch meeting, the Wyatts, and Faith.

"Elle, this is a lot to digest while I'm driving almost seventy miles an hour on my way to pick up Nick," she said, followed by, "look, dude, if you're in such a hurry . . . " and one of those words we never wanted her son to repeat. "Let me call Mom and tell her I'm running late, which I will be by the time we finish talking. I'll pull into a parking lot. I don't want to risk playing bumper cars in this traffic. I'll call you back in a few minutes."

She hung up before I could tell her Logan would be home in the next fifteen or twenty minutes. Calling Mom to ask for special dispensation for late pickup could eat up most of that time.

I stopped planting the flat of impatiens, which, lucky for me, they exactly weren't since they waited quite patiently for almost a week for me to get them in the ground. I brushed the dirt and blades of loose grass off my jeans and debated if now or later was a better time for a glass of Robert Mondavi. I dumped my damp garden gloves at the back door, wiped my mud-caked bare feet against the thick fiber mat, a torture second only to stepping on pine cones, and welcomed the rush of air swept down by the overhead fan as I walked in. My cell phone rang before I even reached the wine cabinet. I settled for a water bottle out of the bar refrigerator and sat in the den to finish my conversation with Cam and also to be able to spot Logan's car.

I dried the sweaty bottle with the hem of my shirt. "Logan's going to be home soon, which means I might not be able to finish talking."

"Elle, you think twelve minutes is enough to resolve this? This isn't a microwave problem," Cam said. "If you're looking for some answer that's going to make everyone happy, then you're as crazy as this whole situation."

I nodded and pictured Cam as she sat in her car, her head down, eyes closed, scratching her forehead. Her classic perplexed pose.

"Cam, what am I going to do? This is insane, right? I mean, I could lose everything. I don't know—"

"No one could have a contingency plan for this. But you didn't call me because you don't know what to do. You knew, from the time you drove away from that restaurant, what you wanted to do."

I drank some water. Too bad I couldn't do one of those Jesus-turn-water-into-wine miracles because I really would have preferred the wine. "But, how? How do I tell Logan? And it's not just my marriage I could ruin. My husband's running for state representative. On the family values ticket, for God's sake. His opponent's going to be orgasmic when he hears this."

"Well, if he is, then maybe you've got something on him," Cam said.

"Not funny."

"Just going for a commercial break, Elle." She sighed. "Do you know how many men are probably raising kids they think are theirs, but their wives would have a stroke if they ever asked for a DNA test? You're not the first wife who's lied to her husband, and I'm certain you won't be the last."

"I never lied to Logan," I said.

"Oh, really? I've been with you this entire trip. Don't play semantics with me. Are you sure you're truly understanding what's about to happen in your life? This isn't we're-all-going-to-hold-hands-and-sing-Kumbaya time. And I can't help you here. Not like I did then. No me, you, and Logan sitting down and talking like we did with Mom and Dad. You've got to do this."

"I don't think I can—"

Cam said, "Did you call me because you wanted me to make the decision for you? Well, here are your other choices. Decide if you're ready to be a single mother because Logan may not buy-in. Or call Holly. Tell her you're a coward. That you won't tell your husband the truth. Tell her she can find a good foster home for Faith to live in for the next three years of her life. Problem solved."

Single motherhood? I wasn't prepared for single not-mother-hood. The other choice, the call Holly one, is the one I wanted to want. On the long road of life, lunch with Holly would be nothing but a speed bump. "Don't be upset with me. I'm trying to figure this out."

"You've had almost sixteen years to figure out how to tell him," she said as matter-of-factly as if she'd just declared the President's name or that today was Wednesday. I supposed truth sounded like an accusation when you chose to avoid it. "I guess if you have to take another two weeks to figure out how you're going to finally end this charade, it's not going to make much difference."

I'm in a car with no brakes gaining speed, and the only way to stop myself is to crash headlong into the wall ahead of me. Assess the damage later.

Before I had time to process my conversation with my sister, Martha called on her way to play auditions to ask if I'd talked to Logan about seeing the properties on Saturday.

"Not yet," I told her. "I haven't talked to him all day. I'll ask him tonight." Other than the note he left this morning, which already seemed like ten mornings ago, and a text, we hadn't had voice contact at all. Not typical Logan phone contact, but since the campaign started, there wasn't much that was typical. I hung up with Martha and tried him again. My call went directly to voice mail. I figured he was in a meeting or on another call.

If he had to be late, he picked a good day. More time for me to rehearse my all-is-well-in-the-world face while chaos squat-ted in my brain, claiming all the territory it could. I walked into my office to find my planner to block off Sunday, and my desk looked like chaos had started there already. Stacked with Junior League information, magazines with design ideas, my laptop in dire need of a battery charge, a coffee cup with some oil-like slick coating the bottom, an avalanche of pens, and an empty tape dispenser, it captured exactly how I felt. Jumbled. I unearthed my planner from a tower of catalogs and wrote "look for center property" across Sunday.

Getting this center built was a dream I'd had since that summer Jenn and I went to the Brookwood Community to visit her sister, Cindy. Almost thirty years old, Cindy had lived there for five years. I'd never been around adults with disabilities, but I didn't want to disappoint Jenn or let her think I was uncomfortable being with Cindy. But instead of being offended or judgmental, Jenn laughed.

"Before Cindy lived there, my parents and I weren't too sure ourselves about how we'd react. Living with someone with a disability isn't the same as being with dozens of people with all sorts of issues."

When Jenn turned down the entrance, I couldn't figure out why this upscale neighborhood was built near Brookwood. Then she told me, it *was* Brookwood. On over 500 acres of lush rolling hills were eight group homes, staff homes, administration and activity buildings, and a steepled church. Jenn drove around and showed me the gift center, the health and dental clinic, the café, and over forty-five greenhouses.

We met Cindy at her home, a red-bricked, white-columned, expansive design that offered porches like handshakes to everyone who entered. Betsy, the house mom who lived there with her husband and their fourteen-year-old daughter, opened the door. While she and Jenn exchanged hugs, I began to understand why Cindy told her parents she wouldn't mind living there. A wide brick fireplace, flanked on each side by tall, pine bookcases anchored the room. The sweeping granite island sat fourteen, and the kitchen could have tiptoed out of *HGTV*. Even the appliances looked happy to be there, all polished and shiny. The house shattered every preconceived idea I had about group homes.

I'd seen pictures of Cindy, a petite young woman whose curls played jump-rope in her short, caramel-colored hair. At first glance, she didn't seem like someone with any sort of disability. But her speech was halting, and she had the voice of someone who'd been congested with a cold for days. But the most delightful part of her, a camera couldn't convey.

She planted herself in front of me, stuck her thumb out in my direction, and asked Jenn, "Who is this you brought?" Cindy pushed her round glasses back up her nose and kept her forefinger on the bridge, pressing it to her face.

"I'm excited to see you, too," Jenn said. "Can you let go of your glasses long enough to hug me?"

"What. Ever," said Cindy, and she allowed herself to be hugged. "You didn't tell me who she is."

Jenn explained we were friends, and I wanted to visit Brookwood.

"Why? You want to live here?" She pinned me with her brown eyes and waited for my response with her hand on her hip. "Because she," Cindy pointed to her sister, "thinks she is going to move in with me. And it's not going to happen."

I cleared my throat to swallow the smile that wanted to escape. "No," I said, "I'm not moving here because Jenn would miss me too much."

"Good. Can we go eat now?" Cindy asked and started for the door. She turned around and stared at me. "You look like my friend Emmie. But she has Down syndrome, and too bad for you, you don't."

That day a longing crawled into my heart that I knew wouldn't leave until I'd found a way to build a center like that close to home.

Five years later, Cindy died from an undiagnosed heart abnormality.

I stood in my office, still barefoot, still smelling like I'd rolled like a puppy in a soup of mud and grass, and I remembered Cindy and her snappy attitude. I unrolled the plans for the café and smiled when I traced the design. Cindy's Café.

I never forgot our lunch together. And no one else will either.

15

Over an hour later, and still nothing from Logan. No call. No text message. Very un-Logan-like. Unless he had a meeting, he was usually home by the time the street lights began to wake themselves up.

I left another message. "TAKING A SHOWER. TOO BAD YOU'RE NOT HERE. WHAT'S YOUR ETA?" I hoped the shower idea might motivate him to call. It's been months since we participated in water sports. He probably didn't remember we used to enjoy that time together.

On my way to grab towels from the dryer, my cell phone rang. But it wasn't Logan's ringtone. The call was from Matt. "You're calling me because my husband messed up his calendar and forgot he had a meeting tonight?"

"No. That's not why he didn't make it home. He's fine—"

"If you're telling me he's fine, then that means he wasn't fine first. What happened? Where is he?" I leaned against the laundry room wall, but my legs were like soggy french fries. I slid down the wall until my butt landed on the floor.

"He had an appointment and was on his way back to the office when the chest pains started. Megan brought him straight to St. Michael's ER. They're still running some tests, but the doctor thinks it was probably stress related."

"Is he still there? Are they keeping him overnight? I need to get to the hospital." I pushed myself back up the wall, but I had no idea what to do next. Do I shower? No. Not enough time. I can't go to the hospital like this. . . . My clothes smelled like old salami. I walked in and out and in and out of the laundry room. "Megan? Who's Megan? Never mind. You can tell me later, I have to get dressed."

"Take your time. We don't need you rushing to the hospital and winding up being a patient too. Is Martha around? Can she drive or go with you?"

"Are you kidding me? No, Martha's not here because she would have already been there while you were still talking to her." I moved to the hall, paced between my bedroom and the bathroom, still unsure which door I'd choose. "And, Matt, don't call her. She's not home anyway. I'll tell her."

"You sure about that?" Matt knew my volunteering to be the center of a dart board would be less painful than what Martha would be throwing my way after she figured out I delayed calling her.

I found a minimally wrinkled sundress in my closet. *Yep. You'll do.* "Yes, I'm sure. And you don't have to cover for me. I'll own it." And why not? After today, I'd be the queen of owning. Possibly a queen without a king or kingdom.

I didn't shower, but I splashed my underarms and neck with enough soap and water to feel clean-ish. I wanted to nix the make-up, but I was going to be Mrs. Logan Butler at the hospital. If I walked in looking like a before photo for an anti-aging cream, then I'd be condemned for not spending more time caring for myself. If I appeared too overdone, then I'd be condemned for spending more time caring for myself than my husband. The Goldilocks syndrome. I had to be just right and never *too* anything.

When enough time passed that we could laugh about this, I'd have to remember to tell Logan to have these inconvenient attacks during the day when I could get by with sunglasses and a hat.

Martha's lights were still off when I drove by. Maybe by the time she was home, she'd think we were lights out for the night. I wanted to talk to Cam, but I thought she'd already overdosed on Elle drama. If Logan hadn't been fine, and I was trusting Matt that he was, I would have called. It wasn't so much that I wanted to talk to Cam. It was more like I didn't want to be with me. I didn't want everything that happened today staging its own little Occupy Movement in my head. It was enough to keep myself from ignoring speed limits and red lights trying to get to the hospital as quickly as possible. One thought that refused to sit in the corner of my brain and be still was Logan's father dying of heart disease before he reached fifty.

I nosed the car into the closest parking spot I could find near the ER, hit the brake too hard, and my open purse slid off the seat. It landed mouth side down, but not before it spewed everything inside. I turned off the car, reached over to grab it, and knocked my head on the glove compartment. *Can one more thing go wrong?* I sputtered a few one-syllable words, massaged my forehead, and tried again. *Is there no weight limit on the emotional trauma loaded on someone in one day?*

Apparently not.

I trudged up the ramp to the double glass doors and waited while two EMS attendants pushed an empty gurney and an empty wheelchair into an open ambulance. Bodies of every shape, sex, and symptom stuffed the waiting room. Kids sprawled across plastic chairs, some with their heads resting in their mothers' laps, others quietly sucking their thumbs and twisting their fingers in their hair. Televisions hung across from one another on the walls, all on different stations. The room smelled like rubbing alcohol and restlessness.

I scanned the room looking for Matt, but he wasn't there. As I walked up to the desk, I realized I'd forgotten to check the damage my forehead might have sustained and hoped a red eye of a bump hadn't grown there. I feathered my bangs across my forehead before I spoke to the admit clerk who was on the telephone giving directions to the hospital. She hung up, then turned to me. "GPS. MapQuest. You'd think people used these things. But, no. It's easier to call from your cell phone and have me tell you every street corner you're supposed to turn on. Do you know my nine-year-old can figure that out?"

"Really? Smart kid," I responded, not knowing if that was an accurate assessment on my part. She seemed young to be the mother of a child that age, but I wasn't sure if she'd consider that a compliment or an insult. "My husband was admitted earlier. Logan Butler."

"Lemme see where your husband is." A few mouse clicks later, she looked up from her computer monitor. "They haven't brought him back from his MRI. He'll be in room E, down the hall to your left. I can let you know when he gets there."

"I was looking for our friend who called to tell me he was here. I don't see him in the waiting room, and I thought maybe he was with my husband."

She stood and scanned the waiting room. "There's who he came in with," she said as she pointed to a woman sitting near the door reading a book.

"Are you sure?" I couldn't see her face clearly, but I knew I'd never met her before. She wore a sleeveless, black and white, color-blocked dress with black platform sandals, and her light blonde hair hung over her left shoulder in a loose braid. Toned arms, body size of a pencil, and long legs. I hoped she was the Megan of the phone call because I didn't want to house other possibilities in my brain.

The clerk shuffled papers on her desk. "Mr. Logan Butler, right?"

I nodded. Someone standing behind me had a cough-sneeze rumba happening, I shifted as close to the desk as possible imagining the possibilities of gunk that could be lurking in my hair. I missed Martha at times like this. She would've already spun around, a mini-lecture on infectious disease prevention and a handful of tissues at the ready.

"Yep. That's her."

I must not have pulled off a credible look of understanding because the admit clerk's eyes darted between the blonde and me, and now the maybe Megan woman closed her book and looked our way as if she suspected she was the topic of discussion. The clerk paused before she sat, a wide-eyed, curling smile on her face. One that said, "Now, this is going to be interesting."

"Thanks," I said and scooted away from the mucous monster. Not so thrilled to approach this mystery woman in my wrinkled sundress, cyclops-bumped forehead, doughy arms, and scantily made-up face. I threaded my way through the ER grab bag of the broken, the bloody, and the bandaged until I reached Megan. Closer, she appeared younger, probably not yet thirty. That roundness of a twenty-something-year-old face still lingered.

I shook her hand because I didn't know the "how to introduce yourself to a woman you don't know, who brought your husband to the hospital when he thought he was having a heart attack" protocol.

"Hi, you must be Megan." I sat in the corner seat across from her. "Thank you so much for getting Logan here—"

"It's not MAY-gan. It's MEE-gan," she said. "I learned it's easier to make the distinction from the beginning." She crossed her legs with practiced precision and clasped her hands in her lap over her book.

She just playground shoved me with those sentences.

"Oh, my. Forgive me," I said and placed my hand over my open mouth for special effect before I continued. "But I do know how you feel. My name, Elle, is sometimes *so* problematic." My tightened jaw muscles would have won an Olympic gold medal for endurance. "But—Logan. In the hospital. What happened? Wait. No. First, I'm sorry. We've never met. What is it you do for Logan?"

The slight twitch of her mouth as I questioned her, along with her sudden need to dismiss non-existent errant threads from her dress alerted me that I'd found the chink in her MAY-MEE-gan armor.

She moved a bit in the chair as if afraid it may have become part of her body and cleared her throat. "Lo . . . Mr. Butler hired me a month ago."

Tick. One penalty point deduction for almost calling my husband by his first name.

"I'm a certified paralegal, and I was told his firm was looking for another paralegal. . . ."

Tick two. News to me.

"I decided to be pro-active, and I made an appointment with Mr. Butler. We also discussed his campaign, and I told him that I had media experience that would be helpful. Essentially, with one salary, he would have the advantage of my expertise in two valuable areas."

Tick three. No wife wanted to hear her husband hired a younger woman with expertise in "two valuable areas." It simply sounded suspect, even if it wasn't.

Megan's voice wobbled less the longer she spoke. I didn't feel altogether comfortable about that. But I had two more questions rolled into one. MEE-gan's expertise at that two-for-one business. "Okay, but what happened to Logan?"

Another precision leg cross. She must have been on dance team in college. "Actually, we weren't *going* anywhere. Log . . . Mr. Butler and I were returning from an appointment with new clients. Well, new potential clients that I'd referred to him. Absolute Logic? Have you heard of them?"

"No, I haven't," I answered, but did it matter if I'd heard of them?

"Anyway," she said, followed by a dramatic sigh, "the appointment took much longer than expected. And, since it was almost past dinnertime, I suggested this fabulous sushi place that wasn't too much out of the way."

"Sushi?" *Logan ate sushi? The closest he'd ever come to eating raw seafood was when I'd first tried to fry shrimp and undercooked them.*

"Like I said, I'd just suggested it. But your husband said he needed to call and check your plans. We pulled into a parking lot, and when I handed him his cell phone, he joked about having indigestion before we even ate. Then he leaned his head on the steering wheel and said he was dizzy and felt like something was stepping on his chest. He told me to call Matt, which, of course, I ignored. I immediately called 911, and based on his answers to the questions they asked, they said it was probably not a heart attack, but I should bring him to the ER."

"I see," I responded, but I didn't, not really. Since my husband escaped death, it seemed shallow and bitter of me to have the urge to kill him at that moment. I reassured myself that MAY-MEE-gan being with him was fortuitous, and I should be grateful because if he had been alone having a heart attack,

I might be sitting in the waiting room of the morgue, not the ER. But as she storied the night's events, I sensed a hint of an emotional intimacy in her voice, like walking into Cam's room after she'd left for a date but a whisper of her perfume lingered.

The desk clerk called my name. Megan stood when I did. I went for the preemptive strike. "I'll be sure to tell my husband that you waited for me to get here before you left. I truly appreciate that," I said and reached out my hand.

"Since he won't be seeing me, he'll probably want these," Megan said, as if I'd just told her she couldn't have dessert even though she ate all her supper. She gave me his suit jacket and in a small hospital-issued bag, his wedding band and watch. "Please tell Mr. Butler that I'm relieved to know that he's better."

"Of course," I said. "But, please, let me call a cab for you."

"No, that's not necessary. My apartment isn't far." Purse in hand, she started to walk away.

"Wait, I'm sure your parents wouldn't want you walking home alone at night. I'll get you a cab."

"No, I'd be more comfortable if you didn't." Megan pulled her cell phone out of her purse and started scrolling. "I'll call. Good night."

I took that as my signal to leave. And I did.

16

On the way down the hall to where I'd finally see Logan, I intended to stuff the small bag from Megan inside one of his suit pockets. But there was already something in the pocket. I stopped a few rooms before him and pulled out a tube of lipstick. Georgio Armani lipstick. Shade: Acid Tangerine. Unless Logan had gender issues about which I knew entirely nothing, it wasn't his. It wasn't mine; I didn't buy lipstick that cost more than my age.

I stood there holding it like I thought it would tell me its life story. *It's lipstick, Elle, not Viagra. One tube of lipstick does not an affair make. Right?* Worse things, delicate, lacey things, had been found in men's jackets and glove compartments and pants' pockets. Things much more convicting than Acid Tangerine. But I didn't know too many men who carried lipsticks for women other than husbands or maybe kind or bullied brothers. It just seemed a tad more intimate than friendship. Maybe my guilt exceeded my sanity.

"Excuse me. Did you need some help?"

Probably a smart question to ask a woman leaning against the wall in the ER fixated on a tube of lipstick. It came from a tall, curly-haired man wearing scrubs and a white coat embroidered with "Dr." followed by something unrecognizable.

"I'm fine . . . just . . . uh . . . stopped to put this . . . " I held up the little silver-tubed culprit, "in my purse." I dropped it in. "My husband's in room E. . . . "

He smiled. Maybe with relief that I wasn't a patient waiting to happen and he'd be stuck with me. "It's two doors down." Dr. Something pointed to make sure I understood spatial concepts and scurried away.

Logan was on his cell phone, sitting on the side of the bed, wearing his suit pants and his hospital gown when I walked in his room. "Hold on, Matt," he said, tossed the cell phone on the bed and held out his arms.

Still holding his jacket and my purse, I hushed the cacophony of women—my mother, Holly, Faith, Martha, Megan—who pulled apart the threads of my life and stepped into his embrace. My head against his chest, I kissed his neck as he softly kissed the top of my head. When death tapped its finger on life's shoulder, whispering it was only a heartbeat away, it reminded us of what mattered most. If only we could warm ourselves with the blanket of these intense moments when life's chilling realities surrounded us.

"Logan? Logan? You okay?"

"I love you, Elle," Logan whispered in my ear before his arms released me.

"I love you more," I said, and he smiled. The "love you more" had been a silly verbal volleyball we played in those early years when saying "I love you" to one another generated more emotional energy than "I'm going to the grocery." It slipped out of our banter when we started focusing more on "stuff" than us. Maybe the presence of that little gold tube reminded me what could have been lost between us. What I hoped hadn't been or wouldn't be lost.

I moved Logan's neatly folded shirt and tie off the swamp-green plastic chair in the room and sat as he picked up his phone. "Sorry. Elle just arrived." He sounded on the verge of surprise. Without his beige hospital wristband and a bandage on each arm where they'd drawn blood, Logan didn't look like a man who'd been the reason for a 911 call. His hair looked confused as to which direction it was supposed to be headed, but tousled worked well on him. The relaxed face he'd greeted me with grew serious as he spoke to Matt. After a few yes and no responses, he said, "Wait, I'll ask Elle." He tilted the mouthpiece up. "Did you tell my mother I'd been admitted?"

My throat snapped even though his tone wasn't the least bit accusatory. I looked at the floor, which was not being at all cooperative in opening up to swallow me, then told Logan, "No. I thought it would be best for me to wait until I saw you. I didn't know, for sure, and—"

"Elle, it's okay. But she already knows, and Matt's just doing some damage control."

"Damage control? She's angry, isn't she?" I tapped my foot and stared at the wall behind Logan. "I'm doomed. She's not going to let me forget this one—"

I heard "No," but he'd started talking to Matt again. "Okay. Will do. And, Matt, thanks."

"Logan, I'm sorry," I said. I checked my cell phone. "I don't have any missed calls. Is she upset? On her way here?"

"She's calling a divorce attorney," he said and laughed immediately. "Matt was able to get in touch with her, and she's home."

"Remind me to buy that man an outrageously expensive gift this Christmas. Maybe an island."

"Would you hand me my shirt?" He untied his hospital gown and pulled his shirt on. "Martha's not the reason Matt's doing damage control."

"What? Then where's the damage?"

He sat on the bed as he finished buttoning his shirt, but something shifted in his posture. In the way he spent too much time rolling his tie around his hand. "Elle, look at me, and wait until I finish explaining. But you have to trust I am telling you the truth. Okay?"

I nodded, but it's a given, "you need to trust me" was the key that opened the door to suspicion.

"The late news reported I'd been taken to the hospital by a young woman, in their words, 'whose identity was yet unknown.' The reporter said the young woman in question and I were seen driving into the Timbers apartment complex, and the 911 call was made after that. But—"

Someone knocked on the door and opened it at the same time. "Mr. Butler, I'm Agnes, the nurse on duty. I have your discharge papers." Cotton candy pinks and blues streaked her blonde hair, and she wore scrubs decorated with Disney characters. She grinned. "Can you tell I usually work pediatrics? I work in cancer care, so I do what I can," she said and held up locks of her hair, "to make them laugh."

Logan and I looked at one another. "Later," hung between us. The worst saved until last. Not the way it should go. I wanted to tug on Agnes's stethoscope and ask if we could have a girl chat outside. I'd tell her my husband was in the middle of explaining what might be an affair waiting to happen. Could this wait? One or both of us might need your services when he's finished. Agnes would *tsk, tsk* and pat my back and tell me how sorry she was, and how I should get on in there and finish this off. And I would waltz in, punch Logan maybe on his cheek, not his nose. He had a nice nose. Then I would sit in the ugly, plastic chair, and he would tell me every detail I never wanted to hear. Instead, I sat in the ugly, plastic chair feeling like an ugly, plastic wife.

"They're lucky to have you," Logan said to Agnes. "That must be a difficult job."

She shook her head. "Not as difficult as theirs," she said. "Let's get you out of here." Agnes sat on a low round stool she pulled from under the bed. "Are you his wife?"

"Yes. Yes, I am," I said. I held up my right hand. "So help me, God."

For years, the idea that I'd ever be introducing myself as Logan Butler's wife battled for the top spot on my list of least likely things to happen during my lifetime along with walking the red carpet at the Oscars with Johnny Depp.

After our month at Leadership Camp, Logan went back home, but returned to LSU in the fall as a freshman.

I returned home to high school and, as all eleventh grade students, contemplated the importance of the upcoming school year. Prom. Spring break. Jake. Sort of.

Jake and I started spending time together at the end of our sophomore year when we both suffered through the same honors classes and student council meetings. A group of six to eight of us at any given time would have study groups or swim parties or hang out at one person's house watching movies, eating. Going to the end-of-year dance was our first real date, as in couple date. Jake and I also saw each other at youth group every Sunday. His father pastored the church, and my dad was a deacon; therefore, choice never factored in to the decision of whether or not we'd attend. Unlike nominal Christian me, Jake was the real deal, but in a way that never made people walk in the opposite direction if they saw him headed toward them. I liked his goofy sense of humor. Whenever he had a cold and I'd ask if he wanted a tissue, his wide-eyed response, almost every time, was, "Elle, tissue? I hardly know you." Of course, that didn't stop me from laughing as if I'd heard it for the first time.

He called me a few days after I'd been home to ask if I wanted to ride with him and some of our other friends to the seafood festival. That next day, as we walked around Fontainebleau State Park trying to decide if we should eat crawfish bread, charbroiled oysters, or shrimp po-boys for lunch, Jake sent everyone off in twos—it was biblically sound, he said—with each couple buying something different, then we'd all get back together and share. The two of us waited in line for crawfish bread, and we weren't sure if we'd even make it to order before the festival ended for the day. He sensed I was different. I saw how he looked at me when he thought I was distracted by something or someone else. Our conversations lurched along, both of us trying to navigate away from the reeling and pitching that came with being familiar strangers.

That night, he brought me home and said that all day, when we talked, it was like trying to talk around someone or something standing between us. And, of course, that was exactly the problem.

I expected that after what Logan and I had shared, we'd find a way to see one another again. But after a few weeks, the e-mails, which were friendly to the point of polite, stopped. As if we were pen pals who lived countries apart instead of cities. I supposed his being at college and my being in high school might as well have qualified as two different countries. I deleted his e-mail address and phone number so I'd stop deluding myself that I mattered to him. And start convincing myself that he didn't matter to me.

Melody and I managed to stay in touch with one another, mostly through my responding to the funny or weird quotes she'd e-mail. Things like, "You won't believe what Werner von Braun said??!!! 'We can lick gravity, but sometimes the paperwork is overwhelming.'!!!!!" She had a torrid love affair with exclamation points. But a cell phone to Melody was like religion to me. We both knew they were around, but neither one of us cared enough to use them. When she called around the Thanksgiving holidays, at a time when I was beyond second-guessing myself about Logan, I was probably working on seventh-guessing by then, I didn't know if I should prepare for Armageddon or for her being on the next lunar launch.

"Elle's bells," an endearment only she could invent, "what's up with our boy-man, Logan?"

My anxiety elevator went to the tenth floor, but left my stomach on the ground floor. "Up with him? Melody, I don't know what's up, down, or sideways with him. Why would I?" *Indeed.* I picked at my cuticles waiting for her answer.

An uncharacteristic pause followed by an okay that was a long string of "o" clipped at the "kay."

"Do *you* know?" I ripped too much skin off my forefinger, which now burned and bled. Melody needed to get to the point before every one of my fingers suffered.

"I think he's practically engaged to that broom-flyer, Cassie, no . . . let me look again . . . Carole. Remember? The one with the legs that started at her neck? She wrote 'almost engaged' on the school's Yahoo group."

My heart constricted and the elevator swooshed to the penthouse, leaving me in the basement. Her news torched the hopeful future I'd built and placed under my pillow every night. I was collateral damage, and no one was going to come to my rescue.

"When . . . when did this happen?"

"Sometime last week, yes, November 21," she said. "I wonder what happened to all their intentions to save the universe, rainforest, and homeless animals or . . ."

Whatever she said next was lost in what sounded like a drum line. Or my throbbing temples or both.

"Sorry," she half-shouted. "Band practice is about to start. I'm going in the building."

The rhythmic thunder of the drums receded, a door squealed, then Melody, accompanied by quiet, said, "Is this better? Good. I was trying to say they blustered about their social conscience during the summer, and by fall they're bragging about their social lives?"

My fingers pressed against my lips to forestall blubbering, I mumbled, "Guess so."

"It was a rhetorical question," she said. "Hey, do you think maybe she's pregnant and that's the rush?"

The conversations Logan and I shared those nights we were together curdled in my mouth. Pregnant? Did he change his mind? Did *she* change his mind? I pinched the corners of my eyes, but the tears slipped through anyway.

"Hey, Elle, are you still on the line?"

I grabbed a crumpled tissue off my desk, wiped my nose, and demanded a performance from my cheeriest voice. "Yes. Nose running. Getting sick, I think."

"What do you think? Think they're trying to make it to the altar before the delivery room?"

"Melody, I honestly don't know what to think. Guess you'll have to keep checking the Yahoo group." And don't update me, I wanted to add.

I woke up a few hours later, on top of my comforter, covered by the bottom half that I'd pulled up over myself. I checked the time on my cell phone. Not even noon. Now what?

Wrapped in my loneliness, I stared out my bedroom window and wished I could float out on the streams of sun that broke through the clouds.

Of course, then, I had no way of knowing that two years later, Logan Butler would boomerang into my life.

17

Agnes said I should drive home, so we left Logan's car at the hospital. Maybe it still being in the parking lot would be a diversion for the people with cameras and ambition, until Logan's leaving the hospital posted on Twitter, Facebook, or some other social media sites. Which probably happened ten to fifteen seconds after we walked out of the ER.

The truth sat between us the entire ride home. Lumpy and large, it pushed against Logan and me, vying for space, making it impossible for us to see one another.

It didn't stir when Logan called Martha, who wanted it to make noise, but he told her he would explain everything in the morning. He wanted her to know he was fine, we were going home, and she didn't need to worry.

Was his mother the only person exempt from worrying? Or was there a free pass for the rest of us?

Since we hadn't eaten, I drove through the nearest fast-food place for burgers and fries to eat at home. As I pulled onto the street, I asked Logan if he needed me to stop anywhere else on the way.

He leaned toward me, but he didn't try to kiss me. Just coddled my cheek with his warm hand and looked at me as if he'd won first prize at the fair. For anything. On a better night, the steam emanating from his eyes might have landed both of us in the back seat. "No. I have everything I need. Right here," Logan said. "I know we didn't finish—"

"And we're not going to now. Not while I'm driving." That was when I plopped that load of truth between us.

Logan nodded and said, "You're right. I'll wait." He reclined his seat and seemed to be asleep before I'd driven a mile. He might have pretended to be sleep. I wasn't sure since he faced the window. Either way, it gave me time to think. I believed him. Because why would he have told me the version that made the situation more, not less, suspect? And why would Megan narrate a story she knew wasn't honest? Especially since she worked for a law firm.

It might have taken years for Logan and me to find our way back to one another, but when we decided to date one another exclusively, I never doubted his faithfulness. After we married, and he decided on this foray into politics, I wasted time waiting for the other shoe to fall. It seemed to be the fallout of even what we thought were "good" marriages. We watched too many politicians stand behind the podium with their wives and admit to indiscretions, some of which provided entirely too much information.

Logan was faithful to God, and though I didn't consider myself a God groupie by any means, I knew Bible-justice smite. And God's vengeance, I was sure, wasn't an idle threat. It provided another layer of security in believing my husband would never bed another woman, and I'm certain it wasn't because he lacked invitations or opportunities. We'd been invited to a fund-raising dinner for the governor, a black-tie event with mediocre food and enough fawning to make Bambi sick. I'd returned from the bathroom to find a woman at our table, in my chair, whose cleavage started at her neckline. She proudly displayed the "girls," having shoved them into a dress made for women who wore training bras.

I walked over, stood behind Logan, ignored her, and practiced the performance art of tousling his hair while barely touching it with one hand and smoothing my other hand over his shoulder. Logan reached for my hand, but before he could speak, I moved closer to him, looked at the woman as if she was a dress hanging on the sale rack. "We haven't met. I'm Mrs. Butler, and you're sitting in my seat." She patted Logan's knee and said, "I'll just be one more itty-bitty minute, sugah."

It was then I suspected this "sisterhood of women" was a sham. And while I hated bashing those close to home, as I later told Camden on one of our visits, "Southern women are the worst. They've watched *Gone With the Wind* too much, and they all think they're Scarlett O'Hara. I think they must have forgotten that she ended up alone at the end."

I wondered, as I turned the car into our driveway and waited for the garage door to open, if doubt buzzed around my head like a mosquito, did I truly, completely, and ever-after trust Logan?

And if I did, then why had I waited this long to tell him about Faith?

I trusted Logan to be faithful as far as not straying from our marriage bed or sofa or whatever. What scared me was that if I told the truth, as in the whole truth and nothing but, it wouldn't set me free. It would set him free, and once again, I'd have disappointed someone who loved me. I'd already watched relationships turn to dust when stabbed with the truth.

After I told my parents I was pregnant, nothing was ever the same between us. For some families, a teenage pregnancy was a flood, not a tsunami like it was for mine. Had my parents offered even the slightest support, I could have survived whatever people said about me. But they wouldn't, and I couldn't.

Cam and my mother were the only ones who saw Faith after she was born. I wanted her to hold what she desperately wanted me to give away. My father never saw Faith, never held her, and never would. Weeks before my due date, my father collapsed in the garage. My mother, thinking he lost track of time piddling with his tools, thought she'd surprise him with lunch. While she was spreading mustard on his ham sandwich, he'd started sweating. By the time she'd scooped potato salad on his plate, his heart cells gasped for air while he rubbed his aching arm. She poured his unsweetened iced tea, not too much ice, and his heart had stopped beating entirely. When the tray my mother carried in fell from her hands and splattered on his tool bench and the concrete floor, his brain cells had already started to die. She saw him crumpled, a cold, wet, grey-blue towel. Elton John tunes streamed from a radio on the floor next to him.

The paramedics provided more help for my mother than my father. They reassured her his death from heart failure likely happened in five minutes, maybe fewer. I didn't know if or when she stopped replaying his last minutes on an endless loop in her head. What I did know was she made it clear that she and Dad had been talking about me. About what they were going to do when the call came that I was on my way to the hospital to deliver. Do? Stay home or go to the hospital. Jabs about my father's disappointment or sadness or humiliation became sheets of paper my mother cut me with at every opportunity. Unexpected stings that sliced into my heart.

I didn't need her to remind me what I'd done to my father. His voice when we spoke was taut, his sentences clipped, and his words marched out with military precision. I would have chosen standing on a platform in the middle of the city while people gawked instead of the emotional distance that separated me from him.

I failed his heart before it failed him.

⁂

I walked into darkness at home, since I'd forgotten to leave lights on when I left. Logan walked in after me, and while I slapped the kitchen wall in search of the light switch, he wrapped his arms around my waist and tugged me toward him. He pushed my hair aside, kissed me behind my ear, and was on his way to making a soft trail of them down my neck.

"Really? You want to do this now?" I squirmed and flipped on the lights. *I might be more interested in ripping your clothes off if I hadn't just picked you up from the hospital after you had an almost-heart attack while you were with another woman.*

His arms stayed around my waist. "Why not now? I've missed you. Every part of you." His lips grazed my hair. "You smell like peaches . . . and it's making me hungry . . . for you."

Every place he touched me, my body responded and ached for him. But, I wasn't going to be seduced into forgetting what we started at the hospital. I didn't want to close my eyes and see my husband tangled in the sheets with some other woman. I loosened his grip enough that I could turn around to face him. I cupped his face with my hands and drew him toward me until our foreheads touched. "I love you, and I want you." I let the urgency of my kiss convince him that I meant what I said. "But for now, I want you to finish the truth you started at the hospital."

139

He smoothed my hair back with his fingertips. "You're right. We'll talk while we eat."

We sat at the kitchen table and unwrapped our burgers. As I divided the fries between us, Logan said, "This isn't going to turn into a food fight, is it?"

I handed him a napkin. "You're making what we need to discuss sound as if it's not a big deal. And it's definitely not *Animal House* kind of amusing."

"Lighten up, Elle. I know that." Logan moved his burger aside. "Let's just get this over with. We're both tired. And tomorrow might be more stressful than tonight. For both of us. Look, nothing happened between me and Megan beyond what I told you. Of course, the press is going to manipulate that. Especially since they're looking for any opportunity to discredit the Conservative Family Values candidate."

"Then why didn't Megan tell me the same story you did?" I swirled my fries in ketchup and waited for his answer.

"What? I don't understand. What did she tell you?"

I skipped commentary on Megan's attitude and repeated the details she'd given me. I reached for my purse, found the lipstick case, and placed it on the table. "And I found this in your suit pocket. Maybe this can help you understand why I'm not thinking that this is amusing. You know, this is one of those times when it's not the thing itself, it's what the thing suggests. It's a tube of lipstick. Expensive lipstick, but what-ever. But, Logan, I don't know too many women—no, I really don't know any women—who'd ask their bosses if they'd mind carrying their lipstick in their pockets. It's the kind of thing a wife asks her husband to do. Trust me, it's in the unwritten code of womanhood."

He leaned forward, elbows on the table, hands clasped. For a moment, I wondered if he might be praying. If he felt he needed to pray, I didn't find that consoling.

"I should've listened to Matt and fired Megan a week ago."

I drank tea to wash down the fries stuck in my throat. "Excuse me?"

"It's complicated. . . ."

"That's a Facebook status update. Not something you tell your wife about another woman." I pushed my own plate aside. This conversation was not conducive to eating.

He held up both hands as if under arrest. "No, no. I meant it's complicated only because I'm an idiot, and I don't expect people to have an agenda. Matt tells me it's admirable to always want to see the good in people, but it's not wise to let it blind you."

I nodded. How could I not?

Logan explained that weeks before, one of the investors in the real estate deal, the one that necessitated that second mortgage on our house, called to ask him if he had any openings for paralegals. He didn't, but since it was the man's daughter who was looking for a job, he agreed to meet with her. "I'll admit, Megan impressed me. Smart, professional, assertive, confident, young—"

"Young, attractive, long-legged, well-dressed . . . "

"Well, yes, but that had nothing to do with why I decided to hire her," he said. "I thought she could summarize depositions and free Jenny to work on discoveries and pleadings. . . . " He stopped. "And don't give me the eyebrow."

"At least you're admitting you noticed."

"Why do you think that would matter to me? Is that what this is about?"

I stacked our plates and slid my chair back to carry the dishes to the sink.

Logan held my wrist. "Sit down, Elle. You can do that later. What's going on?"

I hated that he said it like he really wanted to know. If he'd sounded annoyed or condescending, I could have dismissed him with one of my "Nothing, I'm fine" responses. My passive-aggressive way of saying "everything." But the sincerity in his voice and his expression was real, which made being a brat difficult.

"Do you really feel that insecure about our relationship?"

"No. Maybe." I busied myself with straightening the stack of dishes. "It's me. I feel that insecure about me," I said, but I couldn't lift my eyes to look at him.

"Elle," he said, his voice like warm sheets. "Have I made you feel that way?" He lifted my head, his hand under my chin. "Because if I did, I promise you, I never meant to."

The kitchen symphony overtook the quiet between us. The ceiling fan creaked as it turned, the ice crashed into the freezer bin, even the air conditioner trembled as the thermostat kicked on.

"No," I whispered. "It's not you. It's everything that takes you away from me. Sometimes, there's just not enough of you to go around." I wiped my nose with my napkin. "Then tonight, I'm rushing to the hospital, trusting you're fine because Matt told me you were. And instead of meeting Matt there, this woman I don't even know is telling me she's been riding around with you all afternoon and you're about to go to dinner with her, then you tell me you're in the parking lot of her apartment complex . . . and her lipstick's in your pocket . . . and then there's the truth, the lie, something in between. . . . " I looked at Logan. "It's a recipe for crazy."

"You're right. You're absolutely right. But I had no idea Megan wouldn't tell you what really happened. Matt told me, though, after he'd met her that he didn't trust her. He thought she seemed too smooth, too eager to make herself available for anything that required my attention. I told him to stop being cynical when I'd tell her, sometimes, that she looked nice. But, I tell Jenny that too. I'm not going to invite a sexual harassment suit. I'll admit, at first some of the things she said fed my ego. I'm not proud of that."

"Let me guess. She asked how you stayed in such great shape and said you must have graduated at the top of your class because you were smart and you looked much younger than she expected . . . should I go on?"

"How did you know?"

Poor man, he sounded genuinely surprised. "If women aren't careful, it's a genetic predisposition," I said.

He smiled. "Really? That's one Martha never warned me about."

I wondered what she had warned him about and when, but not enough to ask. "Back to Megan. Why were you at her apartment?"

"I wasn't. First, I didn't ask or need her to go with me to the client. It was a business her father, not her, referred me to. And, yes, we talked about dinner, and I told her I wanted to check to see what your plans were. I hadn't felt well all afternoon, but I figured I was hungry. She asked if we could stop by her apartment, that she wanted to change. When I parked, she asked if I wanted to come in, and I remember thinking, 'Why would I want to do that?' and I started to tell her I was going to call you when the pain started—"

"And this?" I held up the lipstick.

"Elle, I honestly have no idea how that ended up in my jacket."

"I believe you," I said, threw it away with our dinner leftovers and reached for Logan's hand.

"Where are you taking me?"

"To a place where breathtaking things happen. A place we've neglected."

We walked out of the kitchen and down the hall, with Logan fully cooperating by not letting go of my hand. I opened the door to our bedroom. I patted the top of our bed. "This is not just for sleeping," I said. I walked to the closet, removed a black lace teddy and showed it to Logan. "And neither is this."

Logan unbuttoned his shirt on his way to me. "Lesson over. Time for the test."

I woke up the next morning to Logan kissing my bare shoulder. "Hey, sleepyhead. Breakfast time. What are you hungry for?"

I rolled over and lifted my face to his. "You."

We decided late breakfast would do just as well.

18

Two coffees, one newspaper." Logan set one mug on his nightstand, the other on mine, and handed me the paper. "Anything else?"

"Not yet, Prince Charming," I said as I patted the empty space next to me. "Back in bed. You need to relax, remember?"

"Oh, that's what we're calling it now? 'Relaxing'? I'm willing for my coffee to get cold, if we need to relax again," he said and leaned on his pillow propped against the headboard.

I laughed. "Kiss me, for now. We have all day."

His lips were warm, and he tasted like coffee. When his face moved away from mine, his eyes seemed to still hold me close. "I love you, Elle Butler."

"And I love you more, Mr. Butler. Now, hand me the entertainment section, and you read the front page. Or maybe they buried the story about you inside."

I turned the first page of my newspaper when the doorbell rang. "It's 8:30. Do we want to know who this is?" But before Logan could answer me, it rang again.

We said to each other, "Martha."

"Stay here," said Logan. "I'll go talk to her and tell her we had a very long night," he winked, "and we'll call her about going out for lunch." He pulled on his jeans and almost had his T-shirt on when she rang again.

"I might as well get up. She has her own key, and she's not afraid to use it." I set my coffee back on the nightstand, closed the newspaper, and reached for my silk robe, which had been tossed to the floor at some point the night before. I tied the belt on my robe and told Logan, "You're the one she wants to see anyway. Go make her a cup of coffee, and I'll be right out."

I expected to smell freshly brewed coffee as I neared the kitchen, not an entire breakfast of bacon, eggs, and biscuits. It was like walking on to the set of *The Adventures of Ozzie and Harriett* with Martha standing at the stove, an iconic 1950s wife and mother in her tailored dress and sensible pumps.

"Good morning, Elle. Aren't you relieved that Logan is fine? I thought you might stop on the way home from the hospital, but Logan explained how tired he was and he didn't want to chance waking me up." I couldn't decide if her stream of conversation kept pace with her egg scrambling or vice versa.

"Good morning, Martha," I replied. I glanced at Logan as she bent to check the biscuits in the oven. An almost imperceptible head nod, but his eyes shifted to the right. I followed their direction to see the Bailey's on duty next to the coffeemaker. He rolled his eyes, and I had to cough to cover my laugh. The wire whisk scraped the bottom of the frying pan with such speed and force, I wouldn't have been surprised if she'd ended up starting a fire inside the pan. "You're so . . . energetic this morning," I said and poured myself a cup of coffee.

She stopped stirring for a moment and looked off into space, then glanced around the room. "I am, aren't I?" Before the whisk could take a breath, she started again. "How could I be anything but full of pep? My son escaped what could have been a nightmare. And . . . " she turned off the fire under the exhausted eggs and tapped the whisk against the pan, "I have an announcement."

I lowered myself into the chair next to Logan as she closed her eyes for a moment. He and I looked at one another with equal confusion. Mine was tinged with dread.

Then, wide-eyed and animated, her arms spread, she curtsied and said, "You are looking at the next Blanche DuBois in the upcoming production of *A Streetcar Named Desire*."

I didn't know if Logan meant to kick me under the table or if it was truly a knee-jerk reaction to her news, but our delayed response sucked the joy out of her like air in a deflated balloon.

"I thought you'd be excited," she said and turned back to take the biscuits out of the oven.

"We are, Martha. We truly are. I know how much this role means to you," I said and elbowed a comment from Logan.

"Exactly. I . . . we didn't realize that the auditions were already over. You just caught us by surprise," he said.

For the second time this morning.

"Are you sure? I don't want this to be a problem because I know it's going to take time away from my being able to help. You with the campaign and Elle with her center."

"Mother, it's not a problem at all," said Logan as he walked over to hug her. "I'm very proud of you. Putting yourself out there and risking rejection takes courage. It says a lot about your character. How could I not be excited?" He took the spatula out of her hand. "Now, you go sit down next to Elle, and I can serve my two leading ladies."

"Oh, now, son, stop blowing smoke." She swatted him on the arm, but her broad smile and faint blush suggested she was delighted.

"Congrats, Martha," I said and hugged her. "I can't wait to see you on stage."

I had been on stage for over fifteen years, in a role I didn't want to play and I didn't want to give up, and the curtain was closing. Soon. But in the past twenty-four hours, Logan and I reconnected emotionally and physically, and why would I want to pull the plug on that? And Martha was so happy . . . I could ruin it all. And after what Logan said to her, I didn't have to wonder about his reaction to me.

Holly said I had two weeks. I still had time. For years I had time. But the right time and the truth were two trains running on parallel tracks that just never arrived at the intersections together. I could have thrown the switch that would make them adjust course. But it could've derailed one or both of them, and what would have been the point? Leaving them alone protected everyone. Until now. In a few days, one of those trains would run out of tracks.

⸺⸺

Martha wasted no time in capitalizing on Logan's unexpected free day. During breakfast, she asked if we could still make the appointments to see the properties.

"Now all three of us are going to have busy calendars, what with my having to add rehearsals. And Elle, you and I will still have those committee meetings, oh, and don't forget to keep track of your volunteer hours for Junior League, and whatever you need to do with my son. . . ."

After that, I purposely kicked Logan under the table, hoping he caught that his mother had just granted me permission for "whatever" I needed "to do" with him. Since his hand massaged my right leg, I took that as a yes. But while Martha walked off to call Dootsie and Logan went into his office to return Matt's call, I looked at the date circled on my calendar. My husband and my mother-in-law spoke about next month, and the month after, and the month after that, and I smiled and nodded and lied. But it was, for now, the only way I could protect them for a few more days.

"Dootsie said she can meet us in a half hour at the first property. Is that too soon?" Martha leaned against the kitchen counter.

I told her it was fine for me and Logan should be off the phone by the time I finished emptying the dishwasher.

"Will that be enough time for you to get ready?" Martha opened her compact, a vintage, pearlized-green clamshell that belonged to her mother, and used the mirror to dab on lipstick, not Acid Tangerine, more like Christmas red.

I inspected my fresh from Ann Taylor, mint, scalloped-laced blouse for breakfast residue. Clear. Nothing on my linen capris. "Sure, that will be plenty of time." I opened the silverware drawer and starting returning utensils to their places. "Martha, we've not ever talked about this. The scare with Logan yesterday made me wonder." I suddenly wondered myself why I was about to even venture into this territory, but it was too late. I dropped in the last few spoons and pushed the drawer closed.

"Wonder what, Elle?" Martha and I didn't discuss much that required anything more than a garden rake to sift through. I was about to ask a shovel-kind of question. She was understandably baffled.

"I wouldn't ask you this in front of Logan. I can hardly believe I'm asking now. And, please, if you don't want to answer, it's okay. I'm kind of putting you on the spot here. But, does it bother you that Logan and I don't have children? That you'll never be a grandmother?"

Martha looked at her hands, moved her watch around her wrist, and shifted until we faced one another. "Well," she said, "I'd be dishonest if I said it didn't matter. Most of my friends are grandparents, and they tell me their lives have been blessed in ways they never anticipated. In ways their own kids didn't. I'm sad I won't know that, sure." She looked over her shoulder and, like me, saw that Logan continued to talk to Matt. "I'm not all that surprised, though. I guess Logan's like his father that way. Though I never told him."

"Like his father?" I shook my head. "I'm confused."

"Daniel never really wanted children. He thought the two of us would be enough. We could travel, have money to do what we wanted to do, when we wanted to do it. When I told him I was pregnant, he accused me of tricking him. I refused to have an abortion. I had Logan instead. And I thank God for him everyday."

Martha Butler surprised me. She was, in fact, a woman whose character, compassion, and tenacity I had underestimated. Logan had no idea that he was as genetically predisposed to not wanting children as he was to heart disease. Of course, it wasn't as much a matter of genetics as it was his fearing he would be the kind of father to his child that Daniel was to him.

I understood Martha not telling Logan the truth because she wanted to protect him. But in shielding him from the pain of the truth, she also shielded him from the very information he needed to make sense of his relationship with his father.

But who was I to judge Martha? And what had we done to this man we both loved?

19

Matt straightened out the report. No more mystery woman. He said reporters' elation likely plummeted when Megan was not only identified as an employee, but the daughter of a business partner.

While we were on our way to view the first property Dootsie wanted to show us, Logan filled Martha and me in on his conversation with Matt, who reassured him that there wasn't much his opponent's camp could make of this in terms of negative campaigning.

"It's a shame your life is the definition of boredom, Logan. You're probably making them crazy." Martha chuckled as she sat in the back seat, filing her fingernails, the dust of which settled on the black leather around her.

Logan eyed his mother through the rearview mirror. "I hope so. We need to focus on the issues, get some dialogue going about our platforms. It scares me that politics is becoming fodder for entertainment news programs instead of journalistic news."

"Speaking of entertainment, is Matt going to have a discussion with Megan about fact versus fiction?" I wanted to ask about her employment, but I wasn't sure how much Logan wanted to discuss in front of his mother.

"Also on the agenda," he said.

Martha tapped my shoulder. "Are you sure we have the right address?"

"Well, I have the one she gave us, 765 Lily Lane. Why?"

"Logan, isn't this the way to that country club where your father used to play golf?"

"It does look familiar, but it's probably before or after that, especially since we need commercial zoning."

But less than ten miles later, the navigation brought us to the entry of Maple Hills and directed us to turn left. The median of the two-lane entry was a continuous ribbon of flowering plants for almost a mile, with nothing on either side but wide expanses of grass. "We should be getting close," I said looking at the GPS display and wondering why Dootsie thought we could locate in a residential area. Past the first stop sign, we understood. Still no homes in sight, but a stretch of office buildings, a supermarket, a bank, restaurants. It was a "Where's Waldo" reality show because everything was tucked behind or beside intentional landscaping, and even the signs were chameleon-like to avoid dwarfing the scenery.

A few turns later, Martha spotted Dootsie's Range Rover parked in front of what looked like a church.

"She does know we're not starting a new religion?"

Logan just smiled. "Get out of the car, Elle. I'm sure there's a reason she brought us here."

"Is this your clever way of saving my soul and getting me into a church?"

"No, honey. Maybe it's God's way," said Martha. "Now let's go see what this is."

She and Dootsie did the cheek-to-cheek hug, she introduced Logan and me, and Dootsie gave us the overview. "The church was built about six years ago for a congregation of approximately 400–500 members. They outgrew this location, and I thought this might work for your center without having to do too much build out in the beginning." She showed us the commercial kitchens, a large one used for the congregation and a smaller one on the other side of the building close to the nursery. "The sanctuary could be the activity space, and the rest of the building is existing offices and classrooms, and several of them have these partitions dividing the rooms," she said and pushed one of the floor-to-ceiling walls that folded like a tall gray accordion to open rooms.

"What if we decide we want to open it up to residents?" Logan asked. "We'd need separate facilities for the men and the women, and they each have to accommodate the house parents. Can we do that?" He disappeared into another room. I gave up trying to keep track of him.

She brought us to the back of the property. Near the basketball court was a gym, and on the other side of the gym, an open field. "The gym could be converted to a large residence, and there would be enough space for the residents and the house family. Or, since it's a square building, just add on. You could build another home using the field property or you could build a swimming pool there and convert the back classroom wing into a residence."

Martha flipped through the information about the property. "I don't think we'd have to worry about outgrowing the space with clients. I'm more concerned about how it might limit options like greenhouses and a gift shop. But I do like that groceries and restaurants are within walking distance." She closed the portfolio. "Okay, what's the bottom line? What are they asking?"

"Elle, you've not said much." Logan reappeared in the back of the property with the rest of us. "If you don't think it will work, the price tag doesn't matter."

"We've spent so much time designing plans, I hadn't considered finding something already existing that we could work around." The church's vanilla-shaded brick and its sharp, angular style weren't the exterior I had in mind. Most of what could have been gardens had been poured over by concrete, and injecting softness and color could be challenging. "It definitely has potential, and I'd be interested in the committee's reaction to this as a possibility."

"The asking price is $4.1 million," Dootsie said like she was reading information off a cereal box while the rest of us choked on the cereal. "But, of course, we know that's never the bottom. Let's go look at those other two properties. They're both acreage and more in line with the plans you've been developing. And, chins up, we've just begun to fight." She pumped her fist in the air and waved us on.

The two properties she brought us to see were on the opposite ends of town. The first one was actually outside the city limits and required almost a one-mile drive down a lumpy gravel road. It was an eight-acre swath through land once used for tree farming. Not as in Christmas trees, as in planting trees and then harvesting them for lumber. The property was now devoid of trees with the exception of saplings that littered the acreage. The bumpy gravel road, the treeless property . . . none of it appealed to any of us.

To reach the second property, I'm not sure if Dootsie had us follow her along an especially scenic route or if what we passed would be the apron to the stage that would be the center.

Who knew there were places in South Louisiana where ground would swell enough that we could call it a hill? We drove on tar-topped country roads that swirled through towns with populations the size of high schools and past wide-porched homes lounging under yawning oak trees whose canopies stretched across their rooftops. Sometimes a few cows grazed inside fields marked by split-rail fences and azalea bushes. More than an hour later, we turned down another gravel road, this one a wide, smooth path defined on each side by tall southern magnolias every twenty feet, their creamy-white blooms shining against their broad, dusky green leathery leaves. The tires crunched over three miles of gravel before it curved to the right and wove around a pond the size of a football field edged with purple-blue Louisiana lilies. At one point, Logan slammed on the brakes, surprised by not only Dootsie's having come to a complete stop, but the three spotted deer leaping across the road in sizes small, medium, and large. The gravel road ended, and ahead of us were acres carpeted by lush grass, with soldier-straight pines the clouds reached down to touch and oak trees whose wide limbs seemed to curtsy their greeting.

The four of us stood outside without speaking as if we needed permission to break the spell. I didn't need architectural drawings or virtual imaging to see my dream take shape. It was there, as real to me as standing between Martha and Logan.

"Saved the best for last, right, sweeties?" Dootsie chirped.

We didn't disagree. Logan, standing next to me, wrapped his arm around my shoulder and said, "I see it too, Elle. I can see it. . . . " He stretched his left arm out and pointed as he spoke. "The main building would be built behind those oaks. The gift shop could be on the left between the magnolias standing at the edge of the road. And"—he placed his hands on my shoulders and turned me around—"wouldn't the residents' homes be amazing along that pond? Like at LSU where the fraternity and sorority houses face that lake."

Of course. However could I forget that lake? The one where Logan and I first met. The one, when I started school at LSU, I avoided walking past because it evoked too many memories of him. The one where, years later, he asked me to marry him. "You're right. It would be perfect. We could even build a swimming pool between the two houses and have screened-in porches that connected each house to the pool. There's even enough land for the house family apartments to be a wing off each group home."

"But it's not exactly a high profile area. How are people going to find it? And how are the residents going to not be trapped here?" Every organization needed the practical anchor to ground the dreamers floating in their air balloons. Martha was ours.

"The Department of Transportation has plans to build an interstate exit close to here. It's not scheduled for another five years," Dootsie explained.

"Which could really mean eight to ten," Logan remarked.

"True. But, if the exit already existed, this land probably wouldn't be here as unspoiled as it is now. Plus, the exit might have priced it out of range," said Dootsie. "And, as you know, once businesses know the exit's within a year of completion, they start swooping in. You might be coming back to me in ten years saying it's too busy."

"Martha, remember the place we visited in Mississippi? They transport their residents in those larger vans. And there's one for each house. And, we could do surveys to ask parents how far they'd be willing to drive for the ones who would be day clients only," I said.

"Jenny's sister has a son in his early 30s who's autistic, and there's nothing close by for him. I'll bet she'd be willing to drive fifty miles one way if he'd have a life beyond his house," said Logan.

"Back to the bottom line again, Dootsie," Martha said.

"This tract is 24.5 acres, and they're willing to subdivide it into two parcels if you want less land. But they won't make a section smaller than five acres. If you subdivide, the per acre price is going to depend on the number of acres you want. If you buy the entire tract, the asking price is $235,000."

"Negotiable?" Martha asked.

Dootsie smiled and patted her friend's arm. "My dear, you ought to know. Everything's negotiable. The one factor that could make the sale complicated is that it's owned by a family, three sisters and a brother. They've turned down other buyers before you. Even though this is a commercial zoning, they don't want industry. They're keeping the minimal five-acre plots to prevent contractors from turning this into neighborhoods with lots the size of postage stamps."

"They couldn't have objections to this becoming a center for disabled adults, right?" This property seemed so perfect, I didn't want to let myself fall in love with it if there was a possibility it couldn't happen.

"I don't see that as a problem. But I've learned not to predict what sellers will think about anything," Dootsie said. "I know you have a committee that's working with you. If you want them to visit any or all of the places I've taken you to today, call me. I can make arrangements as long as they're all coming on one day. And, I'm going to keep looking. As ideal as this property might seem, something else could go on the market. Just keep your options open."

"And speaking of options . . ." Logan glanced at his watch. "It's almost one o'clock, and I spotted a seafood place on the way here. Why don't we just finish this conversation over some shrimp po-boys?"

Dootsie and Martha looked at one another. "We have play practice this evening at five o'clock. I have a small part, not a starring role, like my friend, Martha," she said and made a small bow toward my mother-in-law.

"What she's not telling you is part of the reason she has a small role is that she's also helping with the set design. Dootsie is a talented artist," Martha said and then imitated her friend's bow.

"We're trapped with the mutual admiration society," Logan said to me. "Ladies, if we aren't back in time for you to leave for rehearsal, then you've ordered entirely too much to eat."

"We just wanted to be sure because William is picking us up at my house," said Martha, "and I don't want him to wait. Let's get moving. In fact, I'll ride with Dootsie, and we'll follow you."

As they walked off, leaving Logan and me in mild states of eyebrow-raised, amused disbelief, I said to Logan, "Does this mean your mother might have a 'male friend'?"

"Then, I guess we might have to have one of those 'safe sex means no sex' talks with her," he said.

20

Before I enrolled at LSU, Cam assured me that the likelihood of seeing Logan would be minimal. He would be a junior, and I'd be an incoming freshman taking classes far removed from where he'd be. I would live on campus and he'd likely be in an apartment, house, or condo by then. And, the enrollment hovered around 26,000 students, over nine times the size of my high school, and I'd just graduated with people I'd never seen until they appeared in a cap and gown that day.

I moved into Miller Hall with three other girls in my dorm room. We all had opted for potluck as far as roomies. The two of us who were rather low maintenance compensated for the two drama queens, and peace prevailed more often than not. I also learned to take advantage of the dorm's outside sundeck by the lake and Middleton Library when we needed to decompress. One afternoon before exams, we were leaving the library and headed toward the Student Union to meet Stacey when we passed Lauren sitting in the quad watching one of the hacky sack groups. She wanted us to go with her to a debate that night sponsored by the Manship School of Communications. Four candidates for parish mayor would be debating and her boyfriend, Chad, was one of the panelists and was representing LSU Tiger television.

"Please, please. Don't let me suffer through this alone," Lauren pleaded. "He's more interested in the fact that I'll be watching him than he is in my watching the debate."

"We'll go, but if we're about to pass out from boredom, we're going to sneak out as quietly as possible," Stacey said.

The debate was being held at the Cox Building, which was right across the hill from the journalism building. We all met outside and then found seats as close as possible to an exit in a huge classroom that could fit 300. I looked up from turning my cell phone off to find myself staring right at Logan Butler, about four rows ahead, leading a girl by the hand as they made their way to find seats. Not the girl of Leadership Camp Melody had reported him being engaged to. Same color hair, same body type, different face.

"I have to go," I whispered to Stacey. I hadn't seen a flicker of recognition in Logan's face when he looked in my direction. Maybe I was safe. It had been two years. My hair was longer (and shoved under an LSU baseball cap), plus I was ten pounds lighter, even after having Faith. But four rows away, watching him with someone else made me want to jump out of a tall building.

"It's starting in two minutes. We can't leave now. What's wrong?" Lauren asked and looked irritated that I wasn't cooperating.

"You look awful. Do you feel sick?" Stacey stood to go with me.

"Long story, just let me out, and I'll explain later. I promise. I can't . . ."

"Do you need me to go with you? I don't mind." Stacey leaned in closer and whispered, "Remember, I didn't want to be here either."

"No, I'm fine. In fact, I think I'd feel better by myself for a bit." I excused myself past ten people with minimal toe mashing and darted out just as the moderator started introducing the panelists. I closed the door and searched for a nearby bathroom, when I heard my name being called.

"Elle? Elle Claiborne?"

Instead of taking flight, my feet rebelled and refused to move. Which gave the voice behind me time to catch up. When he touched me, even my body betrayed me, as if it hadn't been two years since I last felt the warmth of his skin against mine.

I turned, and it took every ounce of strength left in my logical self to keep the door closed to the emotions that pushed against it. "Logan. What a surprise. How have you been?" *Tell me miserable, broken-hearted. Tell me you've spent two years trying to find me.*

"I've been, um, good. I'm in pre-law, planning to graduate next May," he said and tucked his hands in the front pockets of his jeans.

"That's nice."

"I didn't recognize you at first."

No, of course you didn't. "Sometimes it's hard to see faces under these," I pointed to the cap. *Smooth, Elle. Gave him an out, and played show and tell with a baseball cap.*

He grinned.

I hated that grin. I hated it the way I hated his eyes, his lips, the set of his jawline, and how his hair still had those waves that touched the collar of his shirt. I hated that I couldn't pound his chest until I bruised my fists, demanding that he tell me why I dropped off his radar. I hated that I gave myself to him and thought it actually meant something.

"I didn't think you were a baseball cap kind of girl. But I saw those green eyes and that dark hair and I knew it was you."

My cell phone beeped, and I wanted to sacrifice a phone battery in gratitude to the cell phone gods who provided a legitimate way out of this conversation. It was a voice mail from Stacey asking if I was okay. It was also my opening to leave. "Good to see you again. But, um, study group wanted to know where I was . . . "

"You're not staying for the debate? A few of us are headed to Bogies after, and I thought maybe you might want to meet us there."

Was he freaking kidding me? Why would I want to go to a bar where if you're not a greek, you're a geek? And why would I want to go out with him and the blonde who would probably be running her fingers through his hair—or her own—all night? I could watch the two of them leave together and imagine where they might be going and what they might be doing? I didn't think he was a brainless kind of guy.

"Oh, wow, hate to miss that. I promised this group I'd be there, and, well you know, a promise is a promise," I said and shrugged my shoulders.

I gave him some points for a genuinely disappointed expression when I told him I was leaving.

"Guess I ought to get back before it starts," he said. But he didn't move. "You look great, Elle. Really great. I'm glad I got to see you again." He polished the floor with the toe of his shoe for a bit, then he looked in the general area of my face and said, "Maybe we can get together soon. You know, just catch up with one another."

One of those emotions must have busted past my logical self because, in the corner of my brain, it jumped and clapped its hands at the notion of "get together soon." If Logan's definition of "soon" was another two years, then he'd already be gone. Why not commit to something that you know won't happen?

"Maybe. I know we're both busy. We might be able to work something out, but no biggie if we don't."

We suffered through the "do we hug or shake hands or do the upper arm pat" dance. We did none of them, just smiled awkwardly at one another and went in separate directions. So separate it would be another two years before Logan and I met again.

By the time I earned enough credits to be a junior, I rarely left Baton Rouge. My roommates and I had moved into a three-bedroom condo the year before within bike-riding distance of the campus. I worked on weekends during the semester and as much as possible on breaks and the summer months. I refused to depend on my mother to support me in college. I didn't want her to have another reason to bemoan my ungratefulness or selfishness or foolishness. The only holiday I forced myself home to my parents' house was Christmas. The payoff for enduring my mother treating me as if I'd landed on the doorstep as a refugee from a homeless shelter was spending time with Camden.

The one person other than my sister I saw as often as possible was Mamie. She never failed to make me laugh, and I often thought if late night talk show hosts visited assisted-living homes to find stand-up comics, they might have raised their ratings.

"What's the difference between a man who's in an assisted-living home and a man who's still home with his wife?" she asked me during one visit.

I'd started explaining my answer when she clapped her hands to get my attention. "No. No. No. Elizabeth. It's a joke." She repeated the question and then gave me the punch line. "Nothing. Get it?"

She knew who was sneaking into whose room at night, who always carried extra cards to the weekly gin rummy games and tried to cheat. "Ed keeps bringing cards that don't match the decks we use," she told me and then pointed to her head. "He's not the brightest lamp in the room." Mamie recruited enough seniors to have Zumba and yoga classes. When I saw her over Christmas, she told me her "get up and go, got up and went." By Easter, she'd forgotten my name, and in June, when my mother called me several times while I was at the gym, I knew something had to be wrong.

"Mamie's not doing well. You might want to make plans to see her in the next few weeks. If you don't want to drive back the same day, you can stay here," my mother said. "And, either way, bring some extra clothes. Just in case."

I told her I'd call her when I drove in, and I'd let her know then if I'd spend the night. Losing her husband, and now, on the verge of losing Mamie, my mother wallowed in sadness.

Three weeks later, I sat next to Mamie's bed and brushed her silvery hair, so thin it would barely make a ponytail the size of a pencil. She liked it being brushed, she told me, because it tickled and reminded her of when she was a little girl. The temperature was close to 100 degrees outside, but she wore one of her favorite LSU sweatsuits. She'd grown frail and the only letter fully visible was the S, the L and the U were hanging off on each side. My mother warned me, when I called to tell her I was leaving Baton Rouge, Mamie probably wouldn't look like she did when I'd seen her months before. Knowing my mother's penchant for high drama, I just figured she looked tired. And she did. But like someone who had been tired for years. Every part of her was tired. I barely felt the weight of her hand in my own when I held it.

I lifted the covers on her tray of food from lunch, and I wanted to bang them together like cymbals and have a meeting with the dietary department. "New rule, folks," I'd announce. "When people are weeks and days from death, let them eat whatever they please." Even death row prisoners chose their last meal. Death is death is death.

I called my mother and told her she needed to stop at the grocery before she returned to Mamie's home. "Pick up four different flavors of Blue Bell. The pint-sized. And a small cheesecake. Any flavor. Is there a smoothie place on the way? Great, please stop there and buy one. Yes, a large. It doesn't matter. Who's going to eat all that food? I hope Mamie. And I don't care if she eats a gumdrop size of everything." I walked into the hall and stepped out the glass doors leading to the parking lot. "Because she is dying. Dy-ing. Who cares what she eats? Do we think nutrition matters now?" I paced from one end of the paved lot to the other, crushing my frustration and sadness with every step. "Her lunch was soup that reminded me of muddy water, a square of something pink and gooey, and a small cup of yogurt. That makes *me* want to die. Who wants to hang around for that? Please, just do this favor for me. For her. Okay, thank you."

"Where's your baby?" Mamie said to me as soon as I sat down near her.

A nurse must have come in while I was outside because the lunch tray was gone and Mamie was semi-propped up in her bed.

"Mamie, I'm Elizabeth, your granddaughter, not Nancy. I don't have a baby."

She glared at me. "Don't you think I know who Nancy is? She and John have those two girls. But you had a baby."

Who could have told Mamie about Faith? I almost called Cam, but as soon as I thought of my sister, I remembered coming here when I was first pregnant. I looked bloated, but I didn't think I looked pregnant. It seemed ridiculous to lie to her now. The way she dumped all the decades of her life into a basket and pulled out years, she created new stories almost every time. My story would just become part of the memory stream.

"I don't have the baby, Mamie. She lives with someone else now." *And she will never know you,* I thought. She would never know that part of Mamie was inside of her. But she would carry her great-grandmother with her always.

"Don't cry." She handed me the alarm clock next to her bed. "Here. You go ahead and blow your nose, now."

"Thanks, Mamie," I said and handed it back to her.

"I lost a baby, you know."

I nodded. "I know, I know. My father. I lost him, too." I lost him before he died.

She clapped her hands, though it sounded like leaves in a strong wind. "No. No. No. Not John. Joseph. I lost Joseph."

Maybe she had a miscarriage? A stillborn? I had never heard that name mentioned by either one of my parents. "Mamie, I don't understand. Who is Joseph?"

Her eyes puddled with tears. "I had to give him away. That's what my mother said." Mamie's expression grew stern, her eyebrows closed in on one another and her eyes looked like black marbles. She shook a finger at me. "You can't keep that baby. You can't keep it."

She wasn't telling me I couldn't keep Faith. She was her mother telling her she couldn't keep *her* child. "I understand, Mamie."

"I tried to find him. But he was gone. I married a nice man." She nodded, her eyes closed for a moment, then she waved her hand telling me to come closer. "Shhh! I have this," she whispered. Her frail hands reached around her neck, and she fished a long gold chain out of her sweatshirt and pulled it over her head. A gold heart, the size of a nickel, hung from the chain. "Joseph," she said and handed it to me.

Inside the heart was a tiny lock of brown hair. Joseph's hair.

21

Driving home in time for Logan's mother to make rehearsals, Martha told us that William, the man picking up her and her friend, played Stanley in the production. The pitch in her voice rose when she talked about him, in the way a high school girl says the name of the latest love of her life as she doodles "Mrs. Blahblah" in her notebooks.

She had an impressive collection of information about him that she was eager to share. A retired teacher who loved to go on cruises, William hated his blood being drawn . . . in fact, he couldn't even look at the needle. His yellow lab was named Sinatra. And he had to be careful with his Kindle because the last time he left it in a chair, Sinatra ate it. "Can you imagine calling for a new Kindle because your dog ate it?"

Even Logan didn't miss the admiration in her voice. "Is this someone Elle and I need to check out? Maybe ask Matt to run him through his sources and make sure he's not a serial dater of pretty widows?" He winked at me. "And, Mother, if we see his car overnight in the driveway . . ."

"Good grief, son. That's not an appropriate conversation to have with your mother," she said and touched the soft curls around her ears. "Please, do not mention anything to Matthew. How humiliating that would be . . . for all of us."

"He's teasing, Martha. Aren't you, honey?" I looked at my husband, his grin already answering my question.

"Somewhat," he said and reached out to squeeze my hand as he smiled.

I called everyone on the planning committee the day after we visited the properties and scheduled a breakfast meeting at our house for the next day. Some of the members expressed surprise at the short notice, but I explained the urgency of acting quickly, especially if we intended to buy undeveloped land. The time needed to negotiate the sale, finish the site design specific to the property, and fund-raise meant the sooner we started, the sooner our young adults would have a place to call their own. But I knew, too, that Holly expected a phone call from me, and within the next few days. I needed to settle as much as possible before I talked to Logan. I didn't want to destroy the dream of the center because of what might happen between him and me.

Martha, whose new mission in life was the play production, didn't hesitate to express her irritation at my setting a meeting time without checking with her first. When I told her a majority of the women were able to attend, she grumbled but conceded. It helped pacify her that the meeting wouldn't interfere with her evening rehearsals.

The morning of the meeting, I woke up at the same time as Logan and rushed to Shake Sugary, a local bakery. I walked out with boxes of maple-bacon sweet potato biscuits, orange marmalade sweet rolls, peaches-and-cream scones, and apricot puff pastries that I ordered the day before.

Logan was still home. I warmed a biscuit for him, poured a cup of coffee, and headed to his office where I was apt to find him. The mug trembled and a wave of coffee slipped over the side and burned my fingers. At my "ouch!" Logan looked up, and a warm smile that could have melted icing spread across his face.

"Hey. Is that for me?"

I set the plate down with the biscuit, wiped the coffee cup, and set it on a coaster. "Just for you," I said and kissed him. His hair was still damp from his shower, and he smelled all soapy clean.

He held my face. "I meant this, silly," and his soft mouth found my lips while his hands settled around my waist and led me to his lap.

I locked my fingers behind his neck. "Uh, is this allowed during Bible study? God may not approve of your engaging in a make-out session while you're doing this."

"He would totally approve." Logan flipped pages and read, "'Let him kiss me with the kisses of his mouth!'"

"You are making that up," I said.

Logan pointed to the page. "Song of Solomon, verse 1, line 2."

"This is what you're reading in the mornings? The X-rated version of the Bible?"

"This, my dear, is why I want you to get to know God better. He's not as dull as you think."

"I never thought God was boring. Actually, I think He's a very busy man who just doesn't have time for everyone who needs Him," I said and patted his cheek on my way to standing. "You pray enough for both of us anyway."

He lapsed into serious. "It doesn't work that way—"

I held up my hands. "Not now. I have a meeting. You have to leave for work. God's going to have to wait."

"It's what He does best, precious," he said. "And thanks for breakfast."

Guilt followed me out of the room and burrowed into the bones of my soul. In two days, this man whose body I knew as intimately as my own, whose spirit buoyed me when despair flooded my soul, whose faith kept him rooted in this world, would discover the person he loved had betrayed him.

The bakery pastries lay ravaged on the kitchen table, so while their stomachs were satisfied and they hadn't yet crashed from the sugar overload, I started the meeting. Martha detailed the three properties, and I handed out the copies she'd made of the information Dootsie provided.

"Are we limiting ourselves to these three? It seems premature to make a decision on the first options you've been shown, don't you think?" Cathie sipped her coffee, her eyes peering at the group as she waited for a response.

"We know you specialize in the fine art of rhetorical questions. What you're telling us is that you think it's too soon to take a vote," Amanda retorted. The animosity between these two women had been well-documented Junior League lore after Cathie divorced Amanda's brother. Martha and I didn't intend for them to be on the same committee, but they both had a vested interest in the outcome since Amanda's brother and Cathie had a teenaged son who, because of a brain tumor when he was a baby, was now mentally and physically disabled.

Cathie flipped her hair extensions over her shoulders, leaned forward, and prepared for battle. "Amanda, this is an important decision, not like decorating a house and then deciding six months later that you hate it and start all over again."

"If you have an issue with me, then—"

Martha pounded her wooden gavel. "Ladies, I've known you since your mothers punished the two of you for dying each other's hair purple. Now, get over yourselves, and let's limit our discussions to what's important. Important to our handicapped young adults. Not their emotionally handicapped caregivers."

Cathie and Amanda covered themselves with the mantle of mortification, and the rest of us pretended not to notice.

I took advantage of the lull to make an announcement and braced myself because I'd not prepared Martha for what I was about to say. "One of the other reasons I wanted to meet this soon was to ask if someone would be willing to assume chairing this committee, either temporarily or permanently. With my obligations to Logan and his campaign, I don't think I can devote the time needed to make sure this project is a success. I realize this began because of an issue I'm passionate about. And that's exactly why I want to make sure it gets all the attention it deserves and needs. I'm confident someone here can provide the direction it needs."

Years of being a political wife had taught Martha the fine art of grace under pressure. She held her gavel in her lap, surveyed the room and when no one spoke, said, "I'd like to commend Elle for the thoughtful consideration she's given to what's needed to move this important project forward. If any of you were hesitant to volunteer because you thought I would step in as chairperson, I want to reassure you that's not my intention. I have some recent commitments that would make it difficult for me. Rather than volunteer today, I'm certain Elle would agree . . ." she paused and looked in my direction. I nodded. At this point I couldn't imagine not agreeing with whatever she was about to say, ". . . that we'd both prefer if you went home and thought about it. Please call one of us if you have questions, and if there's more than one person interested, we'll decide what to do then."

After everyone left, I gave Martha a plate of pastries to take home. "These are for you. And thank you for how you handled that. I probably should have discussed it with you before today."

"Let's just say I wish you would've trusted me enough to tell me," she said, minus the caustic coating I'd grown accustomed to when Martha expressed her disapproval. Instead, she sounded wounded. Had I been too self-centered and ignored signals that Logan's mother had shed a layer of emotional armor?

Trusting anyone enough to be honest hadn't worked with my parents, and now I had no choice. Well, I did have a choice. I'd had choices for the past sixteen years. And, every time, I chose based on fear. If the consequence of the truth was abandonment, then why would I make that choice? Every time Logan had entered and reentered my life I asked myself why I would want to risk pushing him out again.

How could I have known our lives would come to this all those years ago? I talked to him for five minutes in the hallway of the journalism building after not having seen him for almost two years. Not exactly prime time for dumping information. After that night at the debate, we didn't stay in touch with one another.

After that, I promised myself I wouldn't allow Logan Butler to control my life. Some days I held to that promise better than others. As weeks became months and months became years, he moved from being a plank to a splinter in my heart. For the most part, I forgot it was there. Then a memory, a whiff of cologne, a laugh squeezed that sore spot, and I recoiled, waited for the throbbing to subside. It always did.

Then we met again in New Orleans soon after Mamie died, and all my resolve packed a suitcase and hitchhiked out of my life.

22

After the last time Logan and I met, we didn't have to wait years to meet again. We married a little over a year later.

The weekend after Mamie's funeral, I met Hillarey and Kendra at Superior Grill, thanks to e-mails from the reunion committee. We hadn't seen one another since high school graduation, and Happy Hour seemed a perfect time to get together again. Especially since, at this restaurant, it was actually a deliriously happy two and a half hours. Some afternoons it looked like a street party. And this was one of those afternoons. After circling blocks for almost thirty minutes to find a place to park, my car held its breath and squeezed into a spot about a bumper away from a tow zone. Kendra had already sent a text that she had snagged a window table facing St. Charles Avenue, so it didn't take long to find her and Hillarey.

All three of us were single, in college, and hoped we ran out of month before money. Kendra faced the daunting $50,000 tuition and assorted expenses of medical school, which gave Hillarey and me a reason to laugh because it was unlikely either one of us would earn that in our chosen career paths for years.

We were on our second round of chips, dip, and drinks when Hillarey asked about Faith and if I kept in touch with her parents.

"I did, at first. I thought I'd be able to handle it better as time went by. But the opposite happened. Maybe every six months, a note. Otherwise, I decided it's best to disconnect."

Kendra twirled the stem of her glass between her fingertips. "Actually, Faith could be with you right now."

"I thought you were in med school, not paranormal activity school," Hillarey said. "Why would you say such a thing to Elle?"

"What are you talking about Kendra? You haven't had that much to drink. I don't think this is your alter ego talking," I said.

"I wouldn't say it if I didn't think it was plausible. Scientists now know that cells from a fetus cross the placenta, and the baby's DNA becomes part of the mother's body. They find them in the mother's blood, bone marrow, skin, and some organs, and they stay with her until, well, for her lifetime. The cells can even help her body recover from certain diseases. There's some thought, too, that there might be cases where the cells aren't beneficial. But, I think it's fascinating that a mother can carry the cells of all of her children, and those cells can generate cells as protection from certain diseases," Kendra explained. "Elle, for the rest of your life you'll be carrying Faith with you, and without her even knowing, she could be helping your heart heal."

The sun was shining when I walked in the restaurant, but the moon had taken its place by the time I left, which meant I should have paid more attention to the cross streets where I parked. Wandering aimlessly in the area during the day wasn't the dance with danger that it was at night. Kendra and Hillarey rode the streetcar home, so if I couldn't locate my car, I'd take the streetcar to their place. I settled in one of the benches in front of the restaurant while I decided whether to call the girls or take my chances. Knowing those two, though, I figured it would be smart to call one of them to make sure they actually went straight home. Busy looking for Kendra's phone number, I paid no attention to the person who'd just sat next to me until I heard my name.

"Elle Claiborne, we meet in the most unexpected places."

I gasped. Or whatever sucked-in-breath sound someone emitted when a stranger sat next to her on a bench in a city she didn't live in and who knew her name. After I yanked my heart back into my chest, I squawked and Logan's name tumbled out. "Logan. Holy crap. Is this your new way of approaching women?"

"That depends. Did it work?"

"Sure. If your intention is cardiac arrest followed by a lawsuit." I didn't see a woman lingering in the vicinity, foot-tapping while she waited for him to finish loitering. I expected she'd stroll up at any moment, do that thing women do to mark their territory by smoothing his hair or his shirt or his lips.

"Are you living in New Orleans now? We come here at least once a week, and I've never seen you."

We. Of course. "No, still in BR. My grandmother died, and I stayed a few days after her funeral. Met some friends from high school who I hadn't seen in a couple years for Happy Hour." And wished I'd dipped my chips with more care because I was fairly certain a blip of salsa had landed on my white skirt earlier.

"I'm sorry to hear about your grandmother," he said. He turned toward me, propped one long leg on the other, his arm stretched along the back of the bench, his fingers a hair space away from my shoulder. The anticipation of his touch like that "tingling tension" my art history teacher talked about between God and Adam in Michelangelo's Sistine Chapel. Though neither Logan nor I qualified as suitable stand-ins, Mr. Garrity would have been pleased to know I not only made the connection, but I understood how waiting for that one small thing, the touch of someone's fingertips can create such holy apprehension. That and the navy blue T-shirt he wore, a stretchy knit, tapered from his chest to his waist.

"How long ago was that debate at LSU where we saw each other? Was that two years ago? Guess we didn't do such a great job of staying in touch, huh?"

"No, but we were both busy . . . you know, things happen, life goes on, and all those other clichés." Still no female in the vicinity. "Are you meeting someone?"

"Not anyone I planned to meet." He smiled, and I wished he hadn't. He wasn't helping my I-want-to-hate-you agenda by increasing his adorable factor. "No, one of my study groups meets here on Friday nights. It's our reward for good behavior during the week." Logan looked around. "They must have gotten tired of waiting for me and moved on. Only ten more minutes before it's full-price margaritas again. I'm sure they're storming the bar."

"They might even be drinking your drinks by now," I said and scooted to the edge of the bench, my prelude to leaving. "I know you need to find your friends. Who knows? Maybe we'll meet again in another two years—"

"Hey, you know what I just remembered?"

There were at least a dozen things I hoped he hadn't forgotten. But Logan appeared too animated to wait for a response.

"That time two years ago . . . you couldn't stay because you had to go meet your study group. How weird is that? Or is it irony? Karma? . . . "

"Nerd-dom, maybe?" I figured if I went for the handshake good-bye, I'd save us both a few uncomfortable minutes. I reached my hand out and said, "Great to see you. Thanks for stopping by my bench. Guess you'll be doing that a lot as an attorney. Stopping by benches, I mean. You know, judges' benches, courtrooms . . . nevermind, poor attempt at a joke." Brilliant. I'd saved myself one awkwardness and created an even worse one.

"Eh, it earned a seven on a ten-point scale," he said. "Wait," and hadn't yet released my hand, "is there some place you need to be? Because, if not, I'd love to buy you a drink. Catch up, like we said we were going to do and didn't."

I slipped my hand out from his, hiked my purse on my shoulder, and ignored every pleading of my body to stay. "No, I was just on my way home, and thanks for the offer, but my friends and I met earlier, and I could barely finish one drink . . . " I stood. *Walk away. Walk away.*

"Well, dinner, then. You haven't eaten already, have you?"

I should say yes. "No, but I don't know anyone you're with, and I don't think they'd want to join us going down memory lane. . . ." No is not yes. I knew that. I needed to listen to my head, not my heart.

Logan laughed. "No, they wouldn't, which would be perfect because I spend too much time with them anyway. Come on. We need more than five minutes every two years. And you'll be headed back to Baton Rouge. If not now, when?"

It was logic my head couldn't argue against and emotion my heart wouldn't.

We lucked into a vacant table. Between the ceviche appetizer and the shrimp fajitas, he asked if I was seeing someone.

I wished I could have answered yes simply to watch his reaction. I told him I didn't have much time for anything serious with all the hours I was taking plus my internship hours for occupational therapy. As if any man could get in the way of my washing, cooking, polishing my toenails, watching *Seinfeld* reruns, which was much closer to the truth than what I said.

"And you?" I held my breath while I waited for his answer and focused on adding sweetener to my iced tea as if I was mixing chemicals to produce a cure for obesity.

"I guess I'd have to say no."

"I'm sorry. I don't understand . . . too many variables there with the guessing, the 'having to say' . . . Let me rephrase. Are you in a serious relationship with anyone at this time?"

"In that case, the answer is definitely no. I've dated the sister of one of my fraternity brothers for a few months. But, I keep feeling she's thinking it's more than just dating. She's always telling me about her friends' engagement parties, where she wants to buy a house, and she wants us to plan vacations for next year. . . ." He pushed his appetizer plate to the side just as T.J., our waiter, slid the sizzling platter of shrimp on our table.

Logan waved away the smoke rising from the shrimp. "Let's put it this way. If you asked her the same question, she'd probably tell you we're in a serious relationship."

"In that case, you might find it amusing that Melody had you almost married your first year at LSU."

"Melody? Weird science-girl? That one?" He passed me the basket with the steamy tortillas. "How did she come up with that?"

I traded the tortillas for the bowl of guacamole. "Something about a message Carole had left on the school's Yahoo group. She'd posted about being engaged, or almost engaged."

Logan paused in his methodical layering of ingredients on his tortilla and seemed to be waiting for some connection between what I said and distant memory.

"Carole. Yeah. That was messy. We dated for a while our first year of college, and she had this idea we were going to be together forever. I didn't think it was the right time in our lives to be making that decision. I tried to explain to her I wasn't saying it couldn't happen at some point in the future. But I knew pre-law school was going to be brutal, and I couldn't handle that kind of serious relationship and trying to make the grades and everything else involved in being accepted into law school. I thought she'd understand and we could date without the pressure of her always feeling like it had to go somewhere. That's what I heard from her every other month, 'Where is this going?' Finally, I just told her we weren't going anywhere. About a month after we broke up, she called me and said we needed to talk. Then, we go to dinner at Chimes. We hadn't even ordered yet, and she told me she was pregnant."

He stopped while the waiter filled our glasses and unloaded more chips.

I wanted to unload myself. But not in the chip basket. While T.J. and Logan traded sports trivia about the Super Bowl, I excused myself and went to the bathroom. I'd underestimated Melody's intuition and overestimated my capacity for detachment. I needed to give the hydraulics in my throat time to subside and occupy a stall long enough to cover my face with my hands. After a few tears, I rearranged my smile and returned to the table. Logan was finishing a call as I sat.

"Everything okay?" I wanted to slap myself for asking a question I truly didn't want to know the answer to.

He nodded. "My friend Paul wanted me to know they were going to the Quarter from here. I told him we were having dinner and not to wait on me."

"Don't feel like you have to keep entertaining me. You can get this to-go—"

"Elle, stop," he said, his words a soft reprimand. "You're not holding me hostage. If I wanted to go with them, I'd be honest and tell you. Or is that your diplomatic way of telling me I'm boring you and you're ready to leave?"

"Not at all," I said. I cringed hearing the enthusiasm in my voice. So much for sophistication.

"I probably shouldn't have dumped that Carole story on you. Or just given you the talking points and not everything in-between," he said. "She wasn't pregnant, which not only showed me her capacity for lying, but that she ignored every conversation we ever had about the subject of children. I didn't see that until after we had dinner that night. She deleted it right after I confronted her about it. Guess Melody found it before I did." Logan pretended to tap his spoon against his glass, then said, "Meeting on Butler drama adjourned. Moving on to update on Elle's career plans."

That Logan could embrace his inner dork made him all the more likeable. If I'd idled at likeable and not throttled up to loveable, I wouldn't have risked crashing into the wall. This dinner was the Indy 500 version of returning to the track after a pit stop, except that the finish line was Logan, and there was only one first place.

<hr />

After we finished eating, I left Superior Grill, again, only this time with Logan, who held the door open and said he'd walk me to my car.

"That's a bit of a problem. In fact, it's the problem I was trying to solve when you saw me on the bench."

"Something happened to your car?"

I shrugged. "I hope not, but I don't know. I'm not sure where I parked. I mean, I know I'm just a few blocks away, but I didn't pay attention to the cross streets."

He coughed, but it didn't look or sound convincing.

"It's okay, you can laugh. I didn't want to admit my directional impairment, but I also didn't want my car found in a ditch tomorrow with me in a hundred pieces in my trunk."

Logan looked like someone who just found half of a worm in the apple he'd bitten into. "Such a pleasant after-dinner-mint of a thought. Maybe you need to reconsider your career choice or add graphic murder mystery writer to your profile."

"I'm flattered, but if I can't find my car, I probably won't be able to figure out who did the crime."

A trio of men, who sounded merry enough to have been marinated in tequila for quite some time, sloshed past us as we stood on the sidewalk. They attempted to wobble their way between Logan and me, but he closed the gap between us and they circled behind him. If it meant Logan would have pulled me closer again, I would have invited them to return.

"It must be getting late if the sidewalk's a dangerous place to be," I said, not minding that Logan's hands were still on my arms.

His eyes searched my face. I didn't know what he hoped to find. I found myself staring at my feet because to look into his eyes burned and if I didn't look away, I wouldn't need my car because I would be a handful of ashes on the sidewalk. "Elle, I . . ."

He wasn't holding on to me now. I lifted my head and ignored my heart whispering in my ear. I broke the silence before whatever he might have said would break my spirit. "This was fun, Logan. Thanks."

"I'm glad. It was nice spending time with you. Look, I . . . um . . . " Logan took my elbow and moved me away from clumps of people gathered outside. Still holding on, his eyes searched my face before he spoke, and I wondered if he wasn't having doubts about what he'd intended to say before. But, he drew me closer and said, "I didn't forget about you after that first summer. In fact, I always thought about you. But I was young and stupid and confused. Now I'm probably just older and stupid and more confused."

"I never forgot you, but I didn't hear from you. I figured you'd moved on," I said. "I guess it's a good thing neither one of us majored in mass communications, right?" He still held me, and the part of me that wanted him to let go was losing the battle with the part that didn't.

"Maybe this is our chance to start getting it right." He leaned in and his lips brush against mine, as if asking permission to linger. I granted it.

When we stopped, he smiled and whispered, "That's a good beginning. Look, I parked across the street. Let me drop you off at wherever your car is. I promise I won't chop you into pieces."

I smiled the way parents smile at their children who talk about Santa Claus. Delighted by their innocence and yet sad because one day they'd have to tell the truth and explain that they lied to protect them.

23

Holly expected a phone call in a few days. A call I could only make after talking to Logan about something that I'd known for almost 6,000 days.

Maybe a dinner first, where the lighting and the mood were subdued. We could talk in the restaurant where drama would be not only déclassé, but politically dangerous. Or we could talk on the drive home because avoiding eye contact would be a safety requirement. Or I could greet him at the door wearing only seduction, and after our tryst and its afterglow, we would talk.

I understood why messengers carried someone else's unpleasant news. But I didn't have a messenger, and I didn't have Camden to run interference for me. I was stuck with the one person responsible. Myself.

Regardless of the elaborate scenarios I imagined, the moment Logan processed the words "I need to talk to you about something," the clothes would be off the emperor. I waited for Saturday. He had an appearance that evening, but that couldn't be rescheduled. I weighed his coming home after a full day of work to be told versus a day when he had a reason to leave. Not that he'd ever need a reason again. I was going to give him that. The reason to come home would be one he'd have to give himself.

Friday I vacuumed, cleaned, polished, waxed, washed, bleached, shined, disinfected, and deodorized every crevice in our house. I was the domestic version of a Western gunslinger patrolling my territory armed with a holster of aerosols, dragging dust mops, vacuum tools, and cords behind me. Hours later, the house had been purged of dust and dirt and grime. But it did nothing to relieve the coil of dread that wound itself around every organ in my body. By that afternoon, even my teeth ached. After the assault on the inside of our home, I carried the battle outside. I ripped weeds out of the garden until my hands felt bruised and my fingers arthritic. In the shower, I scrubbed my nails until my cuticles protested and pinpoints of blood appeared near the edge of the red swollen half-moons.

I ordered take-out from P.F. Chang's and picked up a chocolate hazelnut torte for dessert from the bakery. When Logan called that he was on his way home, I set the table, slipped on a flowered sundress and sandals, and panicked. I was the wife version of the husband walking through the door on an otherwise pedestrian day with a bouquet of roses, a basket of Ghirardelli chocolate, and a diamond, heart-shaped pendant. The sirens of suspicion would break eardrums in a five-mile radius of the house.

When Logan noticed the flower beds had been overhauled, he'd figure I needed one of my outdoor stress-relief days. The house cleaned to sterility might make him wonder if I'd decided we needed to place our house on the market.

Despite the humidity and the temperature pushing toward three digits, I felt like I'd just stepped out of an ice bath. I'd never experienced this kind of afraid. The kind that brought you to the edge of the cliff, but then when you arrived, tapped you on the shoulder and said, "You're taking him with you when you jump." Logan would be blindsided by the woman who vowed to "love, honor, and cherish" for the rest of our lives. I'd lost track of the times I'd said, "I'll tell him. I'll tell him tonight" and then convinced myself that waiting was better. I thought I could outwait the truth.

I sat on the sofa, hugged my knees to my chest, and wondered, now that I'd bought my ticket to being alone, what loneliness would look like when I arrived. I imagined even if Logan stayed, which he was apt to do because doing the right thing was some moral imperative for him, I wouldn't be any less alone. He'd be have-a-nice-day to me kind of nice, like he was to the teenager who checked us out at the grocery. But not the nice that brought me coffee in the morning or split the last brownie with me or lifted the blanket when he was on the sofa watching a golf game so I could stretch my body along his, my back pressed in to his front. He'd tuck the blanket around us and wrap his arm around me so that I knew even if I fell asleep, I wouldn't fall.

I had no idea how Faith would live in a house with strangers who loved each other, much less strangers who only tolerated one another. If Logan didn't stay, then she and I would probably be lonely together. I hadn't called my mother. I wasn't in the mood for the parade of platitudes that would march out of her mouth. "You made your bed . . . " "If you tell the truth, then you don't have to remember anything . . . " "You lie down with dogs . . . " Mamie. She would have understood. After she died, I told Cam the story about Joseph and showed her the locket. We wondered if our parents knew. I suspected Dad did. Maybe I wanted to think he knew he had a half-brother somewhere in the world, one he might never be able to find, and that's what added to his sadness and quiet anger about my pregnancy. Maybe he blamed his mother, and he thought that when I had other children, they'd blame me for Faith being adopted. But, he sided with Mom in not wanting me to keep her. But since Mamie and Dad are both gone now, I may never know.

I pulled the cable knit throw off the back of the sofa and wrapped myself in it. It didn't make much of a difference because the reverberations of fear were not going to be warmed away. What did people do when they didn't know what to do? *They prayed.*

I told Logan I didn't pray because if God was God, then He knew what I wanted or needed. Why did I have to ask when He already knew the question and the answer. "What is He, God of the Rhetorical Question?" We had this conversation on the way to a prayer breakfast sponsored by one of the local churches that had invited candidates and their families. I agreed to attend because he promised me that all I'd need to do was bow my head.

"Prayer isn't handing God your wish list. He likes when we talk to Him. I think we make Him laugh . . . in a good way," he said. "You know I love you, right?"

I stopped checking my lipstick in the overhead mirror and turned to look at him. "Only someone who loved me would bother having this conversation with me." I flipped the visor up and shifted in my seat. "I know there's a point waiting to be found. Where is it?"

"Would it be enough for you to just know that I love you without ever telling or showing you? And I wouldn't have to ever massage your sometimes smelly feet or surprise you with that coffee you order from Starbucks that I have to write down to remember?"

"That's a no-brainer. Of course, that wouldn't be enough. I love you telling me that you love me," I said.

"So does God. Prayer isn't voodoo or some script you have to follow. It's just a conversation."

Logan's explanation demystified prayer, but it didn't motivate me to pray, because I didn't know God the way Logan did. Like God was a golf buddy you called on a Sunday morning to set up a tee time. I understood how that worked because they had a relationship. But for me, God was like the guy who came to our house once a year to spray for termites. He definitely performed a useful service, especially since there were few people who wanted to expose themselves to all those chemicals and crawl into those matchbox-sized spaces if necessary. I recognized him when he rang the doorbell, but I never felt compelled to invite him in for coffee and rolls, and chat about the wife and kids. Neither one of us took it personally. We understood the nature of our relationship and respected the boundaries.

Orkin-man God worked for me. Until now. Because I'd limited God to that role, I certainly couldn't call Him when I needed a painter or a plumber or an anything other than what He was. I didn't need or want any of those. But now I needed and wanted a friend, someone to talk to, someone I knew would listen.

Okay, I get it now. You're not Rhetorical Question or Orkin-man God. I'm still trying to figure You out, but I guess You've already figured that out. I don't think I've ever been good at this, not in the way I used to hear people pray in church. Funny, the deacon's daughter is the one struggling with having a relationship with God . . . but then, the cobbler's children had no shoes. . . . You know what I'm up against here. I don't even know what I should pray for. But this I'm sure of. I love my husband, and I've done some stupid you-know-what thinking that I could protect Logan or myself. Guess I thought I was You. We both see how that's worked out. This could be the beginning of the end for me or for Logan and me. It's not going to be pretty tonight. I've made one big, hot mess, and the only way out is through. I've got to make this right, for Logan and for Faith. Maybe, for now, all I need is to know that You'll be hanging around. Take care of Logan. He's going to need You tonight.

Logan parked his briefcase in one of the kitchen chairs and kissed me on the forehead. "Hmmm. You smell good. Like Spicy Eggplant," he said and read the tops of the take-out containers. "Chicken Lettuce Wraps, Crispy Honey Shrimp, Orange Peel Beef . . . did I forget something? Anniversary? Birthday? Somebody coming over for dinner?"

"No. I thought it would be nice to do something different . . . Why don't you take off your suit, and I'll finish setting the table."

"Sure," he said, and I watched him when he walked past me, scanning the clutter-free counter space, the wood floors without their protective layer of dust, the freezer door on top of the refrigerator that was now visible because the magnets holding expired coupons, menus, newspaper articles, the Saints and LSU football schedules, and "to do" lists had been culled and moved to the side panel facing the cabinets.

I carried plates and silverware to the table, filled glasses with ice, and was getting napkins out of the pantry when Logan came back to the kitchen. He'd traded his button-down shirt for a pullover, but still wore his khakis.

"You must have been on overdrive today. Outside, inside, ordering out." He spotted the bakery box on the counter by the coffeemaker. "Dessert?"

I nodded. "What do you want to drink?" I opened the refrigerator. "Iced tea, water, juice, Coke, there might be a beer back here somewhere. . . . " I leaned in and moved a few containers around. "No, never mind. No beer."

"What's going on, Elle? I don't want to sound insulting, but all this in one night is, well, unusual. And I'm getting this Stepford wife vibe from you. You are still you, right?"

He smiled.

I didn't. I closed the refrigerator. Wiped my damp palms down the sides of my dress. *Do not cry. I forbid you to cry.* The sofa shivering of earlier revisited. *Remember, that's when you had that convo with God. He might be around here somewhere.* My hands rubbed my arms like sandpaper and tried to smooth the tiny spikes there. I should have waited until tomorrow to scour the house. He probably would have left after we talked, like he probably will later, and I would've needed to occupy my time with mindless labor. Then, it might have served as part of my sentencing for this crime I've committed. Then again, maybe this was my way of prodding him to say something first. To unlock the door to let me walk through it. "We need to talk."

"You're scaring me, Elle," he said and moved toward me. His handsome face as crumpled as bed sheets.

I waved him away. "Please, don't. If you touch me right now, I'll not be able to do this."

Logan backed up. "Then talk to me. What's going on? Did something happen today?" He sounded wounded.

"Let's sit down. But not here. Not in the kitchen." We should have eaten first. No, no. Better on an empty stomach. Bad news should be bottled and labeled "Take before meals to avoid agitation of gagging reflex." Of course eating wasn't an option. What was I thinking? I could barely swallow, and my internal body parts were rearranging themselves, squeezing into places they weren't meant to be.

I followed Logan into the den where he perched on the edge of the sofa. He leaned forward, elbows on his knees, hands clenched in front of him. His wedding band, inscribed with "I love you more," like mine, flashed a small search light on the opposite wall. At our wedding, when he repeated, "Take this ring as a sign of . . ." and started to slip the band on my finger, we realized the minister handed him the wrong one. A minute of confusion, Logan exchanged his band for mine, and started over. "No, take *this* ring . . ." If weddings had baby books, we would have written that in as "First awkward but endearing moment."

Tonight was neither one of those. A first event I didn't want to record for posterity.

I dragged the square, leather ottoman over and sat in front of him. I held his clasped hands in my own, and I guessed by his immediate shudder, he hadn't expected my touch to be cold. Instead of a face etched with worry, this would have been less painful if I had to look at the hard set of his jaw, his lips thin and straight. I had to own that I was the executioner responsible for his emotional devastation.

"First, you have to let me get all the way through what I need to tell you. I'm not having an affair, I'm not dying of some inoperable disease, I haven't gambled or drugged away our money, and I'm not addicted to anything requiring treatment."

I felt his hands breathe and saw the furrow in his forehead relax. For now.

"Okay. Then what is this?" he said.

I wiped my hands on my sundress again. I wanted to stand and pace and look at the floor and not at him. I stayed seated and grabbed the edge of the ottoman because I was about to go over the falls. "I've needed to tell you this for a long time. As in almost sixteen years, long time. And I didn't, and all the reasons I didn't made sense to me then, and some of them still do, but it doesn't matter." *Labor pains. That's what this feels like. Like giving birth to her all over again.* And I was.

I took a deep breath.

He stared at me. A study in confusion and worry. His still clasped hands bounced against his legs. His right foot tapped against the floor. An all-too familiar response.

Another breath. A jagged-edged breath. A breath that signaled there was no turning back.

"Before we married. I had a baby. A girl. I gave her up for adoption." The first bullet.

Logan sat straight up, his mouth hung open. His hands slapped his knees. His lips started to form a word.

I held up my hand, and his eyes widened. They spoke for him. *You're kidding me. There's more?*

"Her name is Faith. Her adoptive parents died. She's coming here. To live with us." Second bullet.

This one sent him crashing to the back of the sofa cushion. "Elle—" My name escaped as if it was the last sound made by a strangled man. "How could—"

"I'm not finished," I said, my voice an apologetic whisper.

My husband was drowning in disbelief, sucked in by the undertow of my deceit. Instead of tossing him a life jacket, I was about to slam my foot against his head. "She's yours. Ours. Faith is our daughter."

Bullet number three.

24

I was defenseless. I'd emptied myself of the ammunition of the past. I had nothing. I felt like nothing.

I forced myself to look in Logan's face when I told him Faith was his daughter, our daughter.

If I'd dumped a bucket of fresh manure over him, I don't think his expression would have appeared much different than it did now. His hands shot up in the air with such speed, I reared back because I thought he might slap me. I almost wished he would. That would heal faster. But, of course, he didn't. He surrendered. Logan rose to his feet, as I sat cross-legged on the ottoman, crying, not heaving sobs, just this deep well of sadness that needed to empty itself. He looked down at me. His face a toxic mix of disappointment, sadness, anger, and confusion.

I whispered, "I'm so sorry. I'm so sorry."

"I am too," he said. He looked out the window. "Fifteen years. You've known about this fifteen years." He shook his head, then turned to face me. "But less than a week ago you were upset because you thought I kept a secret from you. What a hypocrite you are, Elle."

He didn't yell, though I wished he had. I would have screamed at me.

I didn't follow him when he walked back into the kitchen. I didn't go in there when the garbage disposal crunched and whirred, when the wastebasket's top opened and closed, opened and closed, and opened and closed like a metal jaw. Not even when the back door slammed and the walls shuddered in response. I wiped my nose with the hem of my sundress because I didn't want to move and risk disturbing the universe.

The back door slammed again, followed by an emphatic crash, accompanied by a shattering of glass that sounded like capiz shell chimes whipped by hurricane force winds.

Logan stepped into the den. "The poster fell off the wall. I have to leave. For now. I may spend the night at the office." He pounded the door frame with his fist. "Elle, don't call me. I'll let you know when I'm ready to talk."

"Okay," I said, but it sounded more like I was gargling. "Logan?"

"What? You remembered something else you'd forgotten?"

"I . . . I love you." What I saw in his face was worse than anger. I saw nothing. It was as if the Logan I knew had disappeared.

"I can't do this right now. I have to leave."

Logan spread the brochures on the table like a fan. "A twenty-one day cruise. Denmark, Germany, Russia, Finland, Norway, Scotland, Sweden."

We'd never had a cruise vacation. I packed half of our closets. Logan emptied the suitcases and made his and my clothes fit into one. "We'll buy what we need. You always drag too much stuff with you."

The ship pulled away from the dock as we waved to our parents. "Where's Faith?" I asked Logan.

"I don't have Faith. You didn't tell me to bring her. I thought you had her," he said as he pulled a life jacket hanging near the rail. "Here, you'll need this."

"For what?"

"Look," he turned my head to the shoreline. The people were thimble-sized. "There she is. You'll have to go get her." He strapped the jacket on me and said, "I'm going to help you." Then he carried me to the side of the ship and threw me overboard.

I screamed and woke up to inky darkness. I'd covered myself with the knit afghan, and my dress stuck to places on my body I didn't know were capable of sweating. I pushed the throw off and reached across the arm of the sofa to turn on the lamp.

I remembered Logan leaving, my debating whether or not to call Cam, turning on Pandora on my iPhone, and laying my head on the arm of the sofa. Where was my phone? Logan might have tried to call me. I checked for it under the throw and on the floor, but I didn't find it until I dug between the sofa cushions. It was three o'clock in the morning, and there were no missed calls. I felt hung over. My body protested not being fed its daily allowance of caffeine, and my stomach complained of deprivation as well. Between my physical conditions and my emotional hollowness, my body approached full-scale mutiny.

I wandered into the bedroom thinking maybe Logan had come home while I was sleeping, and not wanting to wake me up, went to bed. Nope. Not there.

I followed my hunger and my headache to the kitchen where I found the after effects of last night's door slamming.

The limited edition 2006 Jazz Fest Rockin' to New Orleans poster I had given Logan on our third anniversary had crashed to the floor leaving a deep gash in the baseboard. The aluminum frame was all cattywampus and likely unsalvageable. I set the poster and now debilitated frame on the kitchen table and fed all the broken glass to the vacuum cleaner.

As it turned out, the vacuum cleaner had more food choices than its owner. The food I'd bought for last night's dinner had disappeared. Down the garbage disposal, I assumed, because the empty take-out containers had been stacked on top of one another in the sink. I found the fortune cookies, sauces, and napkins in the trash when I threw away the food containers. I wiped eggplant goo and assorted vegetables that had melded to the granite. A sharp aim obviously not a priority in his purge.

I decided to make a pot of coffee instead of trying to go back to sleep, especially alone on that big ship of a mattress. And I was hungry. The white bakery box sat by the coffeemaker where I'd left it. He wouldn't have thrown away the torte and left the box behind. Perfect. Breakfast and coffee.

I grabbed a fork to start in on the torte, but when I picked up the box, I knew I wouldn't need it. It was empty. Logan had either eaten it and collapsed in a sugar coma in his office or mashed it down the disposal with the other food. I found an almost full box of granola in the pantry and ate it out of the box with my hand while I leaned against the kitchen counter and waited for my first cup of coffee for the day. The caffeine didn't stop what felt like nails being hammered through my temples. In my search for Aleve, I found the Xanax the doctor had prescribed for me three years ago. Logan had decided to make the run for state representative, and I wanted to run. Away. Far away, as in "Let me know when this is over, and I'll come back." I couldn't match Martha's diplomacy or finesse or confidence. I had nightmares about Logan losing because I was a loser or making faux pas that would be sound bites for nightly news.

After a few episodes of dizziness, heart palpitations, and chest pains, my doctor suggested an anti-anxiety medication. The side effects of the Xanax weren't much better than the panic attacks. I stopped taking them after two days and replaced them with yoga classes, massages, and an occasional pint of Cherry Garcia ice cream.

But since I had pills left, this seemed as good a time as any to practice preventative medicine. I cupped my hand under the bathroom faucet, washed one down, and waited for my insides to uncoil.

I curled up on my bed, the remote control in one hand and my cell phone in the other. The entire day stretched out before me like a road through a desert. But I didn't have a map, and I had no idea where it might end.

I wasn't surprised when Logan wanted to leave. I'd learned before our marriage that he needed time away from whatever the issue was to be able to come to terms with it. Logan and I almost cancelled our wedding weeks before the date to save ourselves the cost of a divorce based on irreconcilable differences. We fought about how we were going to keep track of our money. We had separate accounts and a joint account. Logan thought we should each have a debit card for the joint account. My opinion was two cards made keeping track of the balance challenging since we'd have no way of knowing who spent what and when. Our intention was to use it as our house account, so I didn't think we needed debit cards for that account at all. From there it escalated to and bounced around from you're a tightwad/you're a spendthrift and you don't trust me/you don't value my opinion to you're a control freak/you're too fly-by-the-seat-of-your-pants. After days and days of this, we compromised. One card for the joint account that we'd use on vacations or for emergencies.

What I discovered, over and above that the most important thing about a debit card was remembering the pin number, was how we fought. I wanted resolution, and if it meant talking for thirty consecutive hours, well, we'd rest later. Logan approached disagreements like Thanksgiving dinner. You stuffed yourself to the point of swearing you'd never allow another smidgen of food pass your lips. Until later, when you didn't feel full anymore because your body had time to process the excess. Logan required processing time, which involved separating himself from the source and turning the issues over in his head like compost. If he stayed engaged in the fight, he reacted to the emotional dynamics, and we'd zoom by DEFCON 2 on our way to level one.

If there was any comfort in what happened last night, it was that he followed his instincts. Generally, that meant on the way to resolution. I hoped for the same. Or I prayed for the same, so God and I could get this relationship going and become BFFs.

⸺∞⸺

I knew for sure that I hadn't slept in our bed since Thursday night. Saturday after my morning nap, I walked past the bedroom a dozen times, maybe even thirteen or fourteen. I imagined that, when I turned away from the room, Logan darted in to surprise me on my next round. He didn't. I would have slept on his pillow just to be able to smell him, except I'd washed the sheets in my cleaning frenzy. I finally just closed the door.

I carried my cell phone with me everywhere, even the bathroom. He wouldn't know I answered his call from the toilet, and I didn't care if he did. The phone slept next to me. I discovered an app that played sounds to sleep by. Crackling fires, metronomes, babbling brooks, crashing oceans, the usual nature symphonies. It also played brown, pink, and white noises. I tried them, but the static zzzzzzzzzssssssssszzzzzssss didn't soothe me. It made me feel more anxious than ever. Fortunately, I had Xanax to help with that.

When I was tired, I slept or I watched television until I slept. I became very involved with a couple on *House Hunters International* moving to Panama, where the American woman's husband had grown up. I hated the wife for choosing the house over an hour away from where her husband worked when there were two lovely condos in the city only fifteen minutes away from his office. I wouldn't have been that selfish to insist on living so far away that Logan would have a three-hour round-trip commute. *The next time names are submitted for sainthood, I'll be sure yours is in there, Elle. Oh, did you notice her little girl was with them. In Panama.*

I tossed the pizza I fixed for lunch because it didn't have the puffy crust I liked. I felt guilty wasting food, so I took the pizza out of the trash can and wrapped it in foil. I slid it onto an open shelf in the refrigerator. It would die a natural death there in a week, then I could throw it away and it would be considered an act of kindness for the pizza and anyone else still hungry.

Friday's mail lingered in the basket by the front door. The basket was our inside mailbox. The outside mailbox was at the end of our driveway, so if I stopped on my way out, I'd shove the mail in my purse or toss it on the passenger seat. When I checked it while I was home, I'd walk back into the house, and it would hitch a ride with me to whatever I happened to be doing next. Logan found mail on the bathroom counter, his office, my office, the top of the washer or dryer, sometimes even on the porch. I was always careful to check for a letter or envelope from Kim.

For the first year of Faith's life, they sent me photos at holidays and notes like, "Faith took five steps by herself this morning" or "She said her first word. We think it was 'poop.'" I thought, while she still tossed and turned inside me like she was on spin cycle, I'd want updates with photos. As time went on, I dreaded the arrival of an update from Kim. Reading about her cuteness didn't bore a hole in my heart like looking at pictures of her. Especially the family ones, with the three of them flashing smiles in front of the Christmas tree or the Easter bunny. I'd share them with Cam, but my mother refused to look at them. "You are never going to be able to let her go if you insist on torturing yourself that way." I left the letters on my desk, and sometimes the envelope would be facing a different way or the pictures inside would be in a different order when I'd come back from school. I suspected my mother waited until I left the house to read the letters.

But it was Cam who finally convinced me that not wanting to see Faith's pictures didn't make me a bad person. "Letting go of this doesn't mean you don't care about Faith. The question you have to ask yourself is why are you maintaining this relationship? Is it because you truly want to be involved in Faith's life? Or is it because you're afraid what they might think of you?" Looking back, I realized that as cruel as I thought my mother was in telling me what she did, she was as right as Cam. After that, I wrote Kim and asked her to send brief updates just a few times a year, and I explained that the pictures were difficult. Cam told me to be honest, and they'd understand. I wondered if they were as relieved as I to be freed from the obligation.

Silly of me, I supposed, but even with the ease of e-mailing, I asked Kim if she minded if we continued our writing the old-fashioned way, pen and paper. Since we wrote to one another about four times a year and my notes were primarily to thank her and to let her know I'd received hers, the writing wasn't a nuisance. Plus, I worried less about Logan finding a letter in the mail, which he never did because he rarely nabbed it before I did, than leaving a digital footprint that could have ramifications beyond anything I wanted to imagine. Now, it no longer mattered.

With Logan now paying our bills online, most of our mail had been reduced to advertisements and invitations. I found the monthly mail-out from Logan's church in the basket, and I set it on his desk. His always orderly desk. The stapler and tape dispenser sit at right angles to the deskpad and there's no half-empty water bottle on top of a stack of unread magazines. On my way out, I spotted his Bible on the lampstand next to his leather chair, the one he left with every Sunday morning on the way to church. One more reminder of his absence. *I suppose he's not coming back for you, which means you're stuck hanging out with me until he does.*

In a plan that, in retrospect, could have only made sense to and been contrived by someone fueled by coffee, dry cereal, two bites of pizza and Xanax, I decided if the man wouldn't come to the Bible, the Bible would be brought to the man.

At the time, I considered myself brilliant.

25

I parked near the walkway that led from Logan's Sunday school classroom to the church. In about five minutes, the Bible study would be over, and the smartly dressed members would stream into the main building. If the church sign had switched to "First Financial Services," the men and women of the congregation would have still been appropriately attired. It still made me nervous that being a Christian required fashion savvy combined with sensible shoes. Hooker stilettos were quite frowned upon, as were men with exposed chest hair.

Before I turned off the car, I checked my makeup, which was subdued from two days' wear, but a little lip gloss went a long way to freshening my face. I used an old water bottle to wet my palms to press the front of my dress. As soon as the sidewalk trickled with the faithful, I slipped on my sunglasses, tucked the Bible in the crook of my arm, and casually approached the walkway.

Logan walked with a silver-haired man I didn't know, whose arm movements must have been an integral part of whatever story he told my husband because Logan laughed as he watched. I hadn't seen him since Friday night, and he didn't leave the relaxed, happy version I now saw. I considered for a moment that leaving might be the most honorable and wiser choice. Clearly, both honor and wisdom vacated my mental premises. Instead, I feigned a casual stroll, waved, and called Logan's name.

If joy sat on one side of a see-saw and however Logan's expression might be defined climbed on the other side, it would have propelled joy into orbit. Logan reached me in three giant strides, the last one so close I stepped backward to avoid being stepped on.

"Elle, what are you doing here?" He surveyed me from head to toe. "You're a mess. Isn't this"—he pinched the sleeve of my dress the way Cam removed snot from Nick Junior's nose—"what you were wearing Friday?"

I swept my fingers through my hair as a last-minute fluffing attempt since he was sure to notice it stuck to my scalp. "This," I said and held up his Bible as if presenting evidence to a courtroom, "is why I came. I knew you always had it with you on Sundays, and when I saw it in your office, I thought you might want it." I hoped I sounded as heroic and selfless as I felt.

"I have another one," he said and showed it to me.

"Oh, well, sure enough. It's right there in your hands." I needed a Plan B pronto. One that didn't include mentioning I sprayed his cologne on his pillowcase because I missed the smell of him. He kept looking over his shoulder. I looked too, but I didn't see anyone I recognized.

"This isn't the time or place for us to talk if that's why you're here. I told you I'd call you." His lips didn't move much when he spoke, and I knew that wasn't a good sign.

"Actually . . . I thought this might be a good time for me to attend church," I said and rocked back and forth on my heels, proud of myself for having devised a new plan on the fly. "I've even started praying a few times since you left."

"Attend church? Now?" He sounded confused instead of delighted and surprised. Was I going to need a Plan C?

Logan lifted my sunglasses to my forehead and examined my eyes. "Are you on something? This isn't like you."

I pushed them down again. "I may have taken a few Xanax every day. I have felt, you know, anxious. Logan, I have been in pain." I covered my mouth with my hand, but it didn't do much to muffle the sniffles and sobs. "I . . . just . . . wa . . . wanted . . . to . . . see . . . you," I shoved the words out between wet hiccups. I wanted to stop crying, but I didn't have the energy to force myself to calmness.

He gripped my elbow and walked me closer to the parking lot and away from the church. He bent down and so did his voice. "Settle down. You're making a scene. I'm calling Matt," Logan reached in his pocket for his cell phone, but didn't release me. He scrolled, pressed Matt's number, and held the phone to his ear. "He'll take you home."

I ripped my elbow away. "I managed to drive myself here, alone. I can certainly get myself home." The walkway traffic slowed behind us, with more faces turned toward our drama than the church building.

Logan placed one hand on my shoulder. I thought maybe he wanted to hug me, but the weight and pressure of his hand suggested otherwise. "Matt. I'm at church, and Elle's here. Uh huh. She doesn't feel well. I hate to ask you this, but can you pick her up for me and drive her home? I've got a committee meeting after the service, and I don't think it's safe for her to drive. Thanks."

"You're just going to have to call Matt back because I'm not waiting here for him," I huffed, folded my arms around the Bible and over my chest, and assumed the posture of a five-year-old who's just been told she has to like her new brother even if he does cry all night.

I saw her coming, but I waited for Logan to be surprised.

"Logan, is everything okay here?" Martha's tone matched her suit. Crisp. "Elle, dear, it's such a surprise to see you. Were you planning to attend today's service?" She scanned me from head to toe. "Did you bring something else to wear?"

Logan answered for me. "We're fine. A misunderstanding. Elle thought I'd forgotten my Bible. She came here to drop it off." He didn't make eye contact with Martha. His eye contact with me meant, "This is our story. Got it?"

Martha pointed to the Bible Logan held. "But you have your—"

"Exactly, Mother. We got our signals crossed. And Elle doesn't feel well, so she's not going to church," he said. "I'll meet you in the sanctuary. Usual place."

I don't even know the unusual place. If Logan thought Martha bought one bite of that bologna, he'd better stay out of courtrooms.

"Hope you feel better soon, Elle. Let me know if you need me to help." She patted Logan's back, we exchanged nods, and she left. If there was a speed-dial for prayer, Martha was on her way to write my name on the list.

"Logan, when are you coming home?" I reached out to smooth anything on his shirt, but he intercepted my hand and returned it to me.

"I'd planned to be there after church today. But I can see now that it would be pointless for us to discuss anything serious. Let Matt take you home. Shower, brush your teeth, get some sleep. Throw the pills away."

"For someone who didn't want to be a father, you sure sound like one right now." I gasped as if I wasn't the one who just hurled that vicious, offensive remark at my husband. "I'm sorry. Logan, I . . . I am so sorry. . . . "

"Stop. Don't say another word. I'm going to chalk that up to whatever it is you've been taking that's making you act like this. Matt just drove up, and I'm going to talk to him. Your choice, Elle. Go with him. Don't go with him. Right now, I don't care what you do. Not at all."

I didn't blame him if he hated me. I hated me too.

Of course, I left with Matt. After what I said to Logan, I would have crawled all the way home.

I slunk into the passenger seat while Logan spoke to Matt, too low for me to hear, which I'm sure he intended. The three of us participated in furtive glances at one another. Their conversation lasted longer than I'd expected. I closed my eyes, leaned against the headrest, and wondered how that forgiveness thing worked with God.

The car door closed, but when I opened my eyes, Logan was gone. Matt wore his running shorts and T-shirt, but he didn't have that musty puppy smell. Guess his mission of mercy postponed his jog. I buckled my seat belt and swiped under my eyes with my fingertips. "Thanks," I whispered, thankful I remembered to wear sunglasses.

"Not a problem. You know I'd do anything for Logan," he said.

Including interrupting his own life to pick up Logan's crazy wife on a Sunday morning. I nodded, but since I stared out my window, I didn't know if he saw me.

"Do you need me to stop anywhere? Coffee? Have you eaten? There's a Starbucks on the way to your house. I can drive through or we can go in."

"No. I just want to go home."

Neither one of us spoke the rest of the way. Matt listened to some sports talk radio station. I tried to silence the voices in my head. The ones that sounded more like my mother than like me.

His car turned into our driveway. Our manicured lawn covered the front yard of our house like a green velvet cloak bordered with flowers. The sky curtsied against the backdrop of homes, its skirt decorated with clusters of clouds. A Norman Rockwell painting ready to be framed. And my life was surrealism.

"Appreciate the ride, Matt," I said and opened the door.

"Elle, I'm not sure what this is all about between you and Logan. I don't pry into personal things unless invited or necessary. But the two of you need to be careful. This kind of negative attention is difficult to overcome, especially the closer we get to the election."

"I understand. Would you wait here a minute? There's something inside I'd like you to give Logan for me."

In a brown manila envelope, I put the bottle of pills and a picture of Faith at her first birthday party. A shiny red bow, the kind used for wrapping gifts, sat on top of her curly dark hair. She was in a high chair, a pink bib tied around her neck that said, "I'm 1!" in thick hot-pink letters. The birthday cake on the tray was cratered. Streaks of pink and white icing ran like tracks over her cheeks and forehead. More icing and cake crumbs oozed from her fists, and she'd raised her arms by her head like she'd just declared herself the winner. She was looking at whomever was taking the picture, and her eyes and smile—Logan's eyes and smile—were excruciatingly bright and beautiful.

I handed the envelope to Matt, walked inside, and did exactly what Logan said I should do. Cam had left a message while I showered. She wanted an update. I sent her a text. "STILL WORKING IT OUT. WILL CALL ASAP. LOVE YOU, E." I found a clean pair of yoga pants and a camisole, slipped them on, and went to cook myself breakfast.

I opened the refrigerator, dumped the foil-wrapped pizza in the trash, and scrounged enough to make myself a decent omelet with cheese and mushrooms.

While I ate, I had another one of those God conversations, so I wouldn't feel alone. *Really messed that one up, didn't I? Going solo isn't working out too well for me. I'm sure You have suggestions, but I don't know how to make this a dialogue yet. If You don't mind, I'm just going to stick to a monologue right now because it's weird enough for me to be talking in my head. Listening in my head is beyond bizarre for me to think about. I slammed Logan with that comment, and it was such an evil thing to say. I don't know if he'll ever be able to forgive me for that. I'm going to have a hard time forgiving myself. Not to mention his forgiving me for not telling him anything about his child for sixteen years. Is that even a forgivable thing? If not, then I suppose we don't stand a chance. And where does that leave Faith? We have to work this out, but then You already know that.*

I finished eating, cleaned the kitchen, and even though it was still only afternoon, I picked up Logan's Bible and headed to our bedroom. The sheets were cool as I wedged myself in on my side of the bed, propped myself up, opened the Bible, and started where every book starts. "In the beginning . . . "

26

My ringing cell phone woke me around six o' clock the next morning. Logan's number flashed on my screen.

"Logan." I said his name like a whispered prayer.

"Elle. Are you home?"

Avoid the snarky comment. "Yes, yes, I am. In fact, I took all of your advice yesterday, and I just woke up."

"I'm at the office. I came in early to finish some work. I'll be there in a couple of hours. Maybe eight or eight-thirty."

Thank you. Thank you. "Great. That's great."

"I'll see you then."

A minute before eight o'clock, I made sure I didn't have lipstick on my teeth, checked that I'd shaved under my arms, and started a fresh pot of coffee. I relocated the poster casualty from the table to my office.

Ten minutes after eight o'clock, my eagerness to see Logan was tempered by the realization I shouldn't have assumed this visit was a step toward our relationship, our future.

Twenty-two minutes after eight o'clock, Logan walked through the back door.

"Can we talk here, in the kitchen?" Logan sat, turned his cell phone off, and did that finger crook in the knot of his tie that I'd noticed was a universal male movement of unknotting and moving their heads as if someone tried to twist them off their necks.

"Of course. Sure. No problem." Synonymous responses were symptomatic of my nervousness.

We were two adults on a blind date tiptoeing around one another's personal space. We volleyed polite, abbreviated conversation about how we were, how the weather was, whether or not one or both of us wanted coffee, and then we arrived at the edge of the cliff. We had to decide if we'd cross the bridge to a new, unfamiliar, and likely challenging landscape. Or not.

The small talk ended, which meant time for the big talk. Actually, Logan's turn for big talk. A few nights ago, I'd ripped through small, medium, large, and extra-large. I wanted to reach across the table and pull him toward me. I wasn't sure he would want me to.

"The night you talked to me, you asked me to listen without interrupting. I'm asking you to do the same. I know how difficult that is for you, but you must know how difficult this is for me."

"I understand. But I need to say one thing before you start, and I promise, zipped," I ran my fingers across my lips as if I was closing a zipper, "I'm done."

The tiniest bit of a grin perched on the side of his mouth. He waved his hand across the table. "The floor's cleared for you. Go."

"Please forgive me for what I said yesterday. My Xanax hangover isn't an excuse because that's an issue all its own. It was cruel, and I've already given you more to hate me for than any one person needs in a lifetime. I didn't need to add to that," I said.

He nodded. "I've never had my heart ripped out of my chest by someone's bare hands before, then again, the past few days . . ." Logan rubbed the back of his neck, sighed, and his frustration rose like steam on a summer sidewalk after rain. "What I don't understand is why in the world you kept this a secret for sixteen years. Almost sixteen years, Elle. It's unconscionable." His voice had grown louder with each word.

I kept my hands curled around my coffee mug where they'd be less likely to shake. He paused, but I bit my lower lip and waited for him to continue.

"When I left Friday night, I asked myself, 'Who is this woman I married?' Everything I thought I knew about you," he stopped and stared at his palms as if he'd lost something, "became a question. You lied about a child. A child. Well, how hard is it to lie about anything compared to that?" His fist pounded the table when he said "that," sending his coffee spoon skittering. He drew it back to his mug. "Ironic, huh?"

Logan talked to the spoon. I knew he wasn't waiting for me to answer.

He leaned back. No, it was more like a slump. His head still tilted at the spoon, he raised his eyes. "Ironic when the lawyer's wife is the unethical partner of the two."

He didn't indicate that it was my turn to talk, so I took this quiet as an intermission. This is why fighters go to their corners between rounds. To get a break from what you've been through to prepare for what you're about to go through. Logan went beyond ego-bruising. He went straight for the superego bruising, but I deserved it. I was guilty of all of that. Lying to save someone from the truth isn't protection, it's deception.

Logan pushed his mug forward. "If Faith's parents hadn't died, would we be having this discussion? Did you ever intend to tell me the truth?"

For the first time, in all the years that Logan and I had known one another, he looked at me in a way he never had before. With mistrust.

I met his eyes without flinching because what I was about to tell him was the absolute truth. "I don't know, Logan."

I waited. The ice clunked into the tray in the freezer. I waited. The dishwasher shifted into its next cycle. I waited. Our next-door neighbor's lawn service tuned up their orchestra of motors. I waited. I felt like I did when Cam and I played the "no blink" game. The loser blinked first. But for Logan and me, there was no winner. It was who lost less.

"I believe you. I might have accepted a no, but an absolute yes, probably not. There's not much in life that's neatly never or always. And I don't think you're trying to split the difference."

"Logan, I can't sit here anymore. My butt is numb, and I'm about to jump out of my skin from having to stay still. Can we move to the porch or the backyard? I'll go get a blanket and we can throw it on the grass, I don't care."

We moved outside. The lawn mowers next door moved to the front yard, muting what sounded like an army of enraged African bees to a whirring buzz. I sat in the glider, and Logan moved a deck chair closer.

"Why didn't you tell me you were pregnant when you found out? If you hadn't sent me that picture," he stopped and cleared his throat and gazed past me as if the photograph was a poster behind me, "I might have asked you—"

"Asked me how I knew she was yours?" It saddened, not shocked me that he fell victim to what sometimes seemed the universal male response to fatherhood by surprise. On some other day, it might amuse him to know I would have been the person voted "Least Likely to Ever Have Sex" in high school.

"That's why I wanted you to see her. I knew you couldn't look at her and not see yourself in her face."

"When I opened that envelope, and the pills fell out, well, I got that. But the picture? I hated you when I saw it. I thought you were playing dirty, you know?" He leaned forward, his elbows on his knees, rubbed his forehead, then looked up at me, his eyes wet. "I understood. There was no way she couldn't be my daughter, unless I had a twin."

Logan didn't try to stop the tears that traveled down his face. Those tears of loss, the quiet realization some things in life we can never recover, were their own grief.

"But I need to understand, Elle, how we ended up here, today."

I closed my eyes for a moment, and the me of all those years ago materialized in my heart. The me who held her breath for fear she'd disturb the universe. The me who, years later, could exhale and find herself still standing. The pain of sharing this was bearable because I knew I could finally close the wound. "By the time I realized I was pregnant, you'd started at LSU and I was still in high school. We'd known one another one month; we had sex once. You couldn't have made it any more clear that you had no intention of ever wanting children. My own parents rejected me after they knew I was pregnant—why would I have expected anything different from you? I figured I was on my own after I never heard from you."

"I did miss you," Logan said, "but I was scared. I let my ego override whatever I felt for you. I knew my family had political plans for me; I thought I'd move on. Guess I expected you would too."

"Those first few months of my pregnancy, every time I planned to tell you, something else got in the way. When Melody called to tell me about your 'almost' engagement to Carole, I was feeling our child kick." I pulled my knees up to my chest and wrapped my arms around my legs. Logan had walked to the edge of the deck while I was talking. His back was to me, and I wondered what he was really seeing when he looked out over the yard.

He turned around, hands in his pockets. Logan said, "Having sex with Carole complicated our relationship. I'm not blaming her. I could have said no, and I didn't. I thought it might make me stop thinking you and I had something special. It didn't. It made me understand that 'special' had to happen before sex."

Behind Logan, angry sprinkler heads popped up from the lawn and the gardens and spit water until, seconds later, they relaxed and ribbons of water swayed back and forth. A reliable, consistent, and efficient system. Everything our marriage didn't seem to be at this moment. He moved back to the deck chair to avoid getting wet.

I lowered my legs to push the glider with my toes and held on to the edge of the seat. "Well, I didn't know any of that. Cam told me I needed to talk to you after we met with the social worker. What was I supposed to do? Call you between your classes and say, 'You know that baby you didn't want? I have one of those.'"

"Is my name even on her birth certificate?" Logan folded his arms across his chest as if he needed to underscore the tone of his question.

I think he already knew the answer, but he wanted to hear me say it.

"No. It isn't. But I thought I was protecting you . . . that burden of Butler politics and all. The vetting we went through wouldn't have even been an issue because you might have never had the chance for this political run." I leaned against the back of the glider, rested my head against the cushion, and stared at the sky. Anything to not face Logan when I said, "But it didn't matter because she was carried out of the hospital by the two people whose names would be on her birth certificate."

When I looked at Logan, his head bent, twisting his wedding band around his finger, I wished for one of those confessionals my college roommate used to tell me about in her church. The small rooms where penitents either confessed their sins openly to a priest or knelt behind a latticed screen that obscured both their faces. Sharp truths were less barbed shared with shadowy faces.

I didn't have that option, but neither did Logan. In the contest between the agony of saying the truth and hearing it, there were no winners.

"After she was adopted, I didn't expect I'd see you again. When I did, Faith was three years old. Not a topic for a five-minute conversation in a Mass Comm building." The backdrop of noises from the neighbor's house ended, but I didn't lower my voice to compensate. The words stomped out as if on a mission. I pushed my hair away from my damp forehead. The mid-morning sun replicated the heat I felt in my gut. And Logan's cool demeanor did nothing to make it subside.

"When we started dating, I thought about telling you. But I thought our dating might not last either. Then we were engaged, and we were married. And I was terrified."

Logan had uncrossed his arms, but his jutting chin relayed the same message.

"I told my mother you were Faith's father before our wedding. But it didn't matter to her that I was finally with the man I loved. Our marriage wasn't going to heal my relationship with my mother. Honesty may be the best policy, but it doesn't always pay dividends. It left me with no one. I lost my father, my mother was an emotional washout, and I lost Faith. Then you came back into my life. And I couldn't bear the thought of losing you too."

I stood and pulled my sundress where it had melted to my thighs. "And here we are. Not exactly prime time for an 'Oh, by the way, there's something I've been meaning to tell you . . .' because your political career would be over, and I could lose everything that mattered to me."

"And that could still happen," said Logan.

27

Growing up in the South, we early learned to differentiate between Nacogdoches, which was a city in Texas, and Natchitoches, which was not. It was in Louisiana. People lulled by some mangled southern pronunciations and over-confidence sometimes confused the two and ended up in the one they never intended to go to.

And when I stopped mid-swing after Logan's last statement, I realized we'd been headed for two different towns, but all the while I thought we'd been traveling the same road. I'd been lulled into a false sense of security thinking that, despite the emotional miles between us, we were finally headed in the same direction.

"Elle, what? You look like I just slapped you in the face. Did you think we weren't going to have to discuss consequences and make decisions about what to do and when?"

"What are you saying? That you don't think Faith should live with us? We went through all of this soul-searching, navel-gazing reflection for you to tell me I could lose you or Faith or both of you?"

Logan shook his head. The you're-not-listening-to-me head shake. "Listen," he said, "how did you think this would play out? I'd go to my next committee meeting and announce, 'Elle has a fifteen-year-old daughter she gave up for adoption, who I also just discovered a few days ago is my daughter, and she's coming to live with us because her adoptive parents died. Now, next item on the agenda.' Or Matt would write a press release and add, 'The Butlers will not be taking questions from the media.' Martha doesn't even know she has a granddaughter. Have you even thought of that? We could add that to the press release? Mrs. Daniel Butler will also *not be* answering questions regarding her granddaughter."

Between the whining of the leaf blowers by the neighbor's lawn service and our own raised voices, neither one of us heard the patio door open and close. We discovered it only when Martha, her hand still grasping the door handle, looked from one of us to the other and said, "Regarding my *what?*"

I turned to Logan. His face and Martha's shared a paleness that made their eyes, already wide open like gasps, appear even more startled. I doubted I looked much different considering my stomach lurched into my throat and I thought I'd stopped breathing.

She pulled the handle toward her. The glass panes rattled in distress as the door slammed against the wood frame. Martha took the few steps to where Logan and I were and planted herself between us. "I heard the word *granddaughter*, and I don't want either of you to pretend I didn't. I'm not that old. And since I have only one child, then this has to involve the two of you." She glared at us, from one to the other, her arms crossed over her snappy, bright lime, shawl collar blouse. In the middle of the morning, confronting her son and daughter-in-law, Martha still managed to look like she stepped off the Talbot's catalog photo shoot.

"Mother, let's go inside and discuss this," Logan said and placed his hand on her shoulder as if he could have steered her away. "No high drama, and we'll have more privacy there, okay?"

Even I backed up on that one. Logan's condescending tone was about to put him in time-out.

"The only high drama is going to be my knocking your head off if you don't tell me what's going on. And don't make this about privacy when the two of you are already outside talking."

"She's got a point, Logan," I said and headed inside regretting having given Matt those pills.

Martha huffed and puffed her way inside, helped herself to my last Coke Zero in the refrigerator, and informed us she'd meet us in the den.

"Mother, we're right behind you. We can see where you're going," said Logan. "And was there some reason you're here? You don't wander over here during the day often." He turned to me. "Does she?" *As in, is this another surprise?*

Martha and I both said, "No," within a microsecond of one another.

"I came here because Matt called me after he couldn't get in touch with either of you. He wants you to call him before you leave the house. He said it's important, but not urgent," Martha explained. "Now. I'm waiting." She crossed her legs, crossed her arms, crossed her patience with us.

Over what seemed like a season change, Logan and I recounted everything up to the point when she found us. She didn't interrupt us, and her silent stoicism surprised me. Her expression would have been no less passive had we been reading aloud assembly instructions for a bicycle. We came to the end of the story as we knew it; as in, where do we go from here?

She looked past both of us, toyed with her pearl necklace with her fingers, uncrossed her legs, and smoothed her blouse.

What are we waiting for—a referee's whistle? She and Logan and their processing needed term limits.

Martha folded her hands on top of one another on her lap, eyed Logan and me, and like we were two applicants for a loan who sat across her broad desk at the bank, said, "Let me make sure I understand all this . . . The two of you made a baby, which you," she pointed at me, "gave up for adoption and which, you," now it was Logan's turn to be the recipient of the point, "didn't know about until this past weekend. And now the two of you are telling me this child's parents died, and if she doesn't live with the two of you, she will have to go into a foster home?"

Logan and I nodded, but it seemed to me Martha had just read us the fasten your seat belts protocol on a space launch mission. If I had nails left to bite, I would have started chewing. Had he been sitting closer, I might have grabbed Logan's. He, however, mirrored his mother's one-size-fits-all face, and between the two of them, I could have been on a tour through the wax museum.

Martha took a deep breath, and I prepared myself for the barrage following her exhale.

"You two both understand what this could mean to the campaign and to everything we've all been devoted to for years? And, you understand, I hope, that if you don't make this public first, the media will do it for you."

"Before you surprised us, I planned to discuss that with Elle," Logan said and added peevish to his wax-persona.

My face contorted into a question mark. "That? To which *that* are you referring?" I stared at my husband, who had paced the room while his mother spoke.

"Yes, please explain," Martha said in a way that suggested she doubted he could.

"We could consider a compromise." Logan looked back and forth between the two of us. "Elle could talk to Holly—that's her name, right? I'm sure she'd understand if we needed to delay Faith moving here until after the election."

Lift off.

"Are you crazy . . . a compromise?" I held my breath and waited for the backlash of having just called Logan crazy in front of his mother. But she sipped her Coke Zero and showed no intention of stepping in to save either one of us. "You're going to call Holly and ask for a foster home sequester? Faith isn't an amendment or some bill you're proposing . . . she's our daughter." I stopped to give my twitching chin muscle time to relax. "That's it? Career first, kid later? Or maybe not at all?" My turn to pace, my hands shoved in my pants pockets and my frustration on my shoulders. Logan's turn to stand and watch me.

"Elle, calm down and be reasonable," he said and stepped in front of me. "We can make this work for all of us. Do you expect me to—"

"Logan, stop talking. Both of you, sit down," Martha commanded.

She stood in front of both of us. "Here's how this is going to go down. Elle, when do you need to call Ms. Taylor?"

"In two days," I said, not trying to disguise the anxiety I felt.

"Logan, you are going to talk to Matt and arrange a time for a family meeting." She pointed at me. "Elle, have you told your mother any of this?" Martha rolled her eyes after I shook my head no. "I figured as much. Call her and tell her she needs to meet us here tomorrow morning. Don't go into details, just make sure she gets here."

She swatted the logistical ball over the net and back to her son. "Logan Butler, you're my son, and I love you. But you need to listen to me, now. I know you and your father barely had a relationship. And, for the most part, what you did have was lousy. I get it. Why would you want to be a father, if that's what you would turn into? But by not wanting to be your father, that's exactly who you're becoming. I'll take responsibility for that because I knew why your father treated you the way he did. I chose to stay, and that's on me as well. But I didn't know then how to tell my son that his father never wanted children. His treatment of you had nothing to do with who *you* were. He never expected to have you, and I had never been more grateful to God that I did." She cleared her throat, but the deep breath that followed and the voice on the tip of tears suggested she tried to clear years of pain. Martha placed her hands on Logan's shoulders as she looked into his eyes. "You are not, I repeat, are not, going to carry that forward."

I barely had time to witness the reverberations of what Martha had just shared with Logan, when she held my face in her hands. "Dear, you haven't allowed yourself to feel like a mother for almost sixteen years. Start now. You did the best you could at the time. I know what that's like." Martha brushed my tears from my cheeks with her thumbs. "I know there's more to resolve, more forgiveness to pray for. But it's time for you to learn what it means to step out in faith. For Faith." She smiled and kissed my forehead. "Got it?"

Logan's cell phone rang and shattered the spell that Martha had cast with her wisdom and compassion. I was in awe of her for the first time in all the years that I'd known her. Not the begrudging admiration of self-confidence, but the respect and wonderment of her ability to rise above circumstances, to dissolve her own ego to accomplish good.

"It's Matt," Logan said and walked away, phone to his ear.

I hugged Martha and when her arms tightened around me, I felt peace. Or at least I thought it must be because I could almost hear the shell that I'd built around myself crack and crumble at my feet. "Thank you," I whispered.

"Of course," she said. "It's what mothers do. You'll see."

Logan left for the office, the two of us now entrenched in the demilitarized zone his mother declared. Martha followed him and scurried out, saying she didn't want to be late for her lunch date.

"Date? As in day of the week or as in 'I have a date'?" I held the door open for her.

"Do women my age date?" Martha shrugged. "Eh. At my age, I guess it shouldn't matter what we call it. We should just be glad we do, right?"

"Anyone we know?"

She patted my cheek. "Tell you all about it later. Besides, you and Logan have enough to process."

I smiled hearing the Butler problem-solving family trait, watched as she got into her car, and closed the door thinking of all the ones I had yet to open.

I sent Cam a text telling her to call me when she had a break after I'd received several texts that consisted of "??????!!!!!!" which was Cam-speak for, "Why haven't you called and/or otherwise let me know what's going on?"

She called a few minutes later. After I'd exhausted myself with the "I said, he said, she said" retellings, she asked me to warn her before I called our mother. "You know I have your back, but you have to have my front first. I don't want to be gearing up for a patient and have to hear her rant. I'm sure the patient wouldn't want to sit in the chair after that either."

She asked me if I'd given any thought to getting a bedroom ready for Faith.

"Okay, so don't I feel like the village idiot. No, I haven't, and I'm sure she doesn't want her bedroom adjoining Logan's office."

"Well, you better get busy. Move your office, and that way she'll have that other side of the house for herself. Just make sure she has a bed and maybe a desk. The two of you can shop together for everything else. That way she'll feel like its her own."

I stood at the door of my office and tried to imagine the transformation. "Cam, I'm scared. Really. What if this doesn't work? She may hate us. Me, especially. And if I can't figure out that she needs her own bedroom . . . what else am I going to be clueless about? I don't know how to make up for all those years we lost."

"I don't mean to sound cruel here, but you're not making up for lost years. She's been with a family, two people she grew up with as her parents. And now they're gone. That's going to be the struggle—helping her through that loss, not your own. At some point, you'll probably want to have someone you can all talk to . . . therapy, baby, therapy. It's what all the cool people are doing."

I promised Cam I'd call her before I spoke to Mom, and we hung up. I felt like I'd been assigned to house arrest the past few days. I pulled out my volunteer sheets for Junior League and found the information for the local Association for Retarded Citizens' Buddy Club. Local high schools paired students with intellectual and developmental disabilities with "buddies," students without disabilities. The teens were matched for the entire school year, and they hung out with one another at lunch and school activities like dances and sports events. The ARC sponsored entertainment for them like movies, bowling, eating out, zoo visits, and socials. I called the program director, Julie O'Brien, to ask if I could come by to talk to her about the center and ideas for the Buddy Club. She said this afternoon was Bowling with Buddies, and I could meet her at Paradise Bowling Lanes.

Worked for me. Any place that wasn't the inside of my house was paradise to me.

28

Furniture stores and office supply stores enticed me more than shopping malls. So when Cam suggested I purchase a bed for Faith, I zipped out before my meeting with Julie to wander the aisles of Taylor's Furniture. Angela and Rodney, the store's owners, inherited the store from Rodney's parents and grew it from one of those shops on the corner to a megastore. At over 120,000 square feet, the display space almost required a GPS and fast food shops to finish browsing from one end to the other.

I told Angela I was thinking about redoing our guestroom, and I wanted to look at pretty beds. We strolled through adjoining displays from traditional to casual to what-were-they-thinking contemporary. One of the displays featured a classic sleigh bed, pine with sculpted moldings and distressed, a quality that already matched our lifestyle. Angela handed me a brochure showing matching nightstands and dressers.

"I think a matching armoire comes with it. Do you want me to check?" Angela rifled through a stack of catalogs while I paid more attention to the comforter than the actual bed. "Hey,

Elle, I know you probably can't say too much, but what does Logan think about his mother and . . . ?"

One of the upsides of having a drama-filled life was learning to not spasm when someone smacked me with unexpected trivia. I traced the paisley design on the vintage-inspired matalassé duvet and summoned my sipping-lemonade-by-the-poolside voice. "You mean all those play practices for *Streetcar*?"

She laughed as she handed me pictures of armoires. "Sure, if you want to call it that."

The "it" rendered amusement and wasn't rehearsal. I tried again. "Oh," as if she jogged my memory, "yeah. Go figure. She and having what she doesn't want to call dates? She left my house for one of those this morning."

Armoires didn't fit my idea of a teenage girl's room. I handed the catalog back to Angela, who eyed me with that wisdom that only comes from knowing the other person has not a clue in the universe what you're talking about. She tucked her hair behind her ears, checked for interlopers, and leaned closer. "No, silly, about she and that man swapping kisses at Tujague's last weekend."

I disqualified "knocked me over with a feather" as a cliché in, of all places, the Paula Deen poster bed display section where she invited me to "curl into her favorite chair," which I promptly took advantage of.

Angela's mouth fell open as if her jaw had just been unhinged. It was a relief she covered it with her hands. "You hadn't heard this?" She gasped with the excitement of one who just earned bragging rights as the first person to leak the Martha-Butler-titillating-at-Tujague's story to another Butler.

"It's pointless now to pretend I had," I said. I wished Paula would materialize to tell the story, replete with "y'all" liberally sprinkled throughout and after she'd create a special dish, Martha's Sweetness, some gooey concoction, with the calories dialed down, of course. Make the whole escapade seem as harmless as I'm certain it was. "Okay, spill it," I said, dropped my purse on the floor, and curled up as per Paula's instructions.

"My aunt is in the play and after rehearsals ended early one night, a few of them wanted to go to the French Quarter. It was somebody's birthday." Angela waved her hand as if the birthday issue was an annoying mosquito in the story. "Carly, that's my aunt, said they'd noticed Martha and William exchanging glances that weren't in the script." She paused to make sure I got that.

I nodded.

"They were at the bar, and you know how Tujague's has that really long bar?"

That stand-up cypress bar had been there since 1856. Generations of people knew about it and rubbed elbows and who knows what else with celebrities, titans of business, and whoever else happened to be hanging out that night. Like Martha.

The closer the story traveled to the punch line, the more forward Angela leaned and the more her hands waved. Had it not been a short story, she might have propelled herself to another display room. "Okay, my aunt and a few people are standing at the bar yapping, and she looks down the other end of the bar and oh-my-goodness. She said they were as lip-locked as two teenagers at a school dance."

"Then what?"

She tilted her head, her eyes squinted like maybe if the question had been in focus, she would have understood it. "Then, well, that's it." Angela shrugged her shoulders. "Carly doesn't think Martha and William knew they'd been seen kissing. I don't know if anybody said anything else."

My underwhelmed response muted her animated enthusiasm. She seemed disappointed. I was too. Disappointed a woman who'd been widowed for over thirty years who'd been seen kissing a man had generated such a frenzy. Kissing another woman? Now, that would be newsworthy. If Martha had been forty years younger or not Logan's mother, would it have generated that much interest? After 150 plus years of existence, I was certain if that bar could talk someone would have killed it by now and that one couple kissing wasn't the most or the least of it.

I sighed. On purpose. "I guess Logan and I will have to have 'the talk' with his mother," I said with a voice as tired as I felt. "Since she might be out of the loop about protection, we'll have to catch her up." I smiled, shook my head. "What are you going to do? Senior citizens today just don't act their ages like they used to."

Angela's lips didn't know what to do with themselves. Smile, frown, a bit of each.

I checked my watch. On purpose. "Angela, thanks for all of your help. I have to dash to an appointment. But I'll be sure to tell Logan and Martha that you asked about them."

"Sure. Yes, thanks for coming in. Let me know what you decide about the bed. I'll be happy to help," Angela said, pulling her sentences behind her like a wagon with a lost wheel.

I closed my car door and laughed. Not even to myself. Out loud. Poor Angela. She thought Martha's story deserved a gossip column mention. She had no idea what the Butler family had in production.

⸎

Logan had called twice while I was at Taylor's. I returned his call, but when he didn't answer, I left a message that I was running late for an appointment and I'd call in about an hour.

Opening the door to the bowling alley, I transported myself to a place whose noises and smells were ageless and predictable. Evidence of the twenty-first century existed in the updated scoring and upscaled designs, but if I'd handed out bottles of Eau de Bowling, we'd all expect the aroma of stale beer, musty carpet, burned coffee, recycled cigarette smoke, and a dab of overwrought perfume. The opera of balls whirring through the returns, the pings and rings from the game room, the soft thumpings as balls travel down lanes, and for those who hit the target, a crescendo of clapping and crashing and cracking as the pins fell to defeat.

I felt comforted by the familiarity that bordered on nostalgia. The dull, orthopedic-like shoes that even gained fashion at one point, racks of balls all wide-eyed and gaping waiting for the right hand, and the constant motion of people to and from and up and around. It was a playground of sights and sounds and smells. Which made it perfect for Julie's teens who, in a subdued environment, were sometimes conspicuous and uncomfortable. Their language lacked polish, their syllables hadn't learned to cooperate with one another. Some of them, for reasons either related to their disability or personality, grunted or squeaked or howled or squealed. Their sounds barely caused a rift in the noisy bowling universe.

Julie's group was easy to locate because a majority of the lanes sectioned off for them were lined with bright blue bumpers to prevent gutter balls. The pits where bowlers were supposed to sit and wait for their turn were like hives where worker-bee students helped their buddies pick up their own bowling balls or made sure they stood in their own lanes or tied their shoes. In Julie's lane, a student took one slow step after another next to her buddy whose body looked as if it had melted and then reformed in angles not meant to be. She held the ball for him because he used a walker and could move it only one agonizing inch at a time. When they reached the foul line, she placed the ball in his hands and guided his arms in the direction of the pins. His swing was more like a thrust, and the ball slammed the lane and galumphed until it smacked a few pins down.

I sat next to Julie, who was keeping score. "I'm exhausted from holding my breath hoping the ball would hit something . . . anything," I said. "Why isn't he excited? Four pins fell."

Julie patted my hand and pointed. The student leaned toward her buddy with a smile that occupied almost her entire face, and whatever she said, he applauded himself, waved his head back and forth, and laughed. "He was waiting for her to tell him how many he knocked down. He's blind."

"I don't know how you aren't a puddle of emotions every day," I told her. Julie started the Buddy program in the city and worked with high schools to start their own.

"You'll see when you're working in the center. Their victories, no matter how small, are cause for celebration. And, sister, if I didn't believe in God, my happy butt would not be sitting here. One day at a time, by the grace of God." She started clapping as the student made his way back. "Woohoo! Proud of you, Harry. Giving those pins a beating."

Julie and I spent the next hour together talking between kids who needed her attention for one reason or another. I wanted her opinion on doing the adult version of her program at the center. Needing volunteer hours for Junior League gave me the idea. Volunteers were always welcomed, but it was the relationships that had a profound effect on the student and the buddy. Not one of the high school kids at the bowling alley looked sullen or acted prissy or demonstrated disrespect.

I wanted the volunteers at the center to benefit from the partnership as much as the clients.

A few of Julie's students said they'd be happy to help our volunteers when we were ready. "I'd love for my mother to be involved in your program. She comes with me sometimes, and I have to stop her from taking over," said Courtney, a petite blonde who'd been a buddy for two years. "I mean, I'm constantly having to tell my mom to find her own challenged person to work with."

Her friend Janine said, "When I first started doing this, I'll admit, I was a little scared. You know, about who I'd be paired with, and what if I couldn't help or if I was overwhelmed by the disability. Of course, when they assigned me Harry, I just about quit on the spot. But, Courtney, here," she swatted her friend on the shoulder, "was my ride home, so even if I quit, I was going to be there anyway. I'm graduating this year, and I almost want to take him with me. I never expected him to, you know," she wiped her eyes with the heels of her hand, "change my life. I think we got the roles reversed. He's the one helping me."

Logan told me he believed God brought people into our lives for a reason, either for us to learn or to teach something. And, sometimes, when the lesson is over, the person moves on. I remember joking about wanting God to bring the person who knew the winning lottery numbers into my life.

I thought about Cindy, Jenn's sister, and the difference she'd made for me, totally unaware of her influence. My career choice, the desire to build this center were all rooted in that one day we spent together, in that one decision I made to take a ride with Jenn when she visited. I wondered what my passion might have been or if I would have even had one, if I'd decided differently.

Maybe God brought that person into my life. Maybe the lottery wasn't always about money, but people. Maybe I'd won, but I was still holding on to my ticket.

29

Logan called before I reached my car. "Hey, did you get my message?" I said. "My meeting just ended—"

"I took a chance I'd catch you. You know that long morning we had?" he asked.

I tossed my purse on the passenger seat. "Today's long morning or some other one? We seem to be collecting them."

"Remember that phone call from Matt that Martha mentioned? He got a call from Sidney Carlyle, otherwise known as Megan's father, who's not pleased his daughter was no longer employed at our firm. We're not sure yet what he wants, but he's suggesting sex discrimination, which is crazy, and not fulfilling his campaign contribution promises. Plus Matt said he has well-placed friends." Shuffled papers and a sigh later. "Do me a favor? Please don't tell me it can't get any worse. It's the universe up-ending cliché day somewhere, and I don't want to participate any more than I already am."

I debated driving through Dairy Queen for some sort of Blizzard with chocolate, caramel, and even more chocolate. I couldn't emotionally deal with my emotional eating. "Would another word for this be blackmail?" At the traffic light I spotted a Starbucks and my emotions informed me a White Chocolate Mocha Frappuccino Light would be sufficient.

The drive-through at Starbucks had more cars in line than a bank before Christmas. I parked and braced myself for more doomsday news from Logan. "Any other tidings of joy?"

"Did you call your mother?"

I skipped the "Light" when I ordered. At least I had that going for me since there wasn't going to be anything light about calling Nancy Claiborne.

I stopped at the grocery on my way home partly to overcompensate for my sugar splurge by buying fruits and vegetables and otherwise healthy things. I thought I'd seen Lucy Wiggins turn into the frozen food section. Supermarket stalking wasn't one of my proficiency skills, but I couldn't pretend like I hadn't seen her. Ever since Logan announced Chad dropped out of the race, I wanted to send Lucy flowers or a note or something more than what I did, which was nothing.

She just closed the freezer door when I skittered up to her. "Lucy?"

A speed bump of no recognition before she said, "Elle Butler. I haven't seen you in a long time. How are you?"

Other than her complexion a bit more washed out and the silk scarf of pink and red peonies tied around her head, Lucy didn't appear or even sound like a woman whose body hosted a despicable visitor.

"I'm fine. Great, really," I said. "What about you? You look amazing." *For someone going through chemotherapy.*

"Well, other than this cancer thing, I'm good." She said "this cancer thing" the way someone would talk about an annoying relative who stayed a bit too long. "The chemotherapy's ree-dic-u-lous. You'd think medical science would've figured out a way I could keep my hair *and* stay alive."

Our conversation made us aisle-buggy nuisances, and the tragic grumblings of not being able to reach frozen corn or okra started. I scooted my cart away from the freezer door after a woman who reminded me of Mamie, the younger years, LSU sweats and all, tapped my shoulder and said, "Uh, excuse me, you're blocking the spinach."

"Lucy, I'm glad I saw you," I said. "Please tell Chad hello for me, and I'm praying for your family." Oh, good grief. I wanted to slap myself for lying to a cancer patient. Praying for her family? I wasn't even praying for my own.

"Thanks, Elle. That means a lot to me. It helps to know on those days I'm feeling puny that my name's making its way to God through the lips of people I don't even know." She hugged me despite the man behind her who harrumphed about her blocking the aisle. "You take care of yourself. Give Logan and Martha a hug from me. I'll see you."

An entire freezer section of frozen vegetables booed me for fibbing to Lucy. "Look, it just slipped out," I said, but the bags of broccoli weren't buying it and refused to budge off the shelf. I'd show them. If I prayed, I turned the lie into a truth. *So take that.*

I was pretty sure I heard, "I'll take it," as I rolled toward the salad dressings.

"I thought you said you were buying steaks to grill tonight," Logan said as he lifted the cover of the pizza box.

"I was. I did. What I mean is, I bought steaks, but by the time I got here, put everything away, listened to your voice mail about being late, it passed." I flopped placemats on the table, handed Logan a plate and a napkin, and opened the pizza box.

"I ran into Lucy Wiggins in the supermarket," I said as I rolled the pizza cutter through vegetables and pepperoni. "The woman is remarkable. She talked about her cancer like it was an inconvenient flu."

"How does she look?"

"She looks great . . . for someone with cancer."

Logan paused on his way to a slice of pizza. "That's harsh."

"Actually, those were her words not mine. She has a sense of humor, that's for sure." I served myself and sat across from him. "Oh, and she said to give you and Martha her regards," I said. "Actually, I think her words were more along the lines of my hugging the both of you for her."

"I'm glad she's doing well," he said as he picked the black olives off his slice and transferred them to my plate.

A few bites of awkward silence later, I asked, "What's going on here? With us. Are we going to pretend this is just another day at the Butler household? I'm thinking we need some sort of baseline—"

Logan chucked his leftover crust in the box and leaned against the chair, a slump of annoyance that said, "You're making me crazy." "Could we have just made it through dinner"—he gave the word *dinner* special snark emphasis—"and then sharpened our swords?"

"I didn't mean we had to engage in verbal warfare. . . . I don't know where I am . . . where we are with one another."

"What do you want from me, Elle? To pat you on the head, say you're forgiven, then you run along like it never happened? You turned my life upside down, inside out. . . . You don't know where *you* are?" He pushed his chair away from the table. "I don't even know what my life is anymore. And we haven't even started the hard part of this, do you even realize that?"

What did I want from Logan? I wanted to know he wouldn't abandon me. I wanted more than his physical presence. To be shunned emotionally was worse. If that's where we were headed, we might as well not be in the same house. The only thing worse than not being with Logan would be seeing him every day and being universes apart emotionally. "That's ridiculous. Of course, I know there's a lot left to work out," I said.

"Really? I don't think you do. No, I take that back. I think you do know here," he pointed to his head, "but you're not ready for it here," and he laid his hand on his chest. "I'm betting you haven't called your mother, and we need her to be here tomorrow."

"No, not yet. But I planned to after dinner." The longer this went on, the more defensive I sounded.

"You waited this entire day to get in touch with her, and if she can't make it because you've called late, it's going to be on her, isn't it? If you ask me, and I know you didn't, I think you've worn this victim role long enough." Logan put his plate in the sink. "I'm going to be working in my office for a while. Don't wait up for me." He walked off.

Instead of another whole slice, I raked the topping off one, and shoveled it onto my plate. Logan was right. I didn't want to call my mother. I hated letting her know I needed her because it gave her power and it left me defenseless. Again and again and again. I finished eating, then cleaned the kitchen. I texted Cam a warning as I promised and pressed my mother's name on my phone.

I gave her the pitch and waited.

"Elle, you want me to drive three hours to your house tomorrow to talk? Why can't we do that over the phone? And you're not giving me much notice."

"I apologize for not calling sooner. I could give you a list of reasons, but none of them matter now. I've already spoken to Cam. She's got some plan in place for the baby for—"

"How is it you had time to call Cam, but you didn't have time to call me? And I'm the one who's supposed to drive?" *And start the engines of guilt.*

"Believe it or not, my talking to her first was to help you. I thought you wouldn't have the inconvenience of trying to make a plan for your grandson."

"Oh," she said. "I still don't understand why I have to be there."

"If neither one of us can remember the last time you were here, then it's been too long. That could be one reason. Another reason is I'm asking you to. Could you trust me enough to know I wouldn't do this if it wasn't important? If we could do this by phone, I wouldn't be calling to ask about coming to my house. Logan and I have to make some important decisions, and no, we're not dying or getting divorced. But we want you and Martha to be a part of this." I didn't mention Matt. That would've started an entirely new cycle of questioning.

"And if you don't want to drive home the same day, you can spend the night here. Or at Martha's. She'd probably love the company."

Silence. Then a long sigh where she breathed out the word, "Okay," like a period ending her sentence. "But I'm not happy about it."

I'm not too happy about it myself. "Great. Thank you. Call us when you leave, so we'll know when to expect you. No, not because I think you're not going to come. Because I want to know by what time I should start getting nervous when you haven't arrived."

Logan's office light was on as I headed to bed. The Bible I'd been reading when I fell asleep the night before was still on my nightstand. It reminded me I had a promise to live up to.

After teeth brushing and face washing, I pulled the sheets over me and rested my head on my pillow. *I'm back. I'm just learning how to pray for myself, but I'm not sure how this works for other people. But, hey, You know what the Wiggins need more than I do. Maybe You could lighten up on this cancer thing with her? And she's so blasé about it all. It's enough to make me sick . . . of myself. The Butlers are gearing up for action the next few days. We're going to need all the help we can get. But take care of Lucy first.*

30

My mother looked in people's mouths. Logan's mother listened to them. A fact which began and ended the similarities between the two.

Martha worked a room like nobody's business, chatted people up, won them over, and calmed them down. Yet, it wasn't until Logan decided to pursue politics that I came to understand Martha donned the persona of Mrs. Daniel Butler the way my mother did with her scrubs, lab coat, and name tag of Dr. Claiborne.

This morning, when the gracious and charismatic Martha welcomed the awkward and unremarkable Nancy, it occurred to me Martha lapsed into her hospitality persona as comfortably as my mother lapsed into quiet in social situations. Neither one of them risked stepping out of the roles others defined for them. I wasn't sure if I'd defined my own role even before this surprise shift in my life, and I'd be adding another undefined one to my list: mother.

My mother and her attitude arrived close to ten o'clock as expected. She must have asked Cam what to wear because she looked uncharacteristically unfrumpy. Cobalt-blue linen pants, white T-shirt, and a scarf with scallop designs of blue, yellow, black, and white. She'd cut her hair to chin length, dyed it a golden brown, and stopped fighting her natural waves. The new look softened her features. But in the six months since I'd last seen her, age had sketched deeper wrinkles across her forehead, set small parentheses on each side of her lips, and loosened her cheeks.

She passed around her signature faux-hug, one hand on your shoulder and enough forward body movement to suggest hugging. Logan, who still referred to her as Mrs. Claiborne, introduced her to Matt, and Martha was ready to rock. I had to admit, she had a gift for taking over meetings, like we'd pleaded with her to relieve us of the burden. She didn't count on my mother, though, being so far out of the loop she didn't know we had thread.

"Elle," Martha said, her hands clasped at her waist, "your mother didn't know why we were meeting today?" She gave me the stern-eye treatment, but her forehead didn't scrunch into that V between her eyebrows. Her forehead was completely oblivious to the mini-crisis it was supposed to have reacted to. *Well, I declare, she's gone and gotten herself Botoxed.* "Elle?"

"I'm sorry," I said. I would have been a lousy trial lawyer. In the middle of questioning, I'd have paused to ask a witness who styled her hair or where she found that chunky Plexiglas statement necklace she wore.

"As am I," my mother said. "Martha, I asked her what this was about and she was purposely vague. Considering how late she called me to be here today, and I'm obviously the only person here who doesn't know why, I'm left wondering why I'm even here."

"Martha, you told me not to go into details, just to be sure my mother was here." If she intended to throw me under the bus, I wanted a running start.

"I thought you would have at least told her we were here to discuss Faith," said Martha.

Here we go. . . .

"Faith?" My mother grabbed the arms of her chair, and I recoiled from the bullets in her eyes. "They know?"

I nodded.

"My mother and Matt found out yesterday. I've known for less than a week," Logan said as if in apology.

She ignored Logan and glared at me. "Is something wrong? Did something happen to her?"

"No. Not to her, but her—" I started to explain when Martha interrupted.

"Logan, it's going to take a bit for us to explain this to Nancy. Would you and Matt go to that little deli around the corner? Ask Mr. Warren to slice some turkey, ham, and roast beef. Get a few loaves of French bread," she said. "Oh, and cheese. And whatever else."

"Seriously, Martha? Matt and I didn't carve out this time to run deli deliveries."

I glanced at Matt. He rolled his eyes and mouthed, "Uh-oh."

Logan's remark summoned hands-on-hip Martha. "You're telling me your time is too valuable to waste getting lunch? It's more valuable if you sit here and listen to me explain what you already know? Then, I suppose Elle and I will turn the reins over to you and Matthew, and we'll drive to Warren's deli." She looked at me. "Ready?"

You will not laugh. You will not smile. You will not even grin.
"Sure."

Logan stood. At attention. "Stay there, Elle. Matt and I have it covered."

After the door closed, Martha smiled at us. "That worked out well, didn't it?"

The real reason, I discovered, was Martha wanted my mother to understand the dynamics in the Butler family. Why she felt responsible for the relationship between her husband and her son. "I don't know if Logan has shared anything with Matthew about that, but even if he knew the entire story, I didn't want Logan to feel uncomfortable having to hear it," she explained.

I let Martha relate the story as she knew it, saving me the initial Holly and Cam involvement. As Martha explained, I watched my otherwise stoic mother shed tears. Real tears that caused her to dig through her purse for tissues. Tears that found their way into those aching hollow places in me. The aching that comes from having to tell someone that the plane she needed to get to her dying father's bedside had taken off or the finish line for the race was just over the hill, but you stopped halfway up. Or the baby you loved cost you the mother you loved.

"Nancy, I know you don't like my son, and until he and Elle told me about Faith, I didn't understand why. It makes sense now why you didn't want your daughter to marry some-one who you thought might hurt her or abandon her again. He's going to have to learn forgiveness, whether or not he ever understands Elle made those choices because she thought she was protecting him."

My mother responded to Martha in almost the same way I did yesterday. Her eyes softened, her face and her battle-ready posture relaxed.

Progress.

—⁂—

"It's all in the refrigerator, and I bought enough for dinner, too," Logan said to Martha after he and Matt returned. "Just in case . . ."

"I got it the first time, dear," she told him. "We're ready now."

"Logan told me he suggested waiting until after the election for Faith to move here," Matt said. "Hold up, ladies, I can see you're ready to tar and feather me. I didn't think the idea was wise—"

"No, you told me it was idiotic," Logan said.

Matt looked at him as if he'd passed gas, then continued. "Discounting the fact that Faith would have to wait in a foster home, which . . . to his credit . . . Logan wasn't thinking that if that information leaked, the consequences would be worse. Whether he won the election or not.

"Once she's actually here, as in living in your house, we'll schedule a press conference. In the political world, this is a gnat. But this is a smaller playing field, and the gnat looks the size of a dragonfly. Elle, we want both of you there. We're not saying or putting anything out until we go over everything with you," Matt said.

"May I say something?" My mother tucked her hair behind her ears, then looked around the room, before she spoke. "We need to remember that this child lost two parents, and I can't imagine how devastating that must be for her. She's grieving, and I think as much as possible, we all need to protect her and not be in a rush to put her in the spotlight."

Matt broke the silence that followed my mother's words. "You're absolutely right, and that's what makes our working together important. Not for us, but for Faith."

"Elle, you and I need to call Holly this afternoon and work out whatever she has in mind. I don't know if she planned to drive her here or for us to pick her up," Logan said. He took me in his arms and kissed my tears away. I tried to form words, but all I could produce was a runny nose. He cradled my face in his hands, and his eyes drank me in. "I love you, Elizabeth

Claiborne Butler," he whispered. "We are going to take this big mess and make it something beautiful."

I kissed him and said, "I love you more, Logan Daniel Butler."

By the time we finished eating, Logan decided to not go back to the office. I overheard some of what Matt asked him, like remembering to call him after we talked to Holly, but I also heard the name "Megan." Since they were both expert at the art of keeping a straight face, I couldn't tell if something positive or negative was attached to the mention of her. I'd ask after Matt left.

My mother hadn't brought an overnight bag and decided to drive home, despite Martha's attempts to convince her to stay. "Nancy, you should come back for a weekend and plan to stay with me. I could introduce you to my friends, and we'd have great fun—"

"Mother," Logan said standing by the table, stabbing cheese with his saber toothpick, "speaking of fun . . ."

"Give me a minute, Logan. I'm telling Nancy good-bye."

He winked at me, then said, "Are you bringing her to Tujaque's? Rumor is, you can have lots of fun there."

If it was possible to grow pale and blush at the same time, Martha had clearly mastered it.

"I'll get back to you on that," she said as she wagged her finger at him. "Come on, Nancy, I'll walk you to your car."

"Who told you?" I said, keeping my voice almost a whisper in case she didn't realize I knew the story too.

His eyes wide, he said, "And who told you?"

"I can't reveal my sources," I said and kissed the tip of his nose. "But you can torture me later, and I might confess," I whispered in his ear.

His hands slipped around my waist. "Me too. Torture me too."

Before she left, my mother told me she hoped, after today, we could start again. "I'm sorry for all the years we lost. I'm not going to give you that 'I'll make it all up to you' business because I know that's not possible. All I can do is start from here."

"That's enough for me," I said, and for the first time in too long a time, my mother hugged me. And I hugged her back.

Logan and I reassured Martha we didn't care that she kissed someone at the restaurant and she was welcome to kiss him again in public.

"Of course, please don't take it a step past that, and if his intentions aren't honorable, I'll be forced to challenge him to a duel," he told her. "By the way, when are you going to bring this guy around to meet us?"

"Stop being silly," she said, but we saw the giggle in her eyes and knew it didn't bother her at all.

She reminded me that the committee needed to start making decisions. "No one's even called me yet to volunteer as chairperson. I'm going to give them until tonight, then tomorrow I'll start calling."

We walked her to the door, and she kissed us both goodbye. "I'm proud of you two. Not so proud of all that had to happen to get you here. But you picked a good mountain to die on. And I think God's going to honor that."

Minutes later Logan handed me my cell phone. "Okay, let's do this."

The phone rang longer than it usually did. I thought I'd have to leave a voice message, but she finally answered. "Holly, it's Elle. Guess you already knew that. Anyway, I'm going to hand this over to someone who wants to talk to you."

"Holly, this is Logan Butler. Elle and I want to talk to you about bringing Faith home."

31

In a surprising spirit of volunteerism, our mother offered to keep Nick Junior overnight while Cam's husband went on a weekend fishing trip, which freed Cam to visit. She drove in Saturday and planned to leave Sunday. When I called to tell her Logan and I would be picking up Faith on Wednesday at Holly's, she offered to help get her room ready. I appreciated her sanity even more than the moving help.

"You know that cliché about the anticipation being better than the possession? That won't happen, right?" I pushed a box of books into the hall outside my office.

"Some days. Not much different from husbands, you know," Cam said. She taped another box and wrote "Books & Stuff" on the top. "Not every day is perfect. If it was, we wouldn't want to get to heaven. I mean, Jesus must have had to pick up his own socks and not leave his hair in the sink after he shaved. I'll bet Mary would have been all kinds of crazy if he hadn't."

I emptied another shelf of books and tchotchkes into a box. "Why did I think I needed these?" I held up a mint-green glass bowl and a ceramic, heart-shaped box.

"I don't have a clue. If you don't want them anymore, ditch them. Or have a garage sale next month."

"Cam, I just had this awful thought."

"About getting rid of your crap? Good grief, Elle, this is like awful thought number thirty-one." She sat on the floor and unwrapped another chocolate from the stash she found in my file cabinet. "But, go on. It gives me more time to eat candy, and please don't tell my patients."

"Sure, I promise," I said. "What if she wants all the furniture she had in her old room? I should have asked Holly about that. How is all of her stuff going to get here?"

"Now, *that* is a good question. You're one out of thirty-one. Maybe you should call Holly on that one. But whether she moves her stuff here or not, we still need to have a room ready."

I called, but Holly didn't answer, so I left a voice message.

"I have no idea what kind of house they lived in or how much space she had. This might even be too small." I joined Cam on the floor. I hated that ants-crawling-up-my-spine sort of frenzy that made me want to move when I had nowhere to go.

"These two-bites-and-they're-gone candy are dangerous," Cam said. She leaned toward me and patted my knee. "Stop tying yourself in knots. It doesn't matter how nice her room is in her old house. As harsh as this sounds, she can't live there anymore. That house will be sold, and the money will be in a trust for her. In a roundabout way, it comes back to her."

"You're right," I said and taped another box. "I have this list of unknowns, like what does she like to eat, what does she like to read." I jumped up and shook Cam's shoulder. "I haven't even thought about school, Cam. I haven't even looked at schools near here. I'm going to need her records and that . . . what's that thing called . . . ?"

"Transcript?"

"Yes, that. Has anyone thought of this except me? Do you think Holly's working on this?"

Cam handed me my cell phone. "Leave a new message."

"What if she just doesn't like us?" I asked Cam while I waited for Holly once again.

"Well, maybe she'll find someone to adopt you and Logan."

The next day, we walked into Faith's soon-to-be room before Cam left. "We accomplished a lot in less than two days, didn't we?"

"We're a great team," Cam said and laughed. "Yea. It was a three-bags-of-candy job."

We'd repainted the walls the palest pale pink, named White Dogwood, which meant, I supposed, that someone in the paint-naming department needed a rest. The door and baseboards were the color of butter, and a large sisal rug with white trim covered the wood floors. On Monday, Taylor's was delivering a white beadboard bed with an over-the-bed hutch and a tower on each side, a matching wide dresser, and a desk. We'd installed wood blinds on the windows. When Faith decided on her comforter or duvet, we'd work on window treatments.

"It's going to be exciting to have her here, Elle. I can't wait to meet her. Again," Cam said as we both stared into a room that waited for its future.

Martha stopped by "on her way out," which we think meant she was on her way to see Mr. Wonderful. That's what Logan and I called him because beyond knowing his name was William and that he played the role of Stanley, she wasn't spilling much else. We were in the back, finally cooking the steaks I bought the night of our pizza dinner. To relieve our guilt about eating carrot cake muffins for dessert, we grilled asparagus and squash.

Martha handed me mock-ups of the play booklet. "The play is in two weeks. Be sure to write that opening date on your calendars. Faith will be here, which means she'll be there with the two of you."

She paused, and we looked at one another with the same dawning awareness that by Wednesday, Logan and I would be three. "You know, it's just about killing me that I can't tell my close friends. I never imagined I'd be able to use the words *grandmother* and *granddaughter* in my own life." Martha waved her hand in front of her eyes. "I need to get going. That smoke's making my eyes water."

Logan waved the oversized fork he was using at his mother. "If that's what you want to blame it on . . ."

She blew us kisses. "Talk to you tomorrow." Martha left. Even with the smoke from the grill, her perfume needed a second or two to catch up with her.

I stared at my cell phone, which I'd been doing ever since I tried to reach Holly, and it wasn't at all intimidated. "She still hasn't called. That's not Holly-like."

"If she hasn't called by tomorrow around lunch, try again. I'm sure there's a legitimate reason. She's not always in situations where she can answer every call." Logan opened the top of the pit. It was like something out of *Alien* had just landed, spewing smoke and crackling. He put the steak and veggies on the platter. "Time to eat. Lighten up, babe. I'm sure when you do talk with her, she'll explain."

I followed him inside. "I just don't want the explanation to involve us."

I'd just plunged my feet into bubbling hot water when the phone rang. *Now I get the phone call? In the middle of the nail salon?* Ti handed my purse to me, and I almost had to turn the thing upside down to find the phone. It was Logan.

"I'm at the nail—"

"Don't blow me off. I have good news. Not yet about Holly. But I just met with Matt about this Megan thing. He went over her résumé, called a few references, one of which turned out to be a tanning salon, not a law practice. The one firm where she actually worked provided underwhelming responses to our questions about her. Lesson learned for me. Due diligence on every résumé, no matter whose sister or brother or son or daughter wants a job."

"That's great. Not great that she lied . . . "

"I know what you mean. It deflates her father trying to press discrimination issues, and it puts him in an awkward situation as far as pulling his money or endorsement. In his defense, he probably doesn't have a clue what she writes on her résumé or job application. In fact, he might be appalled. Or should be. Anyway . . . Matt's going to take care of it."

"Thanks for letting me know. I can scratch it off my list of things to be in a twit about."

He laughed. "Honey, try to enjoy yourself while you're there. I'm sure you'll be the one calling me next with great news."

We hung up, and I almost dropped my phone in the pool at my feet when I turned the massage chair back on. I'd been fiddling with the buttons and must have hit "high" because I was being pummeled by Schwarzenegger in *The Terminator* while I rode a bucking bronco.

Ti hurried over, grabbed the remote, and within seconds, I was back to Anya on the Tahitian beach. "Tsk. Tsk." Her forefinger moved in front of me like a windshield wiper. "Don't touch," she ordered and set the remote next to me in the chair.

She shuffled away, her shoulders rounded, shaking her head like there's no hope for America when its women can't operate a massage chair in a nail salon.

———

Holly called at 11:30 as I pulled into the driveway. The call came in on Bluetooth, so I stayed in the car to talk to her. "Holly, whew, I'm glad to hear from you."

"Elle."

When she said my name, not as a greeting, but as a warning, the doors of my heart slammed shut. My dreams had been packing their suitcases for days, and now they were leaving. "Just tell me, Holly. No lead-ins."

"She doesn't want to leave. She's not sure she wants to live with you and Logan."

32

That's an option? She gets to decide that? I thought her parents wanted her with us?" I gripped the steering wheel until my fingers revolted and I stretched them out.

"They did. I don't know if it's an option, legally, for her to not live with you. But I don't think you want me to shove her in my car in handcuffs to get there."

I rocked back and forth in my seat, my hands over my face. The sun burned my eyes, and the air coming out of the car vents smelled like wet steel. I wanted to go home. Not the house that sat at the edge of my driveway. The home inside my skin, where I felt comfortable and safe and at peace and sometimes even happy.

"Elle? Elle?"

"I'm here. What do we do now? Should we go to her? Maybe if we met someplace first?"

"Let's just give her a few days. I think this is like pre-wedding jitters. She'll come through it, but the kid's lost two parents. And she has to leave a home she's lived in her entire life. I have no idea how difficult this must be for her."

"Tell . . . tell her we have her room ready. We bought a new bed and dresser and desk, they're white. And we repainted. But if she wants, we'll hire movers. They can pack her entire room up at her house and have it brought here. It'll be just like . . . home? But it won't be, will it? I had this feeling, Holly, for days. This sludge that wouldn't move out of my gut. I knew something was going to go wrong. Maybe she wants me to know what it feels like, you know? To not be wanted . . . but that was never it and we could tell her when we talk to her . . ." I had to stop because I couldn't breathe, cry, and talk simultaneously.

"Elle, it's going to be okay. Look how much we've worked through already. God didn't take us this far to have this not happen. But if He did, then we wait for Plan B."

"I don't want Plan B. I want Faith."

"I know. I know. I want her there with you. She'll figure it out. I'll keep you updated. You may not hear from me tomorrow. I'm leaving for Houston this afternoon, I told her the two of us could spend a few days together. I thought having time to decompress might help clear her head."

"Can you do me a favor? Can you please call Logan and tell him? He'll ask me questions I can't answer, and I'll be crying and he won't understand me. . . ."

I opened the car door, but I didn't want to get out. I didn't want to walk into the house alone. I'd be outside of Faith's room, sitting *shiva*, just like the seven-day mourning ritual practiced in Judaism.

I stood, finally, and looked across the street. Martha's car was in her driveway. I don't remember if I ran or walked or both to get to her house.

I knocked until my knuckles felt bruised by the time she opened the door.

Martha's expression of shock echoed what I felt after Holly's call. Somehow, between sobs, "She's not coming, Martha. She's not coming," spilled out.

Logan told me later he left the office right after Holly called, and when he couldn't reach me, he called Martha.

Once we were home, I went straight to our bedroom and crawled into bed. Sometime later, I woke up with Logan's body spooned against mine. He still wore his slacks and starched button-down shirt. Instead of counting sheep, I lulled myself back to sleep counting Logan's breaths.

The next day, when the sunlight squinted through the curtains and found its way to my eyes, I woke up again. But Logan was gone. Some electrical charge hit my heart, and I bolted out of bed, shouting for him. He ran into the bedroom. The panic on his face eased when he realized I didn't know where he was.

"I'm making coffee." He kissed my forehead. "Why don't you shower? By the time you finish, I'll have a fresh cup on the nightstand waiting for you."

"I don't want to shower. It's not going to close the hole in my heart." I leaned into his chest.

"You're right. It won't. But you'll feel clean, and clean is good," he said. He lifted my face to his. "You have to put one foot in front of the other today and trust it's going to be okay. She's processing. It's genetic." He smiled and brushed my bangs across my forehead. His fingertips are cool and soft. "Today's already Thursday, and Holly said she'd call tomorrow. We're almost there."

Martha came over to babysit for the day. After work, Logan had two town hall meetings to attend. Our lives were on hold, but his campaign needed to move forward.

She spent the morning verbally whipping that committee into shape and finally getting someone to chair. The group planned to meet next week.

My mother and Cam called with the same reassurances, but it all sounded like *blahblahblah* to me.

I carried my emotions like a hot bowl of soup across a big, crowded room. Small steps. Steady. Steady. Don't look down. I had to keep all the soup in the bowl because I couldn't bear the pain if it lapped out and burned me.

I wasn't impressed with this God I'd been praying to since He couldn't seem to direct a fifteen year old. *Is the difference that Your son always wanted to go home? Well, that's not working out too well for me. Aren't things supposed to happen when we have these little chats? Good things? This is not a good thing.*

I bypassed the baked chicken Martha fixed for dinner, went straight for the strawberry crème pie, and fell into bed. I pretended it was Christmas Eve and I was five years old. Excited to go to sleep because the morning would be filled with presents and half-eaten cookies and an empty glass of milk. So excited your insides moved like one of those little wheels hamsters run on. You just had to make yourself not think of how wonderful the next day would be and trust it would happen.

And it did. Friday morning. Finally.

I reassured Logan I'd be fine and I could entertain myself for the day. He told me Martha would be on standby and left for the office. I showered, I dressed, I drank coffee, I ate breakfast, I read the newspaper, I drank more coffee, I ate lunch. I did one thing after the other after the other to make the time pass.

After lunch, I forced myself outside where I wouldn't find reasons to pass Faith's bedroom-to-be. I brought a book with me, mostly to shade my eyes from the sun because I couldn't pay attention to all those words at once. Not today. I scooted the deck chair to put my legs in the sun and my face in the shade. I heard myself say, "This is one of those days I wished we had a pool." Brilliant idea. One of those cartooned light-bulb-over-the-head ideas.

We had plenty of space for a pool, and it would be great for Faith to be able to invite friends over. Might even help her make friends.

I left the book on the chair, kicked my sandals off, and stepped off the deck to wander the yard and envision the pool in different areas, different angles. *We might even have room for a cabana.*

That was when I noticed Logan and Martha standing on the deck. Holly must have called. I was surprised I didn't hear the thuds of the weights as they fell off my chest. "Holly called! Holly called. Tell me what she . . ."

I backed up. "What?" I couldn't see Martha's lips; they were drawn and tight on her face. And, Logan's eyes were blood-shot. "What?"

"They can't find Faith," Logan said.

"Can't find her? They can't find her? How do you misplace a teenager?"

"They think she ran away," Martha used the same tight tone as Logan.

"Think? They don't know? How. Can. They. Not. Know?" Every cell in my body stood at attention.

"What that means . . ." Logan paused, "is they don't believe she's been abducted. They just don't know where she is."

Logan and Martha lost their shapes, my arms wouldn't move where I told them to go, my legs started to melt into the ground, and someone made the yard spin too fast. I remembered the blades of grass rushed up and met my cheek and all the lights in the whole world went dark.

33

Logan told me when I started to sway, he tried to catch me before I slumped to the ground. "At least you landed on grass, but you have a marble right here," he said as his finger touched the blossoming bruise. "But, I don't think it's going to grow anymore than it has."

I propped myself on my elbow and washed down the two aspirins he'd given me. "I hope these pills stop the drilling going on in my head."

Martha walked in the den with a tray. "You need to lie down for ten more minutes. I looked it up online, on a medical site. But I brought you some food. You also need to eat."

Brownies, apple slices, and an egg salad sandwich. Must be a bad day in the refrigerator.

"Shouldn't we be doing something instead of sitting around here? How long has she been gone? Where was she? How does Holly know for sure no one's taken her?" I pushed myself to sitting. "Where are my shoes? We have to report her missing. Why haven't you done that?"

"Elle, honey, you need—"

"Martha, please, don't tell me to calm down or relax. I've heard that for two days. Didn't work out, did it?" I zig-zagged through the den and the kitchen. "Logan, where are my shoes? Where did you put them? Nevermind. I'll get another pair."

I raged into our bedroom and tried to find shoes to wear to the police station. That's where we needed to go. How could anyone look for her if nobody's going to tell them she's lost? I opened box after box after box. Wrong. Wrong. Wrong. Where were those Tori Burch sandals? The orange ones with the flower. I know they're here. Stupid expensive shoes. Stupid me for buying them. I stood on my toes, and I pulled a box off the top shelf. My fingertips lost control of it, and it bounced on my head, my leather boots flopped around me like dead black fish.

I sat on the floor, my forehead throbbed, my world throbbed. *I can't do this. I can't do this. This hurts so much. Please, please, please don't let me lose her again.* I cried, gulping wet sobs until I couldn't stand my own ugly animal noises.

I didn't know when he found me. I only knew Logan covered my arms with his own, and I sobbed until I was numb. I wiped my face with a scarf that had fallen on the floor and rested my head on Logan's chest while he held me. The quiet felt like a sanctuary.

I whispered, "Is God punishing me for getting pregnant? Or maybe for not telling you about Faith?"

"He's not that kind of God, Elle. Your father wouldn't punish you when you were ten years old for writing on a wall when you were two. You and I have both had to deal with the consequences of our decisions. That's discipline, not punishment. And God wouldn't put Faith in danger to teach us a lesson."

Martha knocked on the bedroom door as she opened it. "Holly's on the phone. She wants to give you an update." She handed Logan his cell phone, and the two of us watched him as we waited to hear what Holly said.

She told him that she had filed a missing persons report, and since Faith was only fifteen, the twenty-four-hour waiting period didn't come in to play. Holly explained that Faith had asked if they could spend time at her old house on Thursday. She said she wanted to take some things with her, and Holly assumed she meant before coming to our house. That afternoon, Faith asked if she could meet some of her friends at Starbucks. Holly drove her there and said she'd be back in an hour to pick her up.

Not only was Faith not there, her friends weren't either. Holly called the numbers Faith had left her, and not one of the three girls had talked to Faith, much less made plans to meet her. At the time, she didn't think anything about Faith carrying her backpack. She was used to seeing Faith with it but realized that she probably had packed more in there than she thought.

"Holly's checking flight, train, and bus schedules out of Houston to Las Vegas. Faith talked a lot about wanting to know where her parents died. Like it was some kind of closure for her. Holly thinks that might be where she's headed. She said we should have our phones with us, and she'd call with any piece of information she had."

"Logan, text her with my phone number, too. If she can't get it touch with one or both of you, I'd probably know how to find you," Martha said.

When he finished the text, Logan said, "What would you think about going on the news now? If more people know she's missing, then more people are helping to find her, right?"

I asked Martha what she thought. "It makes sense. Plus, the media would have less reason or time to focus on the adoption details while this child is missing."

"I'll talk to Matt. Why don't you call your mother and Cam and catch them up?" said Logan.

Martha reached out her hand to help me up. "Elle, I'll call your mother. You just talk to Cam. Better to not have to talk about it twice."

Best not to have to talk about it at all.

"Matt suggested we wait twenty-four hours because he thinks going to the press with this now will make them even more motivated to start digging. He thinks they'll be all over the angle of what is it about us that made her not want to be here. And that opens the door for more speculation." Logan said as he helped me reorganize the closet.

"You don't look as sure about this as you were before you spoke to him."

"I can't disagree with him, Elle. He's making valid points. But I told him that if anything happened to Faith in those hours we waited, I'd never forgive myself."

"What did he say?"

"That this could be the difference between winning and losing the election and that I needed to think about it and get back to him. And then he also reminded me I might be jeopardizing some of the big money contributors, who even if they supported what I did in principle, may not want to back the candidate who just sabotaged himself."

"When are you planning to call him back?"

"I already did. I told him I'd do this even if it meant dropping out. How could I uphold myself as a man of integrity and faith and sell out my own child? If that's who voters want, then I'm the wrong person for the job anyway."

Being on the morning news show to reveal the news about Faith and to discuss her running away wasn't how I planned to make my television debut. Not that I really planned to be on television as a career choice. But if I did, this wasn't the road I would've taken.

We arrived at the station and met Deirdre Franklin, one of the two early morning news anchors who would be introducing us. "Nice to meet you, though I'm sorry it's under these circumstances. You both dressed perfectly for the cameras, so that's a relief. People show up in the most outrageous clothes sometimes. It's difficult to take someone seriously who's talking about debt reduction while he's wearing a Mickey Mouse tie, suspenders, and a green and brown plaid sports coat."

We were up after the first commercial, which was a relief, knowing that if I fell on the way to the sofa it wouldn't be recorded and live forever in a YouTube video. "After you're finished telling Faith's story, we're going to show this picture for the viewers with a number they can call to provide information."

She handed us a photograph that had been faxed to the station. Tall, willowy, she held a star-shaped glass ornament and appeared to be reaching to place it on one of the high branches of the Christmas tree. Her brown hair fell straight over her shoulders, held back by a bright red headband. Her black tights defined her long legs. I heard whoever took the picture call, "Faith, over here," catching her in that unexpected moment. Her smile seemed comfortable and unforced, and her eyes, I recognized. As familiar as her father's. No one who knew us could look at Faith and not connect the dots.

Logan shook his head. "I can't . . . not right now . . ." he said, the words barely escaping the tightness in his throat.

"That's understandable, Mr. Butler. You don't need to apologize." She settled in the chair across from us. "Just talk to me. Don't pay any attention to anything outside of the three of us.

"We're back with Logan Butler and his wife, Elizabeth. Mr. Butler, an attorney and former city councilman, is presently a candidate for state representative. Elizabeth, a former occupational therapist, is hoping to build a day and residential facility for disabled adults in the community. But they're here today to discuss something entirely different. I'll turn this over to them. First, Mr. Butler."

Logan began. "During my campaign, I've asked people to support and vote for me because of my honesty, integrity, and experience. And that's what brings Elizabeth and me here today, to be people of integrity and to honestly share an experience with you that changed our lives.

"Elizabeth and I have been married for ten years, but we've known one another much longer. In fact, we met about sixteen years ago. Elizabeth was still in high school when we had a baby, a girl named Faith, who we gave up for adoption because it was the best decision for her. The adoption was open, and for some time Elizabeth and Faith's adoptive mom stayed in contact." Logan cleared his throat, then continued.

"Several weeks ago, Elizabeth was contacted by a social worker who told her Faith's parents died in a horrific accident while they were on vacation. We found out that her adoptive parents had made a way, in the event of their deaths, for Faith to live with us. It was their way of making sure that Faith would not have to be placed in foster care. And that's what the social worker called to tell us. We've been making arrangements for her to move from Houston to live with us. We wanted to be up front about what was happening. Since we've not had children in the past ten years, we knew that the sudden appearance of a fifteen-year-old in our household would be cause for curiosity.

She was supposed to arrive yesterday. But that didn't happen, and that's the other reason we're here."

Deirdre nodded. "And, Mrs. Butler, what's happened since then?"

"We waited for a phone call to work out the details of Faith coming to our house. But when the social worker called, it was because Faith was missing. She'd dropped her off at a coffee shop to, as Faith told her, tell her friends good-bye, but when she went to pick her up an hour later, she wasn't there. And neither were her friends." *Live television would never work for me. I want to call a time-out. Consult the coach. Get off this sofa. How do I sit this still when the turbulence inside me requires a life jacket to keep me from drowning in fear?* Logan must have seen me drift into myself because he patted my hand as if it was a reset button. "She's a fifteen-year-old who lost both of her parents while they were away from her. Of course, she'd be devastated and confused. We think Faith might be headed to Las Vegas where her parents died. That maybe she's looking for some sort of closure." I fingered my diamond tennis brace-let, my tenth wedding anniversary gift. The wedding guide said aluminum and tin were the traditional gifts for ten years. I used aluminum foil to wrap a tin can filled with golf balls. I went for clever. Diamonds were considered the contemporary gift. He went for flabbergast.

"Here's a photograph of Faith taken just last year. If you have information that would help the Butlers, please call the toll-free number at the bottom of your screen," Deirdre told the viewing audience.

When our spot ended, Deirdre said, "I'm the mother of two teenage daughters. I know they can be impetuous, ridicu-lous, and rebellious. But when they listen to their hearts, they know what's right. Don't bear the burden of guilt thinking she ran away because she didn't want to be with you. Maybe for

Faith right now, the thought of being close to you scares her. One devastating loss in a lifetime is enough for anyone. If she doesn't allow herself to care about you, then she won't have to deal with that kind of pain again." She glanced at the clock. "I need to get back to the set. I know you didn't ask for a drive-by therapy session today. It was something I felt like you needed to hear."

"Thank you," I said as she clasped my hand in hers. I was so focused on all the reasons Faith might hate us or resent us, I didn't even consider there was a flip side to my guilt.

We said our good-byes, and before we left the building, Logan turned his phone on to discover he'd been inundated with texts, calls, and voice mail. He started to scroll through, stopped, and handed me his phone. "Here, put this in your purse. I'm getting close to my gut-wrenching limit for the morning. I'm sure Matt's already talked to most of them by now. I'll call him later." He held his hand out, and I slipped mine in his. "I think we did okay in there. You?"

"It's not something I want to be an expert at, that's for sure."

Logan opened the French doors, and we stepped into unexpected sunshine.

34

We'd arrived at the station at the dusky part of the morning when overserved bar patrons stumbled into the food and delivery trucks stocking the bars they were leaving. Garbage trucks lurched and growled through some of the city streets. Residents often awoke to the oily squeal of brakes and the angry crunching of whatever the men threw into the huge steel mouths of the trucks. By the time we left the building, the city had yawned and stretched itself awake. Houses emptied as students bent with the weight of backpacks, waiters wearing black bow ties with their black jackets, doctors with their white lab coats flapping at their sides, and bike-riders pedaled furiously through traffic made their way into the schools and businesses they filled.

Logan looked down at my feet as we reached the sidewalk. "Sensible shoes today? Not the red-soled ones we may have to sell later to pay for food?"

"I'm actually sorry I'm not wearing them because they're effective weaponry when necessary, and I could've given you a personal demonstration. But, no, I'm wearing flats. Why are you enamored with my feet today?"

He smiled, a rather creepy smile, and pulled me toward him like he'd heard tango music. "It's not just your feet, my dear. It's your legs, your—"

"It's too early and a wee bit too public for more. Can we just get to the car?"

He untangoed me. "Better idea. Now that I know you can walk a few blocks without risking blisters and possible ankle breakage, I thought we could find a restaurant close by and have breakfast or brunch. I'll even buy."

"Game on, Butler. Let's go."

We'd been seated and served coffee when my phone rang. "We forgot to call our mothers," I said as I opened my purse. "Your guess? Martha or Nancy?"

He lowered his menu, closed his eyes for a moment, and said, "I pick . . . Cam."

I saw the number flashing before I pulled out the phone. "Logan. Logan. It's Holly." A couple seated a table away stared at me. I stared back. "She's important," I snapped.

Logan still clutched his menu, where happy and frantic must have been his choices, and he'd ordered one of each.

I pressed "answer" and reached for Logan's hand. "Holly? If it's not good news, please hang up now. We're in a restaurant, and I don't want to be responsible for breakage."

When she laughed, I put the call on speaker and my heart on standby.

"You're *where*?" she said.

"At breakfast. We decided after we left the station to find—"

"Wait. Martha didn't get in touch with one of you?"

"No," I said and handed Logan his phone and told him to check for a missed call. Logan shook his head. No missed call from Martha on his phone.

"We found Faith—"

Logan and I jumped out of our seats at the same time. I yelped, he yelled, we left a generous tip, and we flew out of the restaurant before the couple at the other table could complain.

"Where was she? Is she okay? How did you find her?"

I never thought I'd be thrilled to be standing on a New Orleans sidewalk, staring at a cell phone while I wiped my tears on a restaurant napkin.

"Well, she found herself. She called one of her friends from Hobby Airport. She did plan to fly to Vegas. She's a smart kid. She had to be sixteen to take a bus or the train, but only fifteen to buy a plane ticket. Anyway . . . she must have had second thoughts and reached out for someone to talk her off the ledge. Her friend convinced her that going to Vegas wasn't wrong, but the way she was doing it was."

"Who's this friend? Can she come live with us too?" Logan said and wrapped his arm around me.

"You'll have to ask her parents that when you pick Faith up. They called me on their way to the airport, which is about a half hour away from where they live. They're picking her up, and either in the car or when they get home, they're explaining to Faith that you and Logan are on your way. I was going to go myself, but I thought you might want to."

"We're almost to the parking lot. I'll call from our car to get the address," I said. "And, Holly, thank you, thank you, thank you."

I checked my cell, and I didn't have a missed call from Martha either. "Logan . . . if you don't have a missed call from your mother and I don't have one either, as Mamie used to say, 'There's something rotten in the state of Denmark, and it ain't me.'"

Logan paled. "You don't think something happened to her? Holly called with great news. That shouldn't have been anything to upset her."

"If she doesn't answer, we'll go to her house."

She answered on the fifth ring. "Elle, I was just getting ready to call you and Logan."

"Martha, we talked to Holly a few minutes ago. Why didn't you call us? You had to have known we were finished at the news station."

She didn't answer, and it sounded like an arctic blast just ripped through her phone. "Martha? Martha? Are you okay?"

"I'm fine. Is Logan with you?"

"That's not answering my question. But, yes, he is, and I'm putting this on speaker phone."

"Oh, perfect. I really wasn't sure when the two of you were off the air because . . . well, because I'd already left my house. When Holly called, I thought I could get an hour's head start, at least—"

"Head start? Head start to where, Mother?" Logan lips did that sideways twist thing, a prelude to, "If she wasn't my mother, I'd have her arrested for impersonating a sensible human."

"Why, to go pick up Faith," she oozed. She must have suspected she'd overstepped her bounds by about three countries because her sweet, Southern magnolia voice dripped through the phone. "And, don't worry, I'm not alone. William, from the play, volunteered to accompany me. We should be there in about three hours. I'll call you as soon as we get there. Bye."

The two of us stared at my cell phone as if we were next in the queue to consult Zeus on Mount Olympus.

"She didn't! Tell me your mother, accompanied by a man we've never met, did not just bogart picking up our daughter?"

"She did. She definitely did."

"Well, she is on grandmother probation when she returns. Indefinitely."

"I agree. Indefinitely."

"And no time off for good behavior."

"Agreed. We'll make her write 'I will not drive over five hours to pick up the granddaughter I've never met without first asking her parents for permission.'"

"One hundred times."

I wanted to be really, really, really angry with her. Instead, I was really, really, really grateful to God. Even though I still really, really, really didn't understand Him.

In our car, parked on North Rampart Street with city buses spewing toxic fumes, painters swaying on ten-story-high scaffolds, and construction workers jackhammering sidewalks, Logan and I laughed and cried and celebrated. Celebrated this new birth of our daughter. Together.

When we got back to our house, I called Cam and my mother to relate the good news of Faith being found and the goofy news of how she'd be arriving home. Cam laughed until she couldn't speak and handed the phone to Nick, which required my retelling the story. He was amused, but not to the point of actually making sounds that could be even confused as laughter. When Cam could breathe again, her husband handed her the phone.

"Don't you wish you'd known ahead of time and been able to plant a bug in her car? Let's hope Faith doesn't jump out when Martha slows down at a stop sign."

"Should I be worried about that?"

"Take your sense of humor out of layaway. That was a joke."

I wanted her and my mother to visit us as soon as possible, but Cam disagreed. "You, Logan, and Faith need to get to know one another. You know, between Martha's visits. Let's hope Martha's boyfriend keeps her too busy to be a pest. If he doesn't, then I'd make him an offer he couldn't refuse. Logan could call him Deputy Person in Charge of the Representative's Mother."

"First, he'll have to win the election. With everything that's happened, his campaigning has been puny. Truth is, if Logan wins or not, we both feel like we've won something that could never be trumped."

"And you have, sister, you have."

We hung up, and I called my mother. Elated about Faith being found and amused by Martha's ride to glory, my mother's tone was tinged with sadness. "I wish I lived closer, Elle. Faith is going to be able to spend more time with Martha . . . "

"If you lived closer to me, you'd be farther from Cam, and where would that leave Nick Junior? She'll see Martha more, but that's not always an advantage because Martha can be a bit high maintenance. Plus, Faith could visit you, and then you'd only have to share her with Cam."

"Never thought of it that way," she said. "I don't want to lose time like . . . like I did with you."

Skype might have improved our visual communication, but until someone discovered a way for us to communicate by reaching out and truly touching someone, it could never replace being there. "I'm trying not to think of it as lost. It was a detour. We know where we're going now. And we'll make sure that Faith knows the way."

At home, I sat in Faith's desk chair, turning from side to side, and looked around the room the way I imagined parents did after readying the crib for their soon-to-be born. I hated waiting.

Logan leaned over and kissed the top of my head. "Hey, what are you doing?" He stood behind me, his hands rested where my shoulders curved into my neck.

"Being," I said. "Being happy and scared. Being scared to be happy." I turned the chair to face him. "It's as if I have survivor guilt. We have Faith, but it's only because the Wyatts died. I feel guilty being happy about her being here because it's like I'm saying I'm happy Kim and Jay died. Is she going to think that, too?"

Logan leaned against the desk. "Maybe it's part of our moral DNA to feel uncomfortable if our joy results from someone else's misery or death. In all those wrongful death or injury suits, the money never compensates for the loss. But people shouldn't have to suffer twice. Those settlements can make huge differences in the quality of life for those families. They loved her, and it was for her future and well-being, not ours, that they chose us. I think that's why those plans were in place, to provide them a sense of peace while they were alive, knowing they'd done all they could do for her. Don't you think they'd want us to be happy about that?"

He bent down until we were eye-to-eye and his hands held my face. "Elle, think about it. Why did you choose the Wyatts before Faith was born? Because Faith was the best child for them or because they were the best adoptive parents for her? When they carried her out of the hospital in their arms, I wouldn't doubt they felt then much the same way you feel today."

"It's crazy, I guess, to think this kind of joy doesn't come without a price."

"But you already paid the price. Maybe that can help you when you're confused about this God thing. We can have joy, too, because He paid the price for us."

35

We estimated Martha, Mr. William the Wonderful, and Faith wouldn't arrive home until after four o'clock that afternoon, and that was if they did drive-through for lunch. I sent Logan to his office to meet with Matt and asked him to do whatever he could to arrange a few days off or at least half-days to allow us time to be with Faith when she first arrived.

The truth was I wanted him here for me as much as for her. On one hand, it seemed unfair of me to use Logan as back-up when Faith was on her own. On the other, maybe Faith would need Logan as back-up. What were we even supposed to call one another? Referring to her as my daughter might upset or offend her. Unlike Martha, who jumped right in to grandmother/granddaughter. The difference, though, was Faith barely remembered her grandmothers and Martha didn't have any other grandchildren who would wonder about this instant affection between her and Faith. But if I didn't refer to Faith as my daughter, what other words were available? When Holly said that Logan and I would need to formally adopt Faith, that only intensified the dilemma. She'd then become my birth daughter whom I adopted.

What would she call me? I'd spent hours reading adoption forums and personal stories about birth parents and adoptive parents, and adopted children and adults. Some studies showed sixty-five percent of American adolescents wanted to meet their birth parents and ninety-four percent wanted to know which birth parent they resembled. Would Faith have wanted to meet us on her own? If she had contacted us, would we have wanted a reunion? One study said of those birth parents who'd been contacted by their child, ninety-five percent wanted a reunion.

Where might I have fallen in all those statistics? Seeing pictures of Faith as she grew became increasingly difficult for me emotionally because I saw so much of her father and myself in her. Though, if at any point, Kim and Jay would have said she was ready to meet us, I wouldn't have hesitated. What chilled me was reading that some birth mothers and their children, once they met, felt absolutely no connection whatsoever to one another.

What then?

I didn't want to know.

Around one, I took a break from unpacking boxes in my new office. Cam and I would never be successful furniture movers or household organizers. Our system made for fast packing but made unpacking like a one-woman scavenger hunt. A few boxes lacked identification altogether. Written across the tops of the others was "Desk Stuff" or "Papers and Stuff" or "Books and Stuff." After opening three boxes, the word *stuff* would have sufficed for all of them.

Because I didn't expect Logan home yet, I indulged in a peanut butter, Nutella, and strawberry preserves sandwich.

Really, the bread was necessary to provide support for the other three ingredients, which I could have just as easily lined up on the table and eaten with a spoon.

Holly called and partially distracted me from a second round. She said that Martha, William, and Faith had just stopped for lunch, then they'd be driving straight back.

"Shouldn't they have already eaten by now?" I comforted myself with a spoon of Nutella.

"Best part of the story yet to come," she said. "I had my come-to-Jesus-meeting with Faith, and I told her she was responsible for talking to you and Logan about her leaving. I reassured her we'd make a plan to collect her clothes and whatever else she wanted. I forgot to mention you and Logan wouldn't be picking her up. A few hours later, I receive a phone call from Martha, who tells me Faith won't leave with her because she was expecting you and Logan. Martha explained the story to Faith and told her she'd call you so Faith could talk to you and vouch for her—"

"I haven't heard that from Martha," I said and screwed the lids back on the jars because this conversation had the potential of making me overdose on preserves and Nutella.

"And you're not going to. Faith told Martha that she had no idea what you sounded like on the telephone and just because Martha dialed a phone number, that didn't mean she could trust the voice on the other end."

"If you had called about five minutes ago, I might have died needing a Heimlich maneuver after hearing this. Martha Butler may have met her match," I said. "Logan is going to love this one."

Holly laughed. "Martha handed Faith the telephone, and I apologized for forgetting to tell her. But I also made sure she knew that you and Logan didn't default and that Martha essentially shut you guys out. She told me she could see how that could happen. This kid already has Martha's number."

"Too bad I don't have a baby book for her. Great first running away from home story," I said. "Or first running away from home story in her second life."

"Actually, that's an idea, Elle. Instead of a baby book, why not keep a journal? Maybe Faith could write one as well. One more reason for a mother-daughter shopping trip."

"Am I going to be that to her? Her mother?"

"I don't know. It's different for every family. Be patient. Don't expect too much from her or from yourself. Focus on your relationship. Everything else will follow."

⸻

I sat on the floor of my office separating paper clips from binder clips and pens and markers and highlighters. A task easily accomplished by a trained monkey, but lacking one of those, I substituted. When I focused on mindless activities, my emotional ninja relaxed and felt less inclined to attack every issue in my life. The added bonus was the sense of fulfillment from having prevented office supply cross-breeding.

My engagement level must have been intense because I didn't know Logan had arrived home until I looked up to find him leaning across the doorframe, arms folded, in all his cuteness, watching me as if I played on the beach building sand castles. "Aha! This is the grueling work you do while I'm away? Little wonder you're exhausted by the time I'm home."

I sighed. "I know. By the time I move on to tape dispensers, glue, and scissors, I can barely move. And you think all that lawyering is hard work," I said.

"Perfect segue," he said and sat on the floor next to me. "What would you think if I removed myself from politics altogether and settled for being Logan Butler, attorney-at-law?"

I dumped the binder clips into a brown envelope. "I think the answer is in the question."

"I'm not the Karate Kid, so don't go all Mr. Miyagi on me. What does that mean?" He put all the paper clips in a plastic zipper bag.

"You said, 'settled for being' an attorney. To me, when people settle for something, they're saying they're either giving up or giving in. Is this because of your meeting with Matt?"

He leaned against the wall and propped his feet on a stack of magazines that probably should have been recycled five years ago. "I'm not sure. You know I try to not make decisions based on feelings, which, with our lives lately, would have meant Armageddon if I did. But, still, there's our relationship, my career, my running for office, and in," he looked at his watch, "a few hours, a teenager in the house. I don't want to do many things poorly, instead of a few things well. At least that's how I feel, which brings me back to how legitimate this decision would be."

"What did he say has been the 'Faith fallout'?"

"Lost some, gained some. A few Christian supporters dropped because we admitted we had sex before we married. And a few Christian supporters jumped on board because we admitted we had sex before we married but realized the consequence of that decision. I never wanted to make being a Christian my platform. It's no more my platform than being a human being. It's who I am, not what I am. It doesn't work that way in politics. Any opportunity to attack what's perceived as sinfulness is an opportunity to discuss my hypocrisy or dishonesty, instead of the issues."

"Which is exactly why you need to stay exactly where you are. Being a politician is who you are. Your passion for doing the right thing and helping people is part of that." I scooted next to him on the wall. "I wonder, though, if some of this isn't related to your father. You've worked hard to not be the man he was outside of politics. But he was a successful politician. Are you afraid if you try to follow his political footsteps they might lead to places you don't want to go?"

"I never thought about it that way. Maybe so. Maybe so."

———

Martha's text came while I was chopping onions for jambalaya. "BE THERE IN 30."

When I showed Logan the text, he hugged me and said the onions made him cry too.

36

"Should I wear something else? The jeans are too tight, aren't they? Maybe a camisole." I stopped halfway to my bedroom and went back to the kitchen. "Never mind, that'll make my arms look flabby."

"If I tell you that you look beautiful, will you believe me?" Logan stirred the jambalaya on the stove.

"What was I thinking making that? Now the whole house smells like onions and garlic."

"I'll take that as a no," he said.

I opened kitchen cabinets, jostled things I hadn't seen in years from one side to the other. "I used to have a diffuser. Where did I put that thing?" I opened the pantry door. "Nope. Not here either. I should have bought chips at the grocery. Isn't that a staple of teenage diets?"

Logan put the spoon on the counter. I picked it up, put it in the spoon rest, and then wiped the granite. He tugged on my belt loop as I started to walk off. "Stop. Look at me. Between your running monologue and your obsessing over flabby arms and garlic, you're making me crazy."

"I'm making you crazy? I don't understand how you're nonchalant about this. The daughter you've never laid eyes on is going to walk through the door in less than eight minutes." I tried to move his hand. "Let go. I need—"

"I'm not letting go of you. You are going to stand right here, right now, and tell me what's going on in there." He pointed at my heart.

"The last time I saw her, she was days old and a nurse was taking her out of my arms. I still remember what she smelled like that day, how her eyelids fluttered when she slept, and how, when she opened her eyes, she looked at me as if she knew who I was. Like she was memorizing my face the same way I tried to memorize hers. Oh, God, Logan, I don't know if I can do this. I'm afraid she'll hate me. And I'm afraid to let myself love her. I've spent sixteen years of my life putting everything I felt about her into this vault in my heart. Once it went in, I didn't let it out because look . . . look what's happening now. I'm drowning in it all."

He handed me a stack of kitchen napkins. "Maybe it's not as difficult for me because I have no memory of her. But I'm scared too. I'm not sure I know how to be a father, and there aren't any do-overs after this. I have this prayer on an endless loop in my head, *God, please help us learn how to be a family.* And I remember she's a fifteen-year-old who lost the two people she most loved in her life, is moving away from her friends, and coming to live with two strangers except for our biological connection."

"And she's been with Martha for over five hours," I said and blew my nose.

"And there's that." Logan blotted my face with a dry napkin. "If she's really savvy, she slept, or at least pretended to."

Logan and I waited in the family room in silence. I'd shortened his prayer to *God, please help us* and answered Cam's and my mother's text messages asking if they were here yet, when they would be getting here, how long did I think Martha would stay, and all the scoop on William the Wonderful. They both wanted pictures. I told them that this wasn't a photo op, especially considering what Faith had been through the last few days, but I'd send something as soon as I could.

When the headlights of Martha's car swept through the room, I sent one word, "HERE." The outside lights were on, and when Logan opened the front door, we saw that William the Wonderful and Martha were just getting out of the car. Martha spotted us and waved and gave a thumbs-up signal as William walked around and opened the back door.

If Faith had taken two minutes longer, Logan and I might have both lost consciousness. Me from holding my breath, and Logan from losing circulation in his left arm from my vise-like grip.

Faith didn't look much different than she did in the picture Deirdre showed us at the television station. No headband, her hair tucked behind her ears, she tugged her peasant top down over her jeans, slipped her feet into flip-flops, and hooked her back pack over one shoulder. She looked around as if to get her bearings, and when she saw the two of us it was, again, as if she needed to get her bearings.

When Martha and William reached the door, she introduced him to Logan and me. He reminded me of a shorter James Brolin. We expected her and William to stay, but to our surprise, she said they had dinner plans. "It's been a long day. Faith slept in the car after lunch, but I'm sure she's still tired." She and William told Faith good-bye, and I watched as Martha simply laid her hand on Faith's cheek and said, "I'm so glad you're here."

Faith sat on the sofa, placing her backpack at her feet. She surveyed the room and then looked back at us.

"Would you like something to drink? Water, tea, diet drink?" I asked. I couldn't stop looking at her.

She nodded. "Water. Water would be great. Thanks."

That was the first time I'd ever heard her voice, and I smiled thinking that was another note for the not-a-baby book.

"And water would be great for me, too," said Logan. He turned to Faith. "I think she might have forgotten I was here for a moment."

"Not a chance," I said.

Faith grinned.

I handed her and Logan their water and told her that we'd made supper, but we understood that she might be more tired than hungry. "I don't know if you like jambalaya, and if you don't, it's fine. We can make sandwiches . . . "

"It's been . . . well, I am pretty tired. Holly said I should talk to you about the whole thing—"

"We can do that tomorrow," Logan said. "Elle and I are just grateful that you're fine. That's enough for us for now."

"Um, tomorrow would be better," she said and her shoulders relaxed as she inched back on the sofa. "Thanks."

Logan appeared as mesmerized as I felt just watching this child, seeing bits of ourselves in her face, her expressions. I almost felt I should apologize for staring at her as if she was an item in the Smithsonian when she looked at us and said, "I look like the two of you."

I was afraid if I spoke, my voice would crack and I'd not be able to recover.

Logan nodded. "Yes, we noticed that too."

She laughed. *Her first laugh.* "It's kind of one of those things you wonder. Which parent you look like or if you look like them at all. Mom told me I did, but you know how moms are . . . " She bit her lower lip and looked away.

"Well, after today, you sure know how my mom is," said Logan. "By the way, Elle and I were quite impressed with your not leaving with Martha until you had someone you trusted vouch for her. It's good self-preservation, and it's good for Martha too. Being right all the time can be a burden for her."

"When she and Mr. William knocked on the door, I was kind of shocked. Holly had told me the two of you were coming, so I couldn't understand how you could be my parents and look that old. I thought somebody must've gotten paperwork messed up or something."

"That was absolutely the right thing to do. And I'm sure Martha knew that too. She's usually the one telling people the way things are going to go down," I said.

"I did need a rest from talking and rehearsing lines. It started out as pretend sleep, but I actually did fall asleep for a little while."

"Rehearsing lines? Wait, don't tell me. She asked you to play Stella," said Logan.

"Yes. Yes, she did. I didn't mind, really, but I needed a break. But she's very sweet. I hope I don't sound mean. I did promise her I'd go to the play," she said.

She yawned, and I sensed she might not be comfortable excusing herself from the conversation, but I could at least head her in that direction. "You've been sitting for hours in the car. I think you might want to stretch your legs a bit. Why don't I show you the bedroom that's yours?"

Logan carried her backpack, and I told her about my sister and I picking out her furniture. "I told Cam if you said you didn't like it, I was blaming her."

When he turned on the light, Faith looked around and froze. She walked over to the bed and ran her hand along the edge of the headboard. Her eyes filled, but she blinked and cleared her throat and seemed to recover.

"Hey, if it's not something you want, be honest. I'm sure we could work out some kind of exchange with the furniture store," I said. "Plus, we didn't buy a comforter because we thought you'd want to pick that out yourself."

"No, it's not that I don't like it." She sat on the bed. "I was shocked because this is almost identical to my other bedroom set. Weird, huh?"

"Good weird?" Logan asked her as he handed over her backpack.

"Yes," she said. "Very good weird."

"The bathroom is through those French doors. It's all yours. I put some towels in there for tonight and tomorrow, but when we go shopping, you can decide on your shower curtain and whatever else you want."

"You really wouldn't mind if I showered and then went to bed? I'm more tired than I am hungry." She unzipped her backpack and set it next to her on the bed.

"Not at all. We might end up bypassing dinner ourselves," said Logan. "If there's something you need, let us know. And I mean it—not just tonight. But for always."

"We're grateful your parents blessed us with you. We know how much they loved you," I said. I was almost afraid to blink for fear she might disappear. I couldn't stop looking at her, fascinated at seeing parts of Logan and myself in her features. She even moved through space slow and deliberate like Logan. I bent down and switched on a nightlight I'd plugged in near the hall. "If you woke up in the middle of the night, I didn't want you to bump into walls trying to figure out where to go."

"Thanks," she said and smiled. Faith reached in her backpack. When she pulled out a worn copy of *Love You Forever* and put it on her nightstand, I squeezed Logan's arm and pressed my lips together.

She ran her hand over the cover. "My mom used to read this to me all the time. It's one of my favorites."

"Mine, too," I said in a throaty whisper. "It's the book I gave her when she took you home from the hospital."

Faith looked at the book, then back at me, and in a movement so fluid I didn't realize what she was about to do, she walked over and hugged me.

I looked at Logan over her shoulder. His eyes were as bright and wide-open as my heart.

"I'll love you for always, and as long as I'm living my baby you'll be."

Epilogue

Two Years Later

The two of you have exactly thirteen minutes. You can't be late to your own ribbon cutting. It's a law." Logan said as he stood behind us in the bathroom and straightened his tie.

"And you," Faith said, shaking the flat iron at him, "have exactly thirteen seconds to leave us alone." She resumed the twists and turns that created long spiral curls that didn't look like mattress springs.

Logan hadn't moved.

"I'm counting . . . one . . . two . . . three . . . " At seventeen, Faith had sprouted past me and was almost eye-to-eye with Logan. "Are you're telling me I can't stand here and admire the beauty of my wife and daughter?"

"You can admire us from afar," I told him. "Aren't you supposed to have John? Where is he?"

"Cam's feeding him," Logan said.

"Not anymore I'm not." Cam's voice made it into the bedroom before she did. Her arms were straight out from her body, and she held our one-year-old son around his chest so that his back was to her. As soon as John spotted Faith he pedaled his legs and yelped. "This kid makes the stinkiest diapers known to mankind."

Faith made kissy faces at him. "Sorry, buddy, I'm busy making your mother beautiful."

"But, look, his daddy already made himself beautiful," I said. "Logan, I think you're up."

"Handsome, I'll take handsome," Logan said as he reached for our son.

"I'll do you the favor of getting him to his room," Cam said, her face twisted. "Ugh. Now tell everyone bye-bye because Auntie Cam needs to fumigate herself before she gets dressed."

John waved his arms up and down, spitting out a string of "b-b-b-b-b-b," and he was on his way to cleanliness.

The ribbon-cutting ceremony for the Wyatt Center, named after Kim and Jay, was this afternoon. We were able to purchase the picturesque property we'd admired two years ago for much less than the asking price.

"You're ready to rock," Faith announced. We both faced the mirror, and she stood behind me armed with a can of hair spray. "If his constituents knew that his wife and daughter were polluting the environment for cosmetic purposes—"

Logan had won his election as state representative, but he'd decided he was only serving one term. He wanted to support Chad Wiggins in the next election, and they'd become close friends. Faith often babysat for his children when the two men met, since Chad had lost Lucy almost a year ago. Lucy had been in remission for six months when her cancer returned and she died three months later.

"Just spray before he gets back and sees us," I said. "He'll never out us. We'll threaten to tell the media he's used it too."

Faith laughed, gave me the same kissy face she gave her brother, and said, "My turn to get beautiful."

"You already are," I told her. "So it shouldn't take too long."

She'd been here for two years, and I still was awed by the gift she was to us. We'd experienced challenges that made us both want to run to the returns and exchanges department. But we found ways to fix what was broken or who was broken. Faith would be leaving for college next year, which meant Logan and I made every effort to spend time with her without being one of those "helicopter" parents who constantly hovered over their kids.

I found Logan in the baby's room having another one of what he called his "man" talks with his son about women. "Always tell them to be ready a half hour before they really need to be, and that way you'll be sure to be on time." He finished snapping John's romper, kissed him on each cheek, and handed him to me. "Every time I look at Faith and John, I think if it had been up to me they would have never been in my life."

"Which is why," I said, "we're not the boss of God." I smoothed John's dark hair, and he rewarded me with a toothless smile.

"Are we ready?" Logan walked into the family room, which now really lived up to its name. I followed him, and John, ever eager to practice his crawling skills, traveled behind me.

My mother, Cam and Nick and Nick Junior, and the newlyweds Martha and William filled every available place to sit.

"Okay." Logan looked around the room. "We're missing Faith. Where is she?"

She popped out of the kitchen. "I've been here the whole time, waiting for all of you."

Discussion Questions

(Spoiler Alert!)

1. How much should information about their pasts should engaged and/or married couples disclose to one another?

2. What about forgiveness? Are there absolute "deal breakers" in secrets revealed by one partner or another?

3. Therapists sometimes say that we are only as emotionally and spiritually "sick" as our secrets. Do you believe this to be true for Elle? For yourself? In what ways?

4. Logan defines himself (found his identity) in both his business and political careers. Do our careers and ambitions mask things about us? How would Logan define himself outside of those careers?

5. By what metaphorical yardstick did Elle measure herself? How did this shape her life?

6. What did you think of Elle's parents' reactions to her pregnancy? How would this compare to how you might have, or perhaps already have, reacted? Does society judge the parents of the pregnant girl and/or the father of the baby?

7. Many unmarried couples in Hollywood have children. Some marry, some never do. Does society judge them differently than it would judge Elle?

8. Elle's parents are involved in their church community, yet Elle did not embrace religion. What contributed to this disconnect?

9. What do you think of Martha Butler and her relationship with Elle and with Logan, both separately and as a couple?

10. What, ultimately, did the Butler family learn about God?

Want to learn more about author
Christa Allan and check out other great
fiction by Abingdon Press?

Sign up for our fiction newsletter at
www.AbingdonPress.com
to read interviews with your favorite authors, find tips
for starting a reading group, and stay posted on
what's new on the horizon. It's a place to connect
with other fiction readers or post a
comment about this book.

Be sure to visit Christa online!

www.christaallan.com

If you enjoyed *Test of Faith*, we hope you'll check out other books by Christa Allan. Here's a sample from *Walking on Broken Glass*.

1

Cruising the sparkling aisles of Catalano's Supermarket, I lost my sanity buying frozen apple juice.

Okay, so maybe it started several aisles before the refrigerated cases. Somewhere between the canned vegetables and cleaning supplies. I needed to kill the taste of that soy milk in my iced vanilla latte. Darn my friend Molly, the dairy Nazi. I blamed her for my detour to the liquor aisle. Decisions. Decisions. Decisions. What to pour in my Starbucks cup? Amaretto? Kahlua? Vodka? And the winner was . . . Amaretto. Perfect for an afternoon grocery event.

Ramping up the coffee seemed like a reasonable idea at the time. I'd left the end-of-the-year faculty party and thought I'd be a considerate wife and pick up dinner for Carl on the way home. He told me before he left for work that morning that he'd meet me at the party. Probably he had one too many meetings, which, since I'd probably had one too many beers, made us just about even. Don't know if we matched spin cycles in our brains, though. That was the point of the coffee. A rinse cycle of sorts.

I'd just avoided a game of bumper carts with the oncoming traffic in the organic food aisle when I remembered that I needed juice. On the way to the freezer section, I maneuvered a difficult curve around the quilted toilet tissue display. My coffee sloshed in the cup in tempo with my stomach. I braked too swiftly by the refrigerator case, and a wave of latte splotched my linen shorts and newly pedicured toes. Ick.

Rows of orange juice. Apple juice was on the third shelf down. I reached in and, like a one-armed robot, I selected and returned can after can of juice, perplexed by the dilemma of cost versus quality. *Okay, this one's four cents an ounce cheaper than this one. But this one's . . .*

My face would have reflected my growing agitation, but the stale icy air swirling out of the freezer numbed it. I held the door open with one hand, tried to sip my coffee with the other, and wondered how long it would take before full body paralysis set in. I stared at apple juice cans. They stared back. Something shifted, and my body broke free from a part of itself, and there I was—or there we were. I watched me watch the cans. The rational me separated from the wing-nut me, who still pondered the perplexities of juice costs. Rational me said, "Let's get her out of here before she topples head first into the freezer case and completely humiliates herself."

I abandoned my cart, a lone testament to my struggle and defeat, near the freezer cases and walked away. If I could fill my brain with alcohol like I filled my car with gas, it wouldn't have to run on empty. It wouldn't leave me high and dry in the middle of a grocery store aisle.

No, not dry this time. High. My brain is either high or dry, and it doesn't seem to function well either way.

So that was my epiphany for sobriety.

Apple juice.

2

Carl was late, too late to watch me as I weaved my way from garage to bedroom.

What was today?

Friday. Forgot.

Carl's poker night. Reprieve.

I opened my bedroom closet door and considered changing into my scrubs, but that would've meant negotiating a path to the laundry room to pull them out of the dryer. Since I'd submerged my internal GPS in an Amaretto bath, I doubted I'd make it. The T-shirt and shorts I wore would do just fine. I peeled away the layers of comforter and blankets on my side and let the sheets tug the weight of my weariness into bed.

Two bathroom visits later, I felt the mattress concede as Carl's body plowed onto his side of our bed. As usual, he reached his arm toward me, his right hand landing on my hip. As usual, I didn't move and waited for the morning.

I woke up a rumpled mess, still wearing my coffee-stained shorts and black tee. I didn't need a mirror to know my flat-ironed hair was smashed to my head, except for the twisted front bangs, which stood off my forehead in a lame salute. The sunlight from the bay window drilled through my eyelids. I slapped my face into the pillow but instantly regretted disturbing what could only be tiny thunderbolts in my brain. I needed to see a doctor. I woke up with far too many head throbs.

I felt the swaddled tightness as I rolled over. Carl always tucked in the sheet on his side of the bed as if to prevent me from rolling out. I turned toward the empty space on the other side of the bed to escape the sharpshooter sun.

I plucked the note left on his pillow. Thin, angular letters: "Golf at 8. Call Molly." At the bottom, smaller print but all caps: "Let you sleep. Can't wait for you tonight." I shoved the note under his pillow and tried not to breathe in the whisper of his musky orange cologne.

Why did I remember what I wanted to forget, yet forget what I wanted to remember?

I stared at the ceiling, my eyes stung by my own thoughtlessness. Molly was probably geared up for major annoyance. Saturday mornings were reserved for our two-mile trek through the greenbelt trails of Brookforest. Late was not a time on her clock. I still wore my watch, and late ticked away: 9:00.

Molly Richardson and I met two years ago at the Christmas party for Morgan Management. Both of our husbands had recently joined the firm. She and I had barreled into the bathroom, about as much as one could barrel in ruffled silk chiffon and elastic-backed, three-inch spiked shoes. We crashed reaching for the door handle.

Molly grabbed the knob, steadied herself, scanned me, and said, "We have to stop meeting like this. People will talk."

A woman with a sense of humor and cool shoes in the midst of granite-faced consultants. Our friendship had expanded since then beyond the boundaries of business. We knew almost everything there was to know about each other. Almost everything.

I willed myself to vertical and plodded to the phone on Carl's side of the bed. One of our concessions after we moved into this house: blinding sun in my eyes; ringing phone in his ears.

I punched in Molly's number.

One ring. "You up?" she said.

"Meet you there in fifteen." I hung up knowing Molly would understand that fifteen meant twenty. I yanked on clean shorts and a sports bra, but kept the leftover T-shirt from yesterday. Yesterday. Apple juice. Was today the day I would practice not drinking? Did I pay for groceries? No bags on the kitchen counter. A half bagel waited on a plate.

I passed on breakfast and grabbed my keys from the top of the washing machine. Carl really needed to hang a key rack. I locked the leaded glass doors, unlocked the wrought-iron gate, and walked through a gauntlet of Tudor and French provincial houses. Molly and I always met at the cul-de-sac entrance to the trails at the end of my street.

Molly was in her ready zone. She alternated long, bouncing genuflects to stretch her legs.

"I'm always amazed that your calves are almost as long as my legs," I said and slid the fuzzy banana-yellow headband hanging around my neck to around my head to tame my disobedient hair.

"Save that for one of your hyperbole lessons." A tint of anger edged her words.

"Hey, Moll, I'm sorry. Carl forgot to wake me up when he left for golf this morning."

"It's his fault you're late?" I knew tone, and her tone definitely indicated she thought exactly the opposite. "Did he wake you up for school too?"

Sarcasm lesson. "Sometimes," I said.

She smiled.

I moved close to forgiveness. "Okay, almost always."

A laugh.

Suffering over.

"Let's get started before the sun sucks the life out of us," she said.

Only a silo-sized vacuum cleaner hose could suck the energy out of Molly. Twenty years younger and she'd be on meds for hyperactivity. Instead, she's on meds for infertility. She and Devin had been baby practicing for almost two years. Practice had not made perfect. Over a year ago, when I told her I was pregnant, I almost wanted to apologize. Carl and I hadn't planned to be parents. But we were. For six weeks. Then Alyssa died. I stopped feeling guilty around Molly. Mostly I stopped feeling.

I bent over, pretended to adjust my shoelace, and hoped Molly didn't see the grief floating in my eyes.

"I'm ready." I popped up. Perky trumps pity. "And wait till you hear what happened."

When I chronicled the latest school dramas, my body didn't feel so heavy as I pounded my way down the path. A paralegal for trial attorneys, Molly didn't share many details about work. We entertained ourselves some days imagining which kids in detention would become lawyers and which ones would need lawyers.

"So, get this, I'm handing out tests, and—"

Her power walk shifted down two gears. She held up her hand and said, "No, Leah. Stop." American manicure this week, I noticed.

I looked over my shoulders thinking some school person had materialized behind us and Molly had just rescued me from embarrassment and possible unemployment. No one.

"Safe. Trail clear of suspects." I rattled on.

Another shift down. We now strolled.

"I have to talk to you about something, and it has to be today." She tucked her shoulder-length cinnamon-shaded hair behind her ears, a habit I'd learned meant she was ready for serious.

I sidestepped a clump of strange goo. "What's up?"

Molly pointed to a bench where the path split to lead to the pool or school. That always struck me as an unfair choice for kids on their way to school in the mornings.

She sat. Scary news was sit-down talk. I paced.

"You drink too much."

My feet stopped, but my soul lurched. My ship of composure pitched suddenly on this wave of information. I willed myself to calmness, "Who are you, Molly? AA's new spokeswoman?" The ten-year-old inside of me rose to the surface. "Oops, gender bias. New spokesperson?"

"I'm serious. No more jokes. I've been praying about this for weeks, not knowing how to say this to you. After last night, I knew it couldn't wait."

"Oh, so God told you to talk to me. Got it." I scattered pinecones with the tip of my Nikes.

"I don't think you get it," Molly said. "God hasn't text messaged me about you." Her cool hand wrapped itself around my wrist. "Would you sit down, please?"

I wanted to walk away—run, really—but her words anchored my heart. I couldn't move. I waited. I waited to breathe again. Waited for the tornado of emotions to stop swirling in my chest. I sat.

"Yesterday, Carrie called to see if you'd made it home. She wanted to drive you, but you absolutely refused. When she asked about whether to call Carl to pick you up, you told her . . . well, that's not worth repeating."

"So I had a few too many. It was a party. People drank. I drank. I'll apologize to Carrie for whatever I said."

"You don't remember, do you? Do you remember that night we went to Rizzo's for the company dinner?" She paused while two tricycling kids and a set of parents meandered past us.

If my brain had a file cabinet of events, the drawers were stuck. Dinner at Rizzo's. Retirement. Somebody retired. I tugged at the memory and tried to coax it out.

"Of course I remember. That guy, what was his name? He retired." I leaned back and wished the wrought-iron bench slats were padded.

"And?" Not really a question.

"And, what? Since you already know the answer."

"Leah," she said and leaned toward me. I still couldn't look at her. "Dinner was late. You grabbed the wine bottle from the waiter, gave him your wine glass, and then told him you two were even. You said if we'd pound our silverware on the table, we'd be served faster. You almost dropped a full bowl of gumbo in your lap. You said it looked like something you'd thrown up the night before."

I wanted a button to zap a force field around me. I wanted silence. A piece of me had broken, and Molly had found it. If I talked too much, other pieces might shatter. I couldn't risk it. I couldn't risk turning inside out.

"You were out of control," she said, the words filed by her softness so the edges were smooth when they pushed into me.

Yes, and out of control was exactly what I'd planned.

I couldn't look at Molly yet. I couldn't admit to my best friend in the universe that Carl told me almost every night something was terribly wrong with me. I thought I'd managed to divide myself quite nicely: Leah in the bedroom and Leah outside of the bedroom.

"I want to disappear," I said to the grass blades mashed under my shoes.

"You are disappearing. That's the problem. You're my friend. I want you here." She slid next to me and placed her hand on my shoulder. "In the two years we've known each other, your drinking has gotten worse. I know you suffered after losing Alyssa. I know you still do. But you need help, or something awful is going to happen."

I wanted to hate her. But how could I hate a friend who loved me enough to save my life?

"I lost my sanity at the apple juice case," I repeated to Dolores, the intake clerk who scribbled information onto whatever form they used to admit the inebriated. She placed her pencil on the glass-topped desk, clasped her hands over the clipboard, and peered at me over her reading glasses.

"Were you buying it to mix drinks?" she asked quietly, as if afraid the question would hurt me.

I'm being admitted into rehab by a woman who clearly failed to understand that apple juice mixed with few, if any, hard liquors. My galloping knees knew *that* was something to be jittery about. Hadn't I explained the twelve-pack of beer in the grocery cart? Why would I be worried about mixing? Did rehab centers hire teetotalers so they'd never have to worry about employee discounts for services?

"Noooo. It just seemed too overwhelming to decide which brand to buy. You know, the whole cost per ounce thing."

No doubt Dolores knew I was ready for admission after that, but she persisted. She asked who referred me.

"This was all my friend Molly's idea. She even made the appointment for me. This morning after our walk. Before my husband's golf game ended." Good grief. My inner child needed a nap.

This information about Molly seemed both unsurprising and amusing to Dolores. "Yes, it often works that way. People see in us what we can't see in ourselves. Don't need mirrors here."

Thirty minutes later, Dolores and I agreed I would voluntarily admit myself the morning of July 4.

Leah Adair Thornton. Age 27. Middle-stage alcoholic.